KT-171-840

THE NEW EASTGATE SWING

A DAN MARKHAM MYSTERY

CHRIS NICKSON

The Mystery Press

Northamptonshire Libraries & Information Service ND	
Askews & Holts	

Original cover photograph © iStockphoto.com

First published 2016

The Mystery Press is an imprint of The History Press
The Mill, Brimscombe Port
Stroud, Gloucestershire, GL5 2QG
www.thehistorypress.co.uk

© Chris Nickson, 2016

The right of Chris Nickson, to be identified as the Author
of this work has been asserted in accordance with the
Copyright, Designs and Patents Act 1988.

All rights reserved. No part of this book may be reprinted
or reproduced or utilised in any form or by any electronic,
mechanical or other means, now known or hereafter invented,
including photocopying and recording, or in any information
storage or retrieval system, without the permission in writing
from the Publishers.

British Library Cataloguing in Publication Data.
A catalogue record for this book is available from the British Library.

ISBN 978 0 7509 6698 6

Typesetting and origination by The History Press
Printed in Great Britain

To the woman whose name I never caught, who told me about her father, a real 1950s Leeds enquiry agent. That conversation was the first spark for this book. Thank you.

LEEDS, 1957

NEW BRIGGATE

QUEEN VICTORIA STREET

KING EDWARD STREET

BRIGGATE

1

KIRKGATE

CENTRAL ROAD

NEW MARKET STREET

STREET

DUNCAN STREET

CALL LANE

VIC

LU

KEY

1. Dan Markham's office
2. Bridge Street tunnel entrance
3. Back tunnel entrance
4. Kirkgate tunnel entrance
5. Millgarth police station
6. Leeds market
▨▨▨ Leeds' underground tunnels

PROLOGUE

East Germany, March 1954

'Killing you would be the easiest thing in the world.' He sat behind the desk, smoking lazily and staring at the other man. 'An industrial accident, maybe. A car crash. Or just a simple disappearance,' he added with a hint of a smile. 'After all, no one would be stupid enough to ask questions about you, would they?'

The '*du*' for 'you', so familiar, a hard reminder of who held the power here. The other man kept his gaze on his lap and shook his head. The words weren't meant to be answered. They were a threat, a little dance of victory. He'd been caught trying to escape from East Germany. Like everyone, he knew the price of capture.

He'd already been beaten in his cell by the time the Stasi officer arrived. Eyes so swollen they were almost closed, his nose broken, five or six teeth gone. Ribs cracked and bruises all over his body. He just hoped nothing was damaged inside. The men had enjoyed their work, making him hurt and yell out. He spat blood into the bucket on the floor and breathed through his mouth. He felt numb, beyond pain.

Failure. Death.

The uniformed men leapt to attention as soon as the officer appeared. He dismissed them, waiting and watching silently as the man slowly sat up. Each tiny movement was painful. He winced and tried to focus.

'Come with me,' the Stasi man ordered finally. There was no compassion in his tone, no feeling at all. 'You look strong enough to walk.' He led the way through a maze of corridors to this plain room, the injured man limping slowly behind, steadying himself with a hand on the concrete block walls. No window in here, just a table and two chairs.

'Do you really think the West is paradise?' the officer asked. He didn't wait for a reply; he didn't need one. 'It's not, although they'd be grateful enough for anyone with special skills. Especially someone from this side of that Iron Curtain they keep talking about. Someone like you.' That *du* again. 'Or perhaps you thought you were so unimportant that no one was watching you?' He leaned forward, elbows on the table, his face close enough to smell the sourness of meat and garlic on his breath. 'Here in the Democratic Republic everyone watches everyone. I'd really hoped you'd be less naïve. And not so stupid.'

The man stubbed out his cigarette and lit another, watching the smoke curl upwards.

'You're a very lucky man today. Very lucky indeed. I'm going to offer you a bargain, and it's one you won't turn down. You're going to go to the West. You're going to see what life is like there.' The man jerked up his head in astonishment. Was this a joke? Was he going to promise the world and then shoot him?

The Stasi officer smiled. 'I thought that would get your attention. Your paradise, just beyond that door.' He inclined his head. 'But you're going to do something for us while you're there. To show your thanks for our mercy. You're going to give us information. Lots of it.' A pause that lasted for a heartbeat. 'You're one of us now, Dieter.'

He laid it out in simple sentences. The freedom, the chances. Then the demands, and finally the threat.

'You won't betray us,' he said quietly, matter-of-factly, counting it all out on stubby, manicured fingers. Not even a trace of nicotine stains. 'You won't run from us. After all, your parents, your sister, her husband and children are still here. If you're ever tempted, just remember that their lives–' he held out his right hand, palm up '–are in my hand.' Slowly, calmly, he closed his fingers to make a fist. 'Always remember that, Dieter.'

CHAPTER ONE

Leeds, November 1957

1957 had been a good year. Plenty of divorce business. The bloom had gone off too many marriages, it seemed; whole bouquets of them shedding their petals. It had kept him busy from January until the middle of October. Now, halfway through November, things were winding down. The petrol rationing that had been in force during the Suez Crisis was a memory. People were thinking ahead to 25 December. Families keeping the peace until Christmas was over. Holding a truce. And that was fine. It would pick up again in the New Year.

Dan Markham sat reading the morning paper, going through every article to tease out the time until dinner. For the last four days no one had come into the office needing his services, and for once the emptiness felt welcome. After so many hectic months he was ready to relax.

He lifted his head as he heard the clump of footsteps on the stairs. A familiar, heavy tread, the ominous, unmistakable sound of a copper. Markham waited as the door opened. Close, he thought when he saw the face; it was an ex-copper. Detective Sergeant Baker, just plain Mr Baker now. He'd retired from the force a year before. But he was dressed exactly the way he always had, an old mackintosh, belted and buttoned up, the trilby pushed down on his head, with a white shirt and striped tie. As portly as ever, maybe even rounder than before, a little more flesh to his jowls. He was carrying a large brown paper bag. Sighing, he settled on the empty chair.

'This is a surprise,' Markham said. They'd ended up working together on a case in 1954. Back then Baker made no secret of his contempt for enquiry agents. The man had been wounded by a bullet and never fully recovered. About the only useful thing to come from it was the uneasy truce the two of them had found. Not friends, but able to rub along together.

'I thought I'd see if you were staying on the straight and narrow.' Baker took off his hat and placed it on the edge of the desk.

'I'm getting by. Enjoying your retirement?'

The man frowned.

'My missus kept going on at me to retire as soon as I could, what with that injury from the shooting, so I had myself invalided out. Now she's on at me to do something and not be under her feet all the time.' He rolled his eyes. 'Women. Never bloody satisfied.'

'You could find something.' He knew Baker had a sharp mind. He was still young enough. And he was honest.

'I daresay,' he agreed. 'It got me thinking, any road. You're on your own here. People tell me you're busy these days. You could use some help. I have plenty of experience.'

Markham smiled. It was the damndest job application he'd ever heard.

'I make enough to support myself. There's not enough to pay two people.'

'Ah, you might be wrong there, lad.' Baker stared squarely at him. 'I've had a quiet word round the stations. They all know me. They'd pass stuff on. Missing persons, little things they don't have the time to deal with properly. Think on. It could more than double your business. Get you out of this divorce lark, too.' He said the words with distaste.

'Are you sure?' Markham said warily.

'I am. I'd not be here otherwise.'

'You always said enquiry agents were parasites,' he reminded the man.

'I did,' Baker admitted and scratched the back of his neck.

'So why do you want to be one?'

'Someone has to keep you honest. It might as well be me.' Baker leaned forward and put the paper bag on the blotter. 'Open it.'

It was heavier than it seemed. Markham slid out a piece of polished brass and turned it over. *Markham & Baker, Enquiry Agents* in bold, solid script. He glanced at the man and raised his eyebrows. He had balls; had to give him that. He did have experience, years of it. Markham was only twenty-eight. And if he did bring in more business …

'If we're going to do it, it ought to look right,' Baker said.

Markham began to laugh.

'We can give it a try. Until the end of the year.'

'Fair enough,' Baker nodded.

'And if it doesn't work, go our separate ways.'

'Can't ask better than that.' He extended his hand and they shook.

'I don't even know your Christian name,' Markham said.

'Stephen.' He shot a warning glance. 'Never Steve. You understand that? I know what you young ones are like. Shorten bloody everything.'

★★★

The next day Baker showed up on the dot of nine, breathing hard from carrying a coat rack. He placed it inside the door, hung up his battered trilby and old mackintosh, taking the *Daily Express* and a screwdriver from the pocket. Then he picked up the brass sign, polished it lightly with a handkerchief and vanished back down the stairs. When Markham went out at eleven it was fixed to the wall by the entry door, proud and shining.

'I tell you what, lad, we're going to need another desk in here,' Baker said later in the day. The next morning he brought in a card table, ugly, scarred wood topped with tatty green baize, followed by another trip carrying a folding chair.

'It's just for the moment,' he said as he set them up. Two days into the partnership and already the office seemed crowded, claustrophobic.

That afternoon they were sitting, listening as gusts of wind blew rain against the window, the drops spattering noisily.

'I'll get a proper desk soon,' Baker promised 'So we look professional.'

'God only knows where we'll make room for it,' Markham told him. 'We're already on top of each other.'

'Get rid of some of those filing cabinets. I had a shufti. They're mostly empty.'

'If you like. And if you can find someone to haul a desk up here.'

Baker smiled and just rubbed the fingers of one hand together.

'A little bit of that is all it'll take. I'll go looking later. We don't have anything on, do we?'

'No. I have to be in court at three, but that's all.' A few minutes of short simple testimony in a divorce case. Markham has discovered the man in a hotel bed with another woman. It had all been set up in advance, of course. A prostitute earning a few easy quid without even having to part her legs.

The telephone rang and he answered with the number, then listened for a moment.

'They want to talk to you,' he told Baker in surprise as he passed over the receiver. It was a short conversation. The man listened, asked a question or two, then finished by saying, 'Why don't you send her over? And thank you, George. I owe you a pint the next time I see you.' He replaced the handset and rubbed his hands together. 'Well, it looks like we have our first case, Dan. A missing person.'

***

The woman looked dowdy. That was the only word for it. A grey wool coat that reached to mid-calf, the fur collar ratty and worn. Brogues on her feet, the laces double-knotted, and small, sensible heels. Greying hair in a tight set under a small black hat. No colour at all about her.

She smelt of old powder and Parma violets, eyes blinking behind her glasses. There was no wedding ring. A spinster whose young man had never returned from the Great War, Markham suspected. One of a generation left on the shelf with not enough bachelors to go around. She certainly looked the right age for it.

'How can we help you, Miss …?'

'Harding,' she replied. A careful, educated accent. 'At the police station they told me you might be able to assist me.' She looked from one of them to the other. 'It's my lodger. He hasn't come home for three days now. That's not like him.'

Markham gave Baker the smallest hint of a nod. Let him take over, he'd probably dealt with cases like this before.

'What's his name, miss?'

'Dieter. Dieter de Vries.'

'De Vries?' Baker asked. 'Foreign, is he?'

'Dutch,' she said. 'He's been with me for two years. Very reliable.' She sniffed and pulled a small handkerchief from her sleeve. 'If he's going somewhere, he always lets me know.' She raised her head. 'That's why I'm worried about him. But the police said that there's not much they can do yet, and they suggested I talk to you.'

'We can look into it,' Baker told her soothingly. Markham sat back to watch. He'd never had a chance to see this side of the man before, the one that gently teased information from someone. And he did it well.

In less than five minutes he learned that de Vries had arrived in Leeds a little before Christmas 1955 from Holland. An engineer, he had a solid job with a company in Holbeck. Kept himself to himself, rarely went out in the evenings. Every few months he'd spend a weekend away, then a week each summer when he went back to Holland to see his family. Very quiet and respectful. Never played the wireless too loud and paid his rent on time every week. Miss Harding cooked his breakfast and tea and he took his dinner at work, she said.

'How did he come to you?' Baker asked when she'd finished. 'Did someone recommend him?'

'I had an advertisement at the newsagent's,' she replied primly. 'But of course I asked for references.'

'Do you remember who vouched for him?'

'I do.' She opened her handbag, brought out two pieces of paper and passed them across the card table. Baker read them quickly.

'His employer and another Dutch gentleman, by the look of it?'

'That's correct. Normally I wouldn't take the chance on someone foreign—' she seemed to sniff again as she pronounced the word '—but he had everything in order.'

'Do you have a photograph of him?'

'No,' she answered in surprise. 'Why would I? He's a lodger, not a friend.'

'Could you describe him, please?' Markham asked. A picture would have been much simpler.

'I suppose so.' Miss Harding closed her eyes for a moment. 'He's about five feet nine inches tall, and I'd say he probably weighs thirteen stone. His face is rather round, brown eyes with heavy bags under them.' She rubbed her own face to illustrate what she meant. 'Pale lips, quite full. And he's bald. The only hair he has is on the sides and back of his head. There are some small scars on his face. He told me they were from the war.'

'What would he have been wearing when he went missing?' Baker had been taking notes.

'A suit, white shirt, and tie, I suppose. Black shoes, well-polished. He was very careful of that, cleaned his shoes every evening.'

'Have you taken a look in his room at all?'

The woman looked horrified.

'Of course not. That's his.'

'It might help us to have a look in there,' Baker said gently. 'There might be some indication as to where he's gone, or why.' He smiled at her. 'If you want us to look for him then we need to be able to do our job properly.'

'I suppose so,' she agreed after a little hesitation. 'If you feel it's necessary.'

'It would be helpful. Why don't you go home and I'll come around a bit later and see what I can find.'

She nodded quickly, comforted by what he said. Baker was old enough for her to take seriously. He looked confident, as if he'd covered this ground before. And he probably had.

'Is there something I need to do to employ you?' she asked.

'Just pay us a retaining fee,' Markham told her with an easy smile.

She delved in her handbag and came out with two crisp five-pound notes.

'I trust this is enough.'

'Of course. More than enough.' He wrote out a receipt. She read and folded it methodically before putting it away. She seemed to be the type of woman who kept a lifetime of paper.

'We'll need to know where you live, too,' Baker said. Miss Harding gave her address, a respectable street in Headingley, and they heard her solid footsteps going down the stairs.

'Well, lad, what do you make of that?'

Markham shrugged.

'More your territory than mine.'

'True enough,' Baker agreed. 'Odds are he's met someone and gone off for a randy few days. That's usually the way it goes. He'll turn up when he's had enough. But I'll stop by on my way home and have a look-see. You never know.'

'You're probably right.' He wasn't giving it much thought, sorting through a folder, pulling out the items he'd need for the divorce hearing later.

'I might take a wander over to Holbeck and have a word at that company he works for. They should be able to tell me something.'

'If they'll talk to you. Remember, you're not on the force now.'

'Don't you worry,' Baker told him. 'They'll talk to me.'

***

He was in and out of court in under half an hour. Called to the stand he said his piece, identified the photographs and the husband, then walked back to the office on Albion Place, cutting down Lands Lane by the afternoon bustle of Schofield's department store. The air smelt fresher, less of the thick, endless smog that used to always choke autumn and winter. It looked as if the new Clean Air Act was doing some good.

When he opened the door, Baker was pacing around, his heavy face set, the pipe clamped in his jaw.

'Something wrong?' Markham asked.

'You could say that.' He stopped and tapped the bowl out into an ashtray. 'I went down to Mortimer's. You know, where de Vries works.'

'Well?'

'They looked at me like I was stark raving mad. No one called Dieter de Vries has ever been employed there.'

CHAPTER TWO

'What?' Markham said in disbelief. 'You're pulling my leg.'

'I wish I bloody well was.'

'Then there has to be a mistake.'

'I was in their personnel department. They should know who works there, and there's not a trace of any Dieter de Vries. Not now, not in the past.' He thrust his hands into his trouser pockets.

'Maybe Miss Harding had the wrong place.'

'Did she strike you as the type to make mistakes like that?'

No, he had to admit it. She was exact. Thorough, scrupulous.

'We'd better go and take a look.' He glanced at his wristwatch. 'I can't take too long, though. I'm meeting someone at six.'

'One of your fancy women?' Baker snorted.

'The only one I have.'

He'd promised to take her out. Nothing special. Something to eat, then down to Studio 20, the jazz club in Leeds. There was a rumour that George Melly might be performing. The man was a bit too traditional for his taste, but he always put on a good, entertaining show. And Georgina was eager to go and perhaps pick up a few tips by watching a real professional at work.

He'd met her one empty Friday evening. Restless, unable to settle, he'd gone to a party. As soon as he arrived it felt like a bad idea. The house was full of people who were too bright, too loud, as if they could will themselves into having a good time.

He sat in the front room, letting the conversations and flirtations ebb and flow around him. A baby grand piano sat by the window. But the only music was skiffle and pop from a record player in the other room. Another ten minutes and he'd go, he decided.

When someone called out, 'George. Come on, give us a song,' he groaned inside and stood by the door to leave without a fuss. The woman who settled on the piano stool and lifted the lid looked uneasy, reluctant, taking a sip of gin and putting the glass down before running her hands over the keys. Then she closed her eyes for a moment and started to play.

At first he couldn't pick out a tune, listening through the haze of voices. But the room quietened as she continued and he understood that she was lulling them, drawing in their attention. The melody began to take shape in the chords of the left hand as the right improvised like George Shearing, hinting and nudging here and there before finally settling so that faces began to smile as they recognised it. 'A Foggy Day In London Town.' The woman opened her mouth, her singing low and languorous, as if it was emerging from a distant dream.

She had something. Not a Billie or a Sarah. But there was a velvet sensuality in her tone, hinting at intimacy and soft memories. Then she let her hands take over again, pushing down on the sustain pedal to let chords hang and fade until it all drifted off into the distance.

The applause was polite. People returned to their talk. She took another drink, looking around and blinking, emerging from somewhere else. As she stood he walked over.

'You're very good,' he told her. She didn't blush, just looked him in the eye.

'It's what I do. At night, anyway.'

'You play well, too. A lot of Shearing in there.'

That made her smile.

'I'm Georgina Taylor.' She extended a thin, pale arm.

'Dan Markham,' he said as they shook.

'And I only sound like Shearing because I'm not good enough to be Monk or Tatum.' She spoke the words like a challenge: did he know what he was talking about or was it all bluff?

'No one else can ever sound like Thelonious,' he answered. 'And Tatum …' He shook his head. 'You'd need two more hands. Are you a professional?'

The woman looked embarrassed.

'Trying,' she admitted. 'I do nightclubs when I can. It's hard to get a gig. Working behind the counter at Boots pays the bills. For now, anyway,' she added with determination.

He tried to imagine her in the nylon overall, selling medicines and make-up, but he couldn't reconcile it with the woman he'd just heard performing.

'How about you?' she asked. 'What do you do?'

'I'm an enquiry agent,' he said and her eyes widened.

★★★

The next night they met for a meal and wandered through town to Studio 20. As they walked she told him a little about herself, short sentences with long pauses. She'd grown up in Malton, married young, a couple of years after the war. The decree nisi had come through in July. Leeds had been a fresh start, a chance for her to do more with her music.

'I've never been here before,' she admitted as they went down the stairs to the club. 'I don't know anyone who really likes jazz.'

'You do now.'

The place was packed, hardly room to stand among the young men and women. In the corner a quintet was playing. Three guitars, bass, and a ragged washboard offering rhythm.

Skiffle. Markham glanced at Bob Barclay, the club's owner, sitting in his booth. He gave an eloquent shrug.

'The Vipers,' he said. 'They're up from London, had a big hit. Brings in the money. You can see for yourself, Dan. I've never had the place so full. Still, it lets me put on other things. There's not the market for jazz there was a few years back.'

Disappointed, they left. She tucked her arm through his.

'I'm sorry.'

'Hardly your fault.' She tried to smile, but it was a weak effort. 'It's the same all over. Everyone wants pop music now.'

He saw her again on Wednesday and the following week-end. Soon she was spending some nights at his flat, or he'd stay over in her bedsit in Hyde Park. Six months later and they were still meeting up a couple of times a week. Going out, his mother would have said. Nothing too serious; more than friends but never likely to end up engaged.

Whenever she performed Markham would be there, sitting in the corner of a club with endless cups of coffee, applauding every song. She had talent, but Leeds wasn't a place where it could ever have the chance to flower.

***

The house was a sturdy Edwardian villa with a postage-stamp front garden and lace curtains on the windows, no more than a stone's throw from the Cottage Road cinema.

'Just what you'd expect,' Baker said as he eased himself out of the Ford Anglia. The rain had started again, a half-hearted, chilly shower. Markham patted the hat down on his head as they approached the door.

At home, Miss Harding seemed more sure of herself, usher-ing them into a dusty front room before offering tea, perching herself on the edge of an easy chair that had been in fashion half a century before. A faded picture of a young soldier stood in a silver frame on the mantelpiece.

Baker went over the details again, confirming where de Vries worked.

'Do you know what kind of position he held?'

'An engineer of some kind. That's what he told me. He tried to explain it once, but it didn't make much sense. It was a technical job, I know that.'

Baker made another note, then said, 'Right, we'd better take a look at his room.'

'Is that really necessary?' She made a face as if a bad smell had wafted through the room.

'If you want us to find him, luv,' he said easily and she nodded agreement after a long pause. 'You're hiring us for what we can do, but we need all the background we can find.'

Miss Harding marched over to the polished oak sideboard and removed a key from the top drawer.

'The second door on the right upstairs. I'd be grateful if you didn't make a mess.'

★★★

It was nondescript. A cast-iron bedstead, the sheets and blankets tucked in place with tight hospital corners. Bright rag rugs on the floorboards. A dressing table and a wardrobe with ornate carved legs. An easy chair sat by the light of the window, a small table next to it. A filled, waist-high bookcase. Baker stood just inside the doorway for a little while, looking around slowly.

'Something's wrong here,' he said finally.

'It seems ordinary enough.'

'Too ordinary, that's the thing. Do you smell something?'

Markham sniffed.

'Brylcreem?' He thought quickly. 'Didn't she say he was bald?'

'Easy enough to check. Take a dekko in the bathroom.'

It was the closed door at the end of the hall. One shelf held a man's toiletries – safety razor, shaving brush, a half-empty tube of toothpaste and a toothbrush. Fixative for false teeth.

'No Brylcreem,' he reported when he returned.

'I reckon someone's been in here having a look around when the landlady wasn't at home.'

'Too neat?'

'Too exact. And don't tell me your place is tidy. I've seen that tip you call home.'

He'd searched the flat once, three years before, when Markham had been a murder suspect and Baker the detective investigating the crime.

'Nothing to find, you think?'

The older man shook his head.

'I doubt it. Not if a professional's been over the place. Still, we'll have a look.'

He was right. Half an hour of going through everything turned up no photographs of the man. Nothing to indicate he might not be who he claimed. No passport or driving licence. A couple of suits hung in the wardrobe, along with some shirts, ties, a sports jacket and slacks. Thirty-eight-inch chest, probably about five feet six tall, size nine shoes. The books were paperbacks, all in English. Standard fiction fare, everything from Ian Fleming to Graham Greene. He flipped through each one quickly; nothing hidden inside.

It wasn't much.

'Are you going to tell her?' Markham asked quietly.

'Tell her what, lad?'

'About where he was supposed to have worked.'

'Not yet.' He tapped the side of his nose. 'Never show your hand too early. Always a good rule, especially when there's something fishy going on.'

Baker returned the key to Miss Harding. She stood by the front door like a mother hen guarding her brood.

'Did you find anything?' she asked.

'No,' Baker told her. 'Has anyone been in there since he left?'

'Of course not,' she answered. 'Mr de Vries always does his own cleaning, every Sunday. I have no reason to enter his private room.'

'Can you remind me what he was wearing the last time you saw him?' The question seemed casual but he was listening intently.

'His overcoat. I remember that, because it was cold out. And a hat; he always wore a hat.'

'What colour was the coat?'

'Navy blue,' Miss Harding said, as if no decent coat would be any other shade.

'Thank you.' Baker stroked his chin. 'We'll have a report for you in a day or so. If he gets in touch ...'

'I'll let you know immediately. Of course. What do you think's happened to him?'

'Early days yet.' He gave her a reassuring smile and patted her hand. 'Don't you worry.'

They stood by the Anglia. Baker brought out a pouch and filled his pipe, lighting it with a match and puffing until he was satisfied.

'So we have three questions about him now,' Markham said. 'Where he's gone, why someone would search his room, and where the hell he works.'

'Four,' Baker corrected him. 'Who is he really?'

'We should give it back to the police.'

'What for? He might not be who he claims to be to his landlady, but that's not an offence. He hasn't tried to profit from it that we know of. Don't you want to know what's going on?'

'Not really.' The last time he'd got involved in dirty business, two fingers on his left hand had been broken. Twice. He still couldn't use them, and probably never would. They were like claws, bent, a reminder to carry for the rest of his life.

'I'm curious, any road. This is the best fun I've had since I left the force. And we don't have anything better to do, do we?'

'I suppose not,' Markham agreed reluctantly. 'But the first sign of it becoming dangerous and we stop.' The man who'd crippled his fingers had also shot Baker.

'Right enough.' He checked his watch. 'You'd better get a move on. Won't do to keep her waiting.'

'Do you want a lift home?'

'No thanks, lad. It'll do me good to stretch my legs.' He knew what that meant – stopping at the Skyrack for a pint before making his way back to Burley. 'We'll talk about it in the morning. Maybe a good night's sleep will bring some ideas.'

***

She was waiting under the Ball-Dyson clock on Lower Briggate, clutching her handbag in front of her. Georgina had changed clothes at work, wearing a knitted top and a slim skirt with seamed stockings and patent high heels, a heavy wool coat over her shoulders.

'Busy day?' he asked as he kissed her on the cheek.

'So-so.' There was never much to say about shop work, unless she had a particularly amusing or awful customer. 'How about you? Things fine with Mr Baker?' She gave an impish grin that reached all the way to her eyes.

'It's getting interesting,' he told her. 'Let's put it like that.'

'Good interesting or bad?'

'I'm not sure yet,' he said after a moment. Tomorrow would tell. 'Where do you fancy eating?'

They settled on Jacomelli's. It was close and always reliable. A chilly wind blew from the river as they strolled up Briggate after the meal. Georgina slipped her arm through his. It was comfortable, companionable. Loving.

The notice on the door of Studio 20 announced that Melly had cancelled due to illness. It was disappointing, but hardly the end of the world.

'Do you want to go in anyway?' he asked.

'Not really,' she decided, looking up at him. 'Do you mind if we just go home?'

He set the choke before the started the Anglia. The motor caught after a second, wheezed, then fired. It was growing old. Maybe the time had come to replace it. A Ford Popular, maybe; he didn't need something that would break the sound barrier. Just a car that would stop and go when he wanted and not cost him a fortune.

'Whose home?' he asked.

'Yours?' She kicked off the shoes and waggled her toes. 'God, that's better. They've been killing me all day.'

There was hardly any traffic on Harrogate Road. The November night was too cold to tempt many people out. A few places showed Christmas decorations in the windows, one tree neatly lit up. He didn't want to think about it. When he was young Christmas had been fun, waking early to check the pillowcase at the end of his bed for presents. But the war had changed all that. The magic vanished. There were more important things than gifts on one day of the year. And there'd been precious little joy for years afterwards, just the bleakness of rationing for so long. Grey lives.

He pulled in behind the house and led the way up the stairs. Inside, the flat was cold. He switched on both bars of the electric fire to heat the place. Georgina began to leaf through his records, still wearing her coat.

'Who was that man you played me the other week?' she asked.

He tried to recall who she meant. It seemed as if half his spare money went on the records he ordered from Dobell's in London. It was the only place in England that stocked American jazz. He'd developed a taste for it during his National Service in Germany, working in military intelligence with an American soldier who'd introduced him to the music.

'You mean Herbie Nichols?' Markham remembered suddenly.

'That's the one.' Her fingers moved quickly and she drew out an LP, reverently placing the disc on the turntable. *The Prophetic Herbie Nichols, Volume 1.* An apt title.

The spare sound of piano, bass and drums filled the flat. It wasn't warm or intimate. Everything was angular, awkward, as if the corners would never fit snugly. She was listening intently; trying to work out just what Nichols was doing, what he was thinking.

He handed her a glass of wine. A mug of coffee for him. Real coffee, not Camp. He'd been given a proper Italian coffee pot and used it every day. Each time, he thought of the woman who'd brought it back from her travels, long gone from his life now. He still saw her name here and there in the papers, one of an upcoming generation of artists.

The second track ended and Georgina shook her head.

'It's lovely, but …'

'But it's not you?' he asked.

She smiled.

'Never in a million years.'

She liked songs, something with definite form and feeling. And she had the voice to do them justice. All she needed was a chance. A couple of clubs aiming for sophistication had offered her early evening slots. Background music for the drinkers who came in after work.

'I can't do that,' she told Markham after she'd turned them down. 'I can't just … be there, like a soundtrack. I want people to listen.'

'Maybe they will,' he suggested.

She just shook her head, dark hair flailing around her shoulders.

'No. And if they started, the manager would sack me. They want something unobtrusive. Something easy.'

A few times she'd broached the idea of moving to London, to try her hand there. He knew it was what her musical career needed. But he'd miss her. She was undemanding, easy. Passionate when they both needed that.

'There are trains,' she told him. 'It's only a few hours away. And there's plenty of jazz to listen to down there.' Georgina raised her eyebrows as she looked at him.

Everything she said was true. Still, he knew the likely outcome. Life and distance would take over. She'd develop new friends, a new career. The visits would dwindle, becoming fewer until they vanished altogether.

***

'Why don't you put on some Sarah Vaughan?' he suggested as the stylus clicked in the end groove. They were curled up together, his arm around her shoulders.

'You do it,' Georgina said sleepily. 'I don't want to move.'

He chose the album with Clifford Brown on trumpet. It was the singer at her best, making each song her own as the horn glided around and about her.

'This thing you're working on,' she said. 'It all sounds very mysterious.'

'Yes, it does,' he replied, and realised he hadn't thought about Dieter de Vries all evening.

CHAPTER THREE

He parked the Anglia on Albion Place, kissing Georgina as she headed off for another day behind the shop counter. She had her shoulders hunched against the winter cold, heels clicking swiftly on the pavement.

Baker was already in the office. The newspaper lay unopened in front of him on the card table. The air was thick with the fog of shag tobacco.

'About time you made it in,' he said. 'I've been here for half an hour.'

Markham looked at his watch. Not even quarter to nine yet. Still early. He lit a Craven A.

'Why so early?'

'This de Vries thing's been bothering me all night,' Baker said. 'Made me dyspeptic. I keep wondering what's so special about him that someone would go through his room? How would they even know he was gone?'

'I still think we should give this back to the police,' Markham told him.

'I don't think there's anything they can do that we can't.' But there was a satisfied look on his face. He'd found something to worry at, something to claim his time and his knowledge. 'Not at the moment, anyway.'

'Then what do you reckon we ought to do? We've got nothing.'

Baker stroked his chin thoughtfully.

'Take a look at what we do have and try to pick up the trail from there. It's what I'd have done on the force.'

Markham unbuttoned his jacket and sat behind his desk. For once, the radiator was working well, churning out heat.

'So what exactly is there?' He pulled a pad and pencil towards him.

'He came here two years ago,' Baker began.

'To Leeds,' Markham pointed out. 'We don't know how long he's been in England.'

'Right enough. I did wonder something, though. Vanishing men and rooms being searched, it's all very cloak and dagger.'

'Go on.'

'That got me thinking he might not even be who he claims,' Baker continued. 'Doesn't work where he said. Perhaps he wasn't even Dutch, I don't know. I'll go and ask her if he ever received any post. He worked somewhere. He had money to live on.'

'True.'

'And from his clothes we know he wasn't a manual labourer.'

Markham added a note to the page.

'So he probably had a bank account, you mean.'

'You're catching on,' Baker said approvingly. 'We took a look and didn't see anything. So either he took all the papers with him, which meant he wasn't planning on coming back for some reason …'

'Or whoever searched the place grabbed them.'

'Exactly. Which means they *know* he's not coming back and there's some covering up going on.'

Markham frowned.

'Who?'

'Spies. The whole thing stinks of them. Like that friend of yours who died.'

He hadn't thought about Ged in a long time, he realised guilt-ily. He'd died, shot in the chair where Markham was sitting now.

'Let's hope it's not,' he said, not trusting his voice to form more words.

'You tell me what's going on, then?' Baker pulled out a box of Swan Vestas, struck one, and started puffing on his pipe. 'That's what we've got to find out.'

The bell of the telephone seemed too loud in the room. Markham waited a moment, lifted the receiver and answered with the number.

'Is that Dan Markham?' A woman's voice. A hint of education in the pronunciation, but it was played down into smokiness.

'That's right. How can I help you, Miss—'

'Fox,' she replied. 'Mrs Fox. And I hope you can help us.' She placed a gentle emphasis on the final word.

'That depends what you need.'

'I work with my husband. Perhaps you've heard of him? Mark Fox.'

Of course he had. Fox was the competition, the only other enquiry agent in Leeds. He had an office in Woodhouse Square, a step up from Markham's, a gently moneyed place.

'Yes,' he replied. 'I've never met him, though.'

'He's out of the country at the moment. But there's something come up where you might be able to assist us. I can offer you some fair money for your time. Unless you're too busy, of course.'

'I'm happy to talk about it, Mrs Fox.' It seemed odd. Who would ever give business away? Fox had opened his office in '55, coming to Leeds from somewhere down south. Yet in two years their paths had never crossed.

'Good.' He sensed her smile. 'How about over luncheon? Let's keep it civilised.'

'Fine,' he agreed. She picked somewhere on East Parade, a restaurant favoured by local bankers and businessmen.

'We'll make it at noon,' she finished. 'I'll book a table and see you then.'

'You look pleased,' Baker said when the call ended. 'On a promise, are you?'

'Maybe some work. That was Mark Fox's wife. They might have a job for us.'

'Him?' He snorted. 'There were all sorts of rumours about him when he first appeared up here. I'd trust him as far as you can throw him.'

'I'll be seeing the wife,' Markham said. 'Evidently he's out of the country. Can't hurt to hear what she says.'

'As long as she's picking up the bill.'

'Always. Still, I'm glad I wore a decent suit.'

'While you're eating I'll go back up to Headingley and ask a few more questions. Maybe have another look in that room de Vries had. See if we can find an answer or two.'

'Two days. We'll give de Vries that long. Then it goes back to the police. Sooner if you discover anything nasty.'

'You're the boss,' Baker said amiably.

Yes, Markham thought. He was. And he wasn't going to be sucked into anything bad again. Once had been too much. Too deadly.

***

'I'm sorry,' she said breathlessly as the waiter pulled out a chair for her. There was a shhh of nylon as she sat. 'Have you been waiting long?' The woman held out a hand and he shook it lightly.

'Not really, Mrs Fox.'

'Amanda,' she told him. 'Please.'

'Amanda,' he echoed as she pulled a cigarette from her handbag and he flicked his lighter. 'Now, what's all this about?'

She'd arrived late, escorted over by the waiter. In her early thirties, he judged, and wearing a close-fitting grey jersey dress that reached to her knees. It flattered her and she knew it, moving easily on high heels. Dark hair in an Italian cut, subtle makeup and a graceful, Audrey Hepburn face.

He'd had time to sit, staring around the restaurant and smoking. The place was new, fitted out in leather and oak, wanting to appear expensive, solid and timeless. The year before it had been different. Another couple of years it would be something else again.

'Let's wait a few minutes for that.' Her eyes were bright, a deep, mysterious blue. 'We'll eat first. I always like pleasure before business, don't you?' It was a gentle tease. 'I'm surprised we've never met before.'

'It's just how things are, I suppose.'

She carried an air of sophistication, assured, in control. Next to her he felt juvenile, provincial. She ordered quickly, as if she knew the menu by heart. He decided on steak and kidney pie. Very English. Very filling and plain.

'Then I'm glad to finally change that.' She flashed a brilliant smile, very white teeth and blood-red lips.

'You said your husband's abroad?'

She nodded.

'Germany. We do quite a bit of business over there, he's gone a few times each year, Bonn, West Berlin.' She shrugged. He tried to place her accent. Somewhere in the Home Counties, a good education. But grammar school, not private he decided. Then plenty of polish.

'I wouldn't have thought there was much for an enquiry agent over there.'

'Oh.' She lit a cigarette and waved the words away in a thick plume of smoke. 'Still the fallout from the war. Tell me about yourself, Mr Markham.'

'Dan.'

Amanda Fox nodded her acknowledgement, staring at him coolly.

'You must have started in this game when you were young.'

'Seven years ago. I was twenty-one.'

'Are you good at what you do?'

'I like to think so,' he replied with a soft smile.

'There was some business a while ago, wasn't there?' She tapped her cigarette in the crystal ashtray. 'Before we moved here.'

'Yes.' He wasn't about to say more. If she knew, she'd already read the newspaper clippings and heard the gossip.

The food arrived and they made small talk – the weather, the way traffic grew worse each month – until the plates had been cleared and coffee sat in front of them.

'Do you know Germany at all?' Amanda Fox asked as she lit another cigarette and blew smoke towards the ceiling. He tried to read her face but she was giving nothing away.

'I did my National Service there.'

'Really?' Her eyes smiled for a moment. 'Where were you?'

'Hamburg, mostly. Some time in West Berlin. I was military intelligence.'

'Mark was there after the fighting ended. Stayed there for a couple of years, then Vienna. He made some good contacts. Maybe you met him?'

'Was he an officer?'

'A captain. Why?'

'We didn't mix too much with them.'

'Of course, sorry. Do you speak the lingo?'

'A little.' He'd learned enough to get by. 'What about you?' Markham asked. 'What do you do?'

'Oh, I just help around the office.' She said it dismissively, as if she was just a secretary or receptionist. He didn't believe a word of it.

'What does your husband do in Germany?'

'Background stuff, mostly. Checking on people that companies want to bring over. The whole denazification process wasn't always thorough, shall we say?' She flashed him another white smile. 'Mark goes into more depth.'

'I thought that would be government business.'

'They farm some of it out. As I said, Mark has contacts.'

He nodded. The old boys' network in action. The way everything was done in this country.

'And what would you want from me?'

'Let me ask you something, Dan. You were in intelligence. Did you have to sign the Official Secrets Act?'

'Of course.'

'Good,' she said with a smile. 'That makes everything much easier.'

'Why?' Suddenly Markham was very suspicious. 'What do you want?'

'It's nothing much. Just keeping an occasional eye on people who end up around here.'

'People?' he asked sharply. 'What people?'

Amanda Fox glanced around the restaurant before she answered and spoke very quietly, 'Germans who would be useful to our defence industry.'

'From the West or East?' That was important.

'East, of course,' she replied coolly. 'We work with the Gehlen people in West Berlin, bring them out, give them new names and backgrounds. I'm sure you can understand why.'

Of course. No one in this country would be happy to have a German around. Not with the war still so close in memory.

'The government knows?' He wanted to be certain.

'It's their idea, Dan. These men all have good skills.'

'I don't understand, why can't you do it yourselves?' he wondered.

'Mark is gone so often. We're pretty much a one-man band. As I said, I just look after the office. What we need is someone who has the skills and background.' Now he was certain she knew all about him; this wasn't lucky dip and hope for the best on her part. 'We pay generously,' she added, 'and it won't take a great deal of your time.' She cocked an eyebrow. 'Does it sound interesting?'

'Maybe. I'll need to talk to my partner. He's ex-police.'

'All right,' she agreed, but he saw he'd sprung something unexpected on her.

'We'll talk about it and I'll be in touch.' He shook her hand as he rose. 'Don't worry, he'll have had to sign the Act, too. I'll give you a ring on Monday, Mrs Fox.'

'Amanda,' she corrected him.

'Of course. Amanda.'

***

He strolled thoughtfully back through town. There was a weekend eagerness in the Friday afternoon crowds. Women squeezed past the top-hatted doorman to spend their wages at Marshall & Snelgrove's department store. An older generation sat upstairs in Fuller's and sipped tea.

He wondered exactly what Amanda Fox and her mysterious husband wanted. More than the job she'd promised, he was certain of that.

Baker hadn't returned yet. He spent a while cleaning up some of the paperwork, filing notes and pictures and cleaning off his desk. The card table sat there accusingly, a paperback book under one of the legs to keep it steady. They needed something more professional if people were going to take them seriously.

By four he was still on his own, desk clean, everything put away. No rain yet, but the skies were as heavy as slate. Should he wait, or simply call it a day and beat the traffic out on Harrogate Road?

He was just emerging on to the street when he heard a shout and saw Baker turning the corner from Lands Lane.

'Let's go and get a cuppa,' he said as he lumbered close, hands deep in his raincoat pockets, eyes serious.

Upstairs at the Kardomah, Markham ordered coffee from Joyce, the waitress he'd known for years. Tea and a slice of Dundee cake for Baker. He waited until the man had poured sugar into his drink.

'You don't look too happy.'

'Well …' he began, taking his pipe from a bulging suit pocket and lighting it. 'I am and I'm not. That Miss Harding was about as helpful as she was yesterday. But I finally got her to let me look at the post that had arrived for our friend in the last few days. She had it locked away in a bureau.'

'And?'

He pulled out an onionskin aerogramme and let it fall on the table.

'Just some "Dear Occupant" bumf and this. She didn't notice me take it. I had a look inside.'

He opened it slowly and carefully. Dutch stamps and a Rotterdam postmark. Markham began to read then glanced up quickly.

'See what I mean?' Baker asked. 'That's Kraut, isn't it?'

'It is,' Markham answered.

'Why would a Dutchman be writing in German?'

Markham let the question hang as he scanned the words. Either his German was rustier than he thought, or half of this didn't make sense. He looked again, taking his time, trying to put a meaning to it all. He could follow a few sentences here and there. The rest was gibberish. 'Did you speak it?' he asked.

'Never learnt. Why? What does it say?'

'That's the problem. It doesn't.'

Baker look confused.

'It's got to say summat.'

'A few sentences do. "Took the train to Magdeburg." Then there's "Across by Salzwedel." They're both in East Germany. A couple more like that, place names in the DDR. The rest is just nonsense.'

'Are you sure it's not just you?'

'Positive.' He folded the letter. 'I tell you what, Stephen, we're in over our heads with this one.'

CHAPTER FOUR

'You're the one who's done all this spy malarkey,' Baker said glumly.

'A long time ago.' Markham rubbed his chin. 'It's funny, though ...'

'What is?'

'The meal I had with Fox's wife.'

'What about it? I've seen her once. She has that look about her.'

'A vamp?' He shrugged. Whatever charm she had was wasted on him. 'Seems her husband spends a lot of time in West Germany. Sometimes he brings people over from the East.'

'What sort of people?' Baker asked sharply.

'She didn't say exactly,' Markham replied. 'But professionals, probably. People companies here need. Scientists. Engineers.' He let the word hang.

'What did she want?'

'They want us to follow up on whichever of them settles locally. Check up on them and make sure they're behaving themselves.' He tapped a nail against the aerogramme. 'Odd timing, isn't it? Right as one of them vanishes.'

'Sounds a little dubious to me,' Baker said.

'Official Secrets Act stuff.'

'I don't know that I like it.'

'We follow up, write a report. That's the limit of our involvement. No skin off our nose if they disappear. The money's good.'

Baker was silent, thoughtful.

'So do you think this de Vries or whoever he really is might be one of them?'

Markham finished the last of his coffee.

'Bit of a coincidence, don't you think?'

'There's no such beast. You ought to know that by know.' He paused, wiping cake crumbs from his mouth with a serviette. 'That changes the whole complexion, doesn't it?'

'Maybe. Maybe not. Like I said, we check up on them and write our report. That's all. I told her I wanted to talk to my partner first.'

'If you want my vote, I say we accept and keep looking into all this,' Baker said finally. 'There's something going on, we might as well know what it is. We have Miss Harding's money, too, remember.'

'I said I'd let Mrs Fox know at the start of the week. No rush, is there?'

'Only for this chap who's missing.' Baker slid the letter back into his jacket. 'Whoever he really is.'

***

He was at a loose end, at home alone for the evening. He picked *Blue Train* from the pile of LPs, John Coltrane weaving magic on tenor sax, working through the sweet, soft changes of the title track. Not blues the way most people thought of them, but an indigo mood that settled in the mind. He stood at the window, staring down at Harrogate Road. Time passed; lights winked out in the shops and the traffic grew lighter.

The record ended and he let silence take over. He could drift down to Studio 20 later, but somehow it didn't appeal. As he grew older he was less eager to be out in the evening. Like the song said, he didn't get around much anymore.

First, though, some Monk. He'd read that Coltrane was playing with the man now. That would be something to hear. But he'd never raise the money to fly to New York. Or the will. Instead he lowered the stylus on *Brilliant Corners*, with its fragmented, elliptical beauty. It was music that tugged perfectly at him, drew him out of himself, like someone thrown into the middle of a complex puzzle of time, harmony and melody.

***

The telephone was ringing. He blinked his eyes and glanced at the clock on the bedside table. Quarter past five, the luminous hands read. Still pitch dark. Who the hell could it be at this time?

There was a chill in the living room, enough to make him shiver as he lifted the receiver.

'I hope this is important,' he said. There was frost on the outside of the window, making the harsh light of the street lamps blurry.

'I'm not calling you at this hour for my bloody health,' Baker answered. 'I'm down at the office. Can you get here?'

'Why? What is it?'

'Just get yourself here.' He hung up, letting the line buzz.

***

Twenty minutes and Markham was dashing up the stairs on Albion Place. He'd tried to imagine what could be so important and come up with nothing.

Baker was sitting at the table, a deck of cards laid out for a game of patience, the pipe clamped tight in his jaws.

'This had better be good,' Markham said.

'Keep your coat on. We're going somewhere.'

'Stop being so bloody mysterious.'

'You'll see,' Baker said from the doorway. 'Are you coming or are you just going to stand there gawping?'

They walked down Briggate and turned on to Call Lane, passing the abandoned warehouses that seemed to creak with age. A ginnel brought them out by the river, a hundred yards east of Leeds Bridge. The air was bitter.

Close by, someone had rigged up some spotlights. Policemen were milling around, uniforms and plain clothes. Markham glanced at Baker, but the man just walked towards the scene, greeting old colleagues he saw.

A fellow of about fifty took him aside and began to speak quickly in a low voice. Baker nodded then waved Markham over.

'George, meet Dan, my new partner. Dan Markham, this is Inspector George Wills. He's the one who told Miss Harding to see us. They pulled a body out of the water a couple of hours ago.'

'DeVries?'

'There's a Dutch label in the jacket. That's what made me think,' Wills explained. 'We're going to have his landlady come to the mortuary in the morning, see if she can identify him. I was wondering what you two had managed to dig up.'

***

They sat in the canteen at Millgarth Police Station. It was hot, steamy as a Turkish bath, and the smell of bacon and fried bread filled the air. A bright chequered oilcloth covered the table. Half-empty cups of stewed tea sat in front of them. Wills stubbed out his third cigarette and immediately lit another. His fingers had bright nicotine stains and his face belonged to a man who'd been awake far too long, the skin drawn tight over the bones.

He glanced at the aerogramme once more.

'You're certain most of this is rubbish?'

'Positive,' Markham said for the fifth time. He'd forgotten a lot of the German he'd learned, but not everything. Not by a long chalk.

Wills rubbed his chin. He was about to say something when one of the uniforms entered and handed him a piece of paper.

'They've done a quick examination at the body. No sign of any violence. Water in the lungs. Looks like chummy drowned, whoever the hell he is. The coroner will likely go with a verdict of suicide. Miss Harding should be over there now. They'll ring if there's a confirmation.'

'And if there's not?' Baker asked.

'Back to square one.' Wills sighed. 'Not that we're much past it even if she says it's him. Why couldn't the bugger have floated to the other side? Hunslet could have had him then.' He stood. 'They won't be doing the full PM until Monday. I'll ring you when I know something, Stephen.'

He walked off, hardly making a sound in a pair of brown suede shoes, head bowed under the weight of it all.

'You think it's de Vries, don't you?' Markham asked.

'I know it is. I can feel it in my water,' Baker answered.

'Then it's not our problem any more.'

'Eh?' Baker turned sharply.

'Miss Harding has her answer as to what happened to him.'

'We can't leave it like that.'

'She's hardly going to pay us to find out more,' Markham pointed out. 'And we don't do charity cases. Anyway, we don't have the resources.' He put the packet of Craven As in the pocket of his sports jacket. 'I'm off. There's nothing more here.'

On the way back to the car he stopped at the market. Fruit and vegetables from the outside stalls. Carrots and parsnips, apples and pears. A pound of King Edwards, dirt still clinging to the skins.

There was no rush. He had all Saturday ahead and no plans.

A couple of chops from one of the butchers, then past the flower seller and up the metal staircase to the cafe. Condensation clung to the windows. He ordered toast and tea and settled by the window, wiping a space clear to look down on the Saturday crowds.

'You'll make someone a lovely little wife doing the shopping like that.'

He looked up to see a man holding a cup of coffee and smirking. Trevor Peel. Clever Trevor.

'Haven't see you in a while, Trev. I was starting to wonder if they'd banged you up again.'

'Nah.' Uninvited, he sat down. Peel was in his early twenties, hair greased into a high quiff, wearing a donkey jacket and American blue jeans. His sallow cheeks still had faint red spots, the hangover of teenage acne. He brought out tobacco and papers and began to roll a cigarette. 'I'd have to be a bad lad for them to put me away. I've been keeping my nose clean.'

That was hard to believe. Trevor had been in and out of Armley Jail, a fortnight here, thirty days there. Three months once. All minor things: shoplifting, a scuffle. Once he'd been caught trying to walk out of the music shop in County Arcade with a guitar under his arm.

'Seriously, Mr Markham. I've got a good job now. You know Cokely's out towards Yeadon? I've got on with them. They're talking about sending me to night school,' he added proudly, and held up a motorcycle helmet. 'Even bought meself a bike.'

'Given up on the music?'

They'd met at Studio 20. Markham had wandered in, hoping for jazz and finding skiffle. Trevor had been bouncing up and down like a lunatic, a broad grin on his face.

'Those are my mates,' he'd said to anyone who'd listen. 'They got it, don't they?'

What they had was the standard tea chest bass and washboard. But the guitarist had rhythm, some basic ability, and a voice that sounded genuinely American.

'They're going to have me with them as soon as I learn to play,' Trevor added. That had been over a year ago.

'Can't get the hang of it, Mr Markham. It's like my fingers don't want to do what I tell them, you know?'

Since the first meeting he'd run into Trevor here and there. A pub, a cafe, twice more at Studio 20. The lad had gone down to listen to some jazz but left before the first set ended.

'It turns me head around,' he complained. 'It just sounds wrong.'

There was no real malice in him, he just liked taking a chance here and there, being a devil. Perhaps he was older and wiser now, settling down a bit.

'You like the job, then?'

'I do,' Trevor answered with an emphatic nod. 'Simple stuff right now, like, but it has prospects. I'm learning things.'

'What about those friends of yours in the group? Are they still playing?'

'Youth club dance tonight. It's working out all right for them. I tell you, Mr Markham, they're going to be big.'

***

Back at the flat he put his purchases away and switched on the immersion heater for a bath. Georgina had a gig tonight at the Trocadero and he'd be there, the way he always was. He'd known the club three years before when it was called the Kit Kat, owned by the man who'd ruined his fingers.

That was history, he told himself. Put it away.

The hot water was already running when the telephone bell started ringing.

'It's definitely him,' Baker said. 'Miss Harding identified him.'

***

He wasn't going to think about it again until Monday morning.

Instead he sat in the corner at the Trocadero and listened to Georgina play and sing her heart out. She looked glamorous in a long black gown, her hair glossy and glowing under the lights. Two sets, finishing the first by looking straight at Markham as she made 'Lover Come Back To Me' into a smouldering fire of sensuality.

During the break she sat with him, sipping a glass of bitter lemon. It kept away the Romeos and allowed her to relax. The audience had quickly warmed to her, applauding and listening intently to each song.

She was playing as well as he'd ever heard her, letting her solos stretch out, teasing and pulling at the tunes, inventive and fluid. By the end of the evening, when she took another bow, her face was flushed with pleasure.

***

The office felt Monday-morning stuffy, as if the radiator had been throwing out heat all weekend. He left the door and window open, trying to cool the place off.

By the time Baker arrived the temperature was liveable.

'DeVries,' the big man said. No good morning, no how was your weekend. Straight down to business.

'It's over,' Markham told him.

'No, it's not,' Baker corrected him. 'I popped up and had a word with Miss Harding yesterday, after she got home from church. She was still upset about having to identify him.'

'Then what else can there be?'

'She wants us to find out who he really was.'

'What?' That was hard to believe. And how would they even start? He lit a cigarette and leaned back in his chair. The window was still cracked, just enough to allow a little frigid air inside. 'Why?'

'She doesn't have anyone. Never married. No kids. Parents long dead and she's an only child.' He shrugged. 'Maybe she took a shine to the poor bugger, I don't know.' Baker brought a leather wallet from his inside pocket and brought out four five-pound notes. 'She paid for four more days.'

'That's fine. But how are we going to find out about him? We've got nothing to go on, in case you've forgotten.'

'George Wills is going to ring me when he's heard from the immigration people. It's a start. And I took a gander at the magazine he got through the post. It's engineering, but quite specialised.'

'Go on.'

'As far as I can make out, it could have something to do with aeronautics.'

'We don't have any aircraft factories around here.'

'Not now, maybe' Baker agreed. 'We used to, though. Blackburn's on Roundhay Road, and that secret Avro place in Yeadon.'

'What Avro place?' He'd never heard of it. Secret?

'Just by the aerodrome. They made Lancaster and Ansons there. All very hush-hush, camouflaged and everything. They called it a shadow factory.' He laughed. 'They even drained the tarn out there to make it hard to spot, then put a false duck pond on the roof and fake cows that they'd move around every day or two. Fooled the Jerries, right enough.'

'But they're not making anything there any more.'

'Not since the war. No need. I've no idea what they do now. It was a huge place, though. I was out there once, someone was nicking bits and pieces as they were dismantling the place. After I was demobbed.'

'That still doesn't help us find out more about de Vries, or whoever he was.'

'We'll get there,' Baker said confidently. 'I've had to deal with worse.'

'And I'll give Amanda Fox a ring. Tell her we're in.'

'Amanda is it now?' Baker raised his eyebrows and smirked. 'Better not let that lass of yours find out about her, Danny.'

***

She asked him to come over to the Fox and Co. office to discuss the details. A winter wind scoured the Headrow, strong enough for him to hang on to his hat at times. He cut through to Great George Street, past the infirmary and up the hill to Woodhouse Square.

It must have been a grand house at one time. These days, though, the building was all offices, and the exterior had an air of genteel decay. Not as wealthy as Park Square, with its solicitors, dentists, and doctors, but still for the moderately well-heeled. He pressed the bell and climbed a wide staircase when she buzzed him in.

Shiny Burmantofts tiles in greens and browns lined the walls of the hall. The office door was open, an invitation. A two-room suite with a bow window that looked down over the city centre. It was intended to impress and it did the trick.

Today Amanda Fox wore a dress in two shades of grey velvet that accented her figure. A knowing smile flickered across her lips. He settled next to her on a leather sofa. A manila file sat on the coffee table.

'I'm so glad we're going to be working together, Dan,' she began. 'I know Mark will be, too.'

'Good.' It seemed like the only answer he could offer. 'How did he end up doing this kind of thing?'

'Oh, he was SOE during the war.' She said it lightly, as if it was of no consequence. But Markham knew better. During his National Service he'd heard tales about the agents of the Special Operations Executive. They were tough, deadly, working behind enemy lines half the time. If Mark Fox survived that and the aftermath when the war was over, he'd have come to know important people. He'd have value.

'I'm interested in the details of the job,' he told her, 'and what you want from us.'

She tapped red-painted nails on the folder.

'That's the bumf on five people who've come over from Germany to work around Leeds. There's everything about each of them in there, including photographs.' She paused a second. 'When you were in Germany did you ever come across the *Fragebogen*?'

'Of course.' It was the long questionnaire all Germans had to fill out to get the card proving they weren't Nazis, the *Entlastungsschien*. He'd seen a few, dealt with a small number, trying to catch men out here and there. By and large he'd never paid much attention to them; it hadn't been his real field.

'They're in there, too. I hope your German's still good enough to read them.'

He gave her a smile.

'I'll manage.'

'We want you to do some background. Ask around about them,' Amanda Fox told him. 'Keep it all on the QT.'

'All right,' Markham agreed. 'But why?'

'Follow up,' she explained. 'Find out if they're all being good boys and write me a little report on each one.'

'Are you expecting a problem with any of them?' He wasn't about to mention de Vries. See if his name was in there first.

'Not really. None of them were Nazis, not involved with the Reds. But I don't have the skill, and Mark is over in West Germany again. He's the one who suggested you, in fact. He asked around a bit.'

Markham riffled through the paperwork. Quite deliberately, he hardly glanced at the pictures, then placed the folder on his lap.

'It seems straightforward.'

'Good.' She placed a hand on his and let it rest there a moment too long. She seemed to veer between the seductive and the professional. It was disconcerting, annoying, as if she was trying to play him like a fish. 'One more thing. You'll find that they all seem to come from other countries, ones the Germans overran. I'm sure you can understand why. We've changed the names in some cases.'

'Of course.' No one was going to admit they were from Germany. Not if they wanted to get by in England.

'Right. Shall we say you report back on Friday?' Businesslike again, a quicksilver change.

'That's fine.'

He hurried back to the office on Albion Place. Only then did he open the folder and draw out one set of papers, everything held together by a paper clip. The photograph was clear enough. He knew the face. He'd seen it on Saturday morning on the bank of the River Aire, lifeless and empty.

Amanda Fox evidently hadn't learnt yet that the man was dead.

Reading quickly he went through the information on Dieter de Vries. Real name Dieter Vreiten; fairly close to his alias. Born in Berlin in 1915. He'd spent the war working as an engineer on several projects connected with aircraft. He'd been a member of the Nazi party, but that meant nothing; it was probably just a condition of his employment and survival.

Much of the language was too technical for him to understand. Something to do with developing lightweight armour for aeroplanes, as far as he could make out. His wife had died during an RAF bombing raid. Brought out of East Germany. Arrived in England 1955. Interesting, he thought.

Quickly, he looked through the other four names. All of them had come out through the Iron Curtain. That made it clear what Mark Fox did in Germany. Still working behind enemy lines.

De Vries – Vreiten – was employed at Cokely's. Not the company in Holbeck he'd told his landlady. Why had he lied about it? Funny, he knew he'd heard that name lately, but couldn't remember where.

He was still going through everything when the telephone rang. He answered with the number.

'Is Stephen Baker there?' A man's voice, weary.

'He's out. This is his partner. Can I take a message for him?'

'Dan, that's it?'

'Yes.'

'It's George Wills, Leeds CID. I just wanted to let you know something odd.' He hesitated. 'There doesn't seem to be a record of that chappie we found coming into England.'

There was an air of defeat in the words.

'Definitely a suicide, though?'

'It look that way,' Wills replied. 'I was talking to the doctor who did the post-mortem. He's convinced.'

'Does it really matter, then? It's not your problem.'

'No.' He seemed to brighten a little. 'I suppose it doesn't. Can you let Stephen know?'

'Glad to.'

He'd glossed the truth a little. But the Detective Inspector would have been worried if he knew what Markham had just learned. In this case at least, ignorance was bliss.

He was still going through everything when Baker returned, clutching a sandwich in a brown paper bag.

'Any luck on de Vries?' Markham asked.

'Not a dicky bird.' He hung up his hat and coat and settled at the card table.

'Take a look at this.' He handed over Vreiten's paperwork.

'A Jerry, eh?' Baker said after a few moments. 'That makes sense. How did you get this?'

'The same place I got these.' Markham held up the folder. 'Amanda Fox. These are the men they want us to check. Dieter was from East Germany. They all are.'

'Well, well, well.' He started to eat and the office smelt of potted meat. 'Sounds like they don't know yet.'

'Your friend George rang. No record of anyone named Dieter de Vries entering the country. But everyone's satisfied that it's suicide by drowning.'

'You didn't tell him …?'

Markham shook his head.

'This is just for us. For now, anyway. He worked at Cokely's.'

Baker snorted, his mouth full.

'Yeadon.'

Now it clicked into place. The factory where Clever Trevor Peel worked.

'Two of the others work there, too. Fancy a run out when you've finished?' Markham asked.

'As long as we stop for a cuppa first. I'm parched.'

***

The road was empty on a Monday afternoon. Through Headingley and Cookridge. Past the newly built semis that lined Otley Road. Then the houses abruptly thinned out, replaced by farms with drystone walls, like skimming back through time.

'Turn left up here,' Baker said. He'd been quiet since they left, his face looking thoughtful and heavy. Markham signalled and headed towards Pool on a quiet country lane. The only traffic was a slow-moving tractor, easily passed.

He didn't know the area well. He'd been to Yeadon Airport a couple of times, but that was all.

CHAPTER FIVE

'That's it.' Baker pointed off down a road.

'Cokely's?'

'That Avro factory I was telling you about earlier. The secret one. Pull off on the verge.'

Markham found a stretch of level ground and came to a halt. He followed the other man's gaze. It was difficult to make out a building. Grass seemed to rise in a short, steep hill to a plateau.

'Are you sure?'

'Of course I am.' The older man turned his face and gave a withering look. 'I might be knocking on but I'm not bloody doddering yet. That grass slope is how they disguised it. It's all covered on the top, too. See it from the air and you'd think it was flat.'

Markham was still looking, trying to take in just how vast it was. It seemed to run on forever. About the length of fifteen football pitches, he thought, but that was no more than a guess.

'God,' he said finally, amazed by it all. It seemed impossible that people could build anything so huge. And then to hide it …

'Remarkable, isn't it?' Baker was all business again. 'Best as I see it, Cokely's should be down on the right. About a hundred yards.'

The car park was half empty. Plenty of bicycles and motor-bikes, though. Idly he wondered which one belonged to Trevor Peel.

The receptionist handed them off to the personnel department. A fussy little manager in a cheap Burton's suit listened as Baker talked. It made sense for him to take the lead. He had the age, the copper's manner that made people help. But this time it didn't seem to work. The manager gave a firm shake of his head.

'I'm sorry,' he said. 'It's terrible news about Mr de Vries, of course. We'll miss him. He was well liked in his department.' The words sounded empty, as if he'd read them from a card. Probably he barely knew who the man was. Then he continued, 'But I can't just go giving out details to every Tom, Dick and Harry. I'm sure you see that.'

'We're working for his landlady,' Baker explained. 'She's the closest person to him in this country.'

'Yes, yes. But she's not *family*, is she? Even then I could only give details to a relative or someone with written authorisation. There are policies to follow.' He smiled, enjoying the chance to exercise a little power. 'I'm sure you understand.' His eyes glittered triumphantly. He wasn't going to give an inch; he had his authority and he was determined to stand on it.

Outside, hands deep in the pockets of his mackintosh, Baker turned and looked at the factory.

'Bloody little Hitler. Wouldn't have been any skin off his nose to let us see de Vries' file.'

'We never had much chance, really.' It had been worth a try. Something to note when he handed everything back to the Foxes. *Subject committed suicide by drowning in the River Aire. Employment file not available.*

He wouldn't have a chance to see the information on the other two from the list who worked here, either. That was fine. He expected it. He'd talk to landladies, local shopkeepers. All told it probably wasn't even a full day's work.

Baker stayed quiet as they drove back into Leeds. Markham pulled over outside the Original Oak in Headingley. The remains of a dead tree rose from the pavement, the slabs pushed up around it at awkward angles.

'We might as well call it a day for now.'

'True. Four of them left to look at, aren't there?'

'We'll take two each,' Markham said. 'We've nothing else on, anyway. Split them up in the morning. And we're getting paid.'

Quite handsomely, too. Twenty pounds for each follow-up, Amanda Fox had promised. The bills taken care of by Her Majesty's government.

'I'll dig around a bit more on this deVries,' Baker said.

'Vreiten.' He wanted to give the dead man his real identity.

The man shrugged.

'I'll give Miss Harding her money's worth. She deserves that.'

★★★

He overslept. The alarm didn't go off. He dashed through shaving and dressing, ignored breakfast, and made it to the office by half past nine.

Baker was sitting, reading the *Yorkshire Post* and puffing on his pipe.

'Decided to get out of your pit, did you?' He grinned.

'Don't,' Markham warned. 'Anything more on Vreiten?'

'A couple of the shopkeepers knew him. Not well, mind, he didn't seem to talk a lot, but you can hardly blame him, I suppose. Everyone's sad that he's dead. Shocked at the suicide, of course.'

The way people always were. Death inevitably came as a shock or a blessed relief, he'd found.

He opened the buff folder that Amanda Fox had given him, took out the two top stacks of paper and passed them over.

'We can probably get these out of the way today.'

Baker checked through the first, then started on the second. He'd barely begun when he put it aside and began thumbing through the newspaper.

'What is it?' Markham asked.

'That name. Maxim Mertens. Or Marius Martin, according to what's in here.' He found the article, folded the page and tossed it on the desk. 'Take a look.'

The man killed in a car crash on Thursday night has been named by police as Maxim Mertens, a Belgian national residing in Leeds. The accident happened in the early hours of Thursday morning on the road between Pannal and Harewood. Investigators believe Mertens, who was driving, skidded to avoid an animal and ran into a tree. He was the only occupant of the vehicle. The police are attempting to locate his family in Belgium.

Markham lowered the paper slowly.

'You already know how I feel about coincidences,' Baker said.

'I think I'd better go and have another word with Amanda Fox.'

'I'll get started on these other names.' He sighed. 'While they're still alive.'

***

'That's impossible,' Amanda Fox told him. She was seated behind her desk, her face showing her disbelief.

Markham sat opposite her and hitched up the knees on his trousers.

'It's happened,' he said. 'That's the problem. My partner's checking on the others. But I think I need to know what's going on here.' He lit a Craven A and blew smoke towards the high ceiling.

She stared at him.

'I've told you what I can. I'd need to talk to Mark before I can say anything more.'

'Then you'd better have a word with him soon. Whatever it is, things are getting out of control.'

She was silent for a few moments, biting her bottom lip.

'I'll get him back here,' she said.

'How well does he know the men he's brought over?'

'Well enough,' Mrs Fox said. It was an ambiguous, neutral answer. He wasn't going to pursue it for now. And he wasn't going to ask who might want these men dead. Not yet. He wasn't even sure he wanted to know. With a quick nod of his head he said goodbye.

***

Baker was checking into all three remaining names. That would keep him busy for the day. Markham returned to the office and sat reading the *Manchester Guardian*. There was a picture of the Prime Minister, Harold Macmillan, on the front page, with his long, basset face. Never had it so good, the man had said earlier that year. Perhaps he was right. There were plenty of signs of prosperity. More motor cars on the roads. People crowded into the shops to buy washing machines and televisions on hire purchase.

The days of rationing and all the deprivation seemed like a bad memory now. Leeds had certainly recovered from the war and the austere years that followed. The new affluence was here. Advertisements for everything under the sun.

At noon he strolled over to the Milkmaid on Commercial Street. A cheese sandwich and a cup of milky tea. It was bland, but it would fill him for now.

By the time he returned, a couple was waiting outside the door. As soon as they saw him they looked embarrassed, as if they'd been caught doing something wrong. Divorce, he decided immediately.

'Sorry to keep you waiting,' he said, extending his hand. 'I had to pop out for a moment. I'm Dan Markham.'

He ushered them in and sat them down. In their late thirties, he guessed. The woman seemed uncomfortable, gazing down and playing with her wedding ring, turning it round and round on her finger.

'I'm John Duncan,' the man began hesitantly. He wore his suit and tie easily, crossing one leg over the other. The first signs of grey in his hair and a carefully clipped moustache. 'This is my wife, Diana. We've …' The words seemed to fail him.

'Divorce?'

'Yes,' Duncan agreed sombrely. 'That's it. We married very young, before the war. The children are grown now and, well …'

He'd heard the story so often he could have told it himself. Marriage had become a stale habit, without joy. Maybe one of them had met someone else – from the blush on Diana Duncan's face, it could have been her. So now they were doing the civilised thing. No rows, no fury. Just letting it all die quietly and legally.

'I understand,' Markham said. 'It's actually quite simple.'

He explained how it worked. Tawdry, but it was a way around the law, and the courts accepted it.

'It does come down to some proof of adultery. But it only has to look that way,' he added to assure the man.

'We've discussed it,' Duncan told him. 'I'd be willing to, you know …'

'Have you seen a solicitor yet?'

'Yes.' Diana Duncan raised her head and spoke for the first time. She sounded nervous. 'We've put in the papers.'

'Good.' Markham smiled at them. 'Then we can get cracking.'

He took all their details and two five-pound notes as a down payment.

'I'll make all the arrangements and give you as much notice as I can. But it shouldn't be more than a few days. After that I'll give your solicitor my statement and the photographs.'

There was a bed and breakfast place off Harehills Lane, close to Potternewton Park, that appreciated the extra business. And a prostitute who liked a few quid without having to perform. Money for old rope, she called it, but she still didn't lower her rates.

Half an hour later he saw them out, hearing their footsteps clatter down the linoleum on the stairs. They seemed a little happier. Or perhaps it was relief. It was still a long road to a decree absolute but they'd taken the first steps.

He made two telephone calls, setting everything up for Friday afternoon, then wrote a quick note to Mr Duncan.

Markham was putting on his coat, ready to go to the post box, when the phone rang.

'Are you in the middle of something?' Baker asked.

'Not really.'

'I'm up in Moortown, on the parade. Could you come up?'

'What's happened?' Another mysterious summons. He hoped it didn't mean another body.

'Nothing too bad. Maybe just something you should see, that's all.'

'All right,' he agreed slowly. 'I'll be there in a little while.'

***

The Anglia stalled twice on the journey, once at the top of Chapeltown Road, the next time outside the Kingsway cinema. He needed to take it in. Maybe the garage had something he could use in the meantime.

He spotted Baker leaning against the phone box, reading his newspaper. A north wind bit down from Harrogate and the Dales.

'So what do you want me to see?' he asked.

'We might as well get in your motor. It's along Street Lane.'

A good mile along Street Lane, as it turned out, down in the Romans, on a street of neat three-storey terraced houses that had probably been villas at the beginning of the century. They still had an air of solidity and permanence.

He turned off the engine, hearing the soft clicks as it began to cool.

'Right,' Markham said, 'what do you want me to see?'

'Second house from the end.' He pointed with a stubby finger. 'Morten Blum's lodgings. He's supposed to have come from Denmark.'

'Go on.'

'We know he's from East Germany,' Baker continued. 'His real name's Manfred Blum; close enough, isn't it? I had a chat with his landlady. She let me have a look around his room.' He opened the door of the Anglia. 'Come on, I'll show you. Let me do the talking, all right?'

The woman smiled when she opened the door, happy to see Baker once more.

'I'm sorry to bother you again, luv,' he said, 'but this is my colleague. I was thinking a bit and I'd like to have him see everything, too. Is that fine?'

'Of course it is.' She was a thin woman, like a tall stick covered with a heavy cardigan. Her dark hair was gathered in a bun, her eyes hidden behind a pair of thick glasses. She took a key off the table in the hall. 'You know where it is.'

Baker leaned close to her.

'Like before, not a word.' He tapped the side of his nose with a finger.

'Don't you worry.' She seemed to simper.

★★★

The room was upstairs, at the end of the hall. The key turned soundlessly in the lock. It was a large room containing a double bed covered with a burgundy candlewick, a small dressing table, easy chair, table and bookcase without seeming crowded.

'What did you tell her?' Markham asked.

'I might have mentioned the police.' Baker's eyes were twinkling. 'Didn't say I was one, mind. She just chose to think so. Very happy to help the boys in blue, is Mrs Thompson. That's why I said you should let me talk.'

He went over to the bookcase and picked out a book. *Roget's Thesaurus*. Common in so many English households. He had a copy in the flat.

'Take a glance through that and tell me what you see,' the man continued.

He looked, paying attention as he leafed slowly through the pages. After about twenty seconds he began to notice something. Tiny pinpricks under letters. As soon as he knew what to look for, he kept opening the book at random. Some pages had nothing, others had two or three. It wasn't an accident. There was some method behind it.

'You did well to spot this,' Markham said.

'It was an accident, really, but I thought there was something to it. Any idea what it means?'

'It's a code pad of some sort, from the look of things. They taught us a little bit about it in military intelligence. All beyond me, though.'

'The question is why an engineer who's been brought out of West Germany would have something like this,' Baker said.

'There's only one reason anyone would need it.'

Baker took it from his hands and replaced it carefully in the bookcase.

'That's what I thought, too. Something for you to pass on to that Fox woman. You understand why I wanted you to see it?'

Morten Blum, or whatever his real name might be, was spying for the East Germans. That meant the Russians. What the hell were they getting mixed up with? Two dead men and now this.

'Have you been to any of the others?' He was driving along Princes Avenue, through the broad expanse of Soldiers Field.

'One. He seemed clean enough. One more to go.'

'Where's he?'

'Down by Potternewton Park.'

'I'll drop you off.'

***

Back in town Markham wandered over to the Kardomah for a coffee and a chance to think. He'd write up the report for Amanda Fox, put the cheque in the bank, and that would be the end of it. Baker could poke around more into Vreiten's life if he wanted. There wasn't going to be much for him to discover about it in Leeds, that was certain.

As he came back out on to Briggate he heard the sound. Trumpet, trombone and more, playing some Dixieland. He had to stop to be certain he hadn't imagined it. Then he walked up the street, moving between people, following the noise. What the hell was it?

***

Standing at the corner of the Headrow everything became clearer. A procession, like the New Orleans funerals he'd read about. The jazz funerals, they were called, music sombre and dark on the way to the graveyard, joyful as the musicians made their way home.

He waited as they passed. A group of students, looking like this was the most fun they'd had in their lives. The young man out in front had a stick like a regimental sergeant major leading a parade. Behind him, a cornet and a saxophone, someone with a trombone, a banjo player, and finally a man playing a tuba, feet splaying from a pram as someone pushed him along. A girl walking beside them was handing out sheets of paper. Markham took one as she passed. It was badly mimeographed, faint and blurred, the music and lyrics for a song. *The New Eastgate Swing*, the title read. He smiled and pushed it down into his pocket.

The whole spectacle was unlikely. It was impossible. But it was there. Traffic had stopped, people were gawping in disbelief. There'd certainly been nothing like it in Leeds before. A beautiful, strange joke. The music was ragtag, the players struggling, but that didn't matter. He followed them down the Headrow and on to Eastgate. The leader moved his stick faster, like a baton, and the tune sped up to double-time, turning into a raucous, enthusiastic version of 'When The Saints Go Marchin' In'.

If he hadn't seen it, Markham wouldn't have believed it. He wished he'd had a camera to capture it all. Eastgate swung. For the first time and very likely the last.

It had brightened his day. The wonderful unexpected. He made his way back to the office with a smile on his face; all the worries about dead Germans vanished from his mind for a few minutes.

CHAPTER SIX

Baker arrived a little after five, shrugging off his mackintosh and hanging up his hat with a long sigh.

'Did you find anything on the last one?' Markham asked.

'Nothing in his room. He's the other one who works at Cokely's. He feels clean enough to me.'

A copper's hunch. It was probably good enough.

'Just write a few lines. I'll take it over to Fox before I go home.'

'I had a word with a couple of neighbours and the local shops. Nothing unusual.'

'We'll pass that on.'

★★★

Amanda Fox read the reports, staring briefly at him before she looked at the sheet on Morten Blum again, going slowly over everything.

'Are you sure?' she asked after a long silence. 'He's a spy?'

'I think it's very likely.' Markham chose his words carefully. 'That's two dead and one spy. The other two seem clean. It's all in there.'

'I'll have to ring people in London,' she said.

'You haven't before?'

'When I talked to Mark he said to leave it until he was back. But with this ... if Blum's a spy ...'

'When do you expect your husband?'

'He'll be back here tomorrow. The day after at the latest.' She crossed her legs and the soft, crackling sound of nylon filled the air for a moment. 'He's going to ring you as soon as he's here.' She reached into a drawer and took out a cheque-book. 'One hundred pounds. That's what we agreed.'

He waited quietly. For a woman who looked so seductive – lemon yellow silk today, with just the hint of cleavage, hair held down by an Alice band – she was precise in her actions. Carefully blotting the ink, tearing out the cheque with small, intent moves.

Markham folded it and placed it in his wallet without even checking the amount.

'I look forward to meeting Mr Fox.'

Six. The banks had been closed for over two hours; he'd deposit the money in the morning. As he made his way back to Albion Place, Leeds seemed empty, only the people heading for a meal or the cinema out and about.

Baker had left. The undercurrent of typing from the secretarial agency downstairs had vanished. He had the building to himself.

The whole Fox business was a mess. Good pay, but it all nagged at him. As soon as he'd mentioned the two deaths she should have been talking to MI5. Anyone could see that the pieces didn't add up properly. Never mind, he told himself as he locked the door. They were out of it now and he was glad. He'd never wanted to be part of the cloak and dagger set.

***

'Leave it?' Baker said in surprise. He was surrounded by a fog of pipe smoke, the raw smell of shag from the tobacconist's in County Arcade.

'Yes. As soon as this Fox bloke shows his face. We'll bring him up to speed and that's it.' He paused. 'It's what they've paid us for. The whole thing's gone out of our league.'

'We've done the spadework. The landladies know us.'

'Fine,' Markham said. 'Do your bit for Miss Harding and call it a day. We'll let the people with the right clearances and authority take care of the rest. Divorce, frauds – that's our speed. Just forget about it.'

'You sound like you got out of the wrong side of the bed this morning,' Baker told him.

'No. I just had time to think it all through last night.'

He'd smoked cigarette after cigarette, considering every avenue they'd begun to explore on this. None of them looked appealing. And every single one seemed to have danger at the end of it.

'Maybe you're right,' Baker agreed finally and turned the pages of the newspaper. 'There's something here. Sounds right up your street, jazz, happened on the Headrow.'

'I know,' Markham said with a smile. 'I saw it. Bloody wonderful.'

***

They were about to leave for dinner when the telephone rang.

'Is this Dan Markham?' A man's voice, easy and cultured.

'Yes.'

'Hello, this is Mark Fox. I just arrived in Leeds a few minutes ago.'

'Yes, Mr Fox.' He looked at Baker, his eyebrows raised, signalling the man to wait. 'I think we need to have a chat, don't you?'

'Yes, I believe you're right. The Victoria Hotel on Great George Street?'

'That's fine. A quarter of an hour?'

***

The Victoria had probably really been a hotel when it was built; there were enough storeys rising up from the street to offer rooms. These days most of the pub's trade came from workers at the Town Hall. It was a big barn of a place, still with the original etched glass, wood, and brass. But it was uncared-for, the carpets threadbare, no polish on anything, all the old beauty hidden under an air of neglect that hung heavily on the place.

The main bar was busy, men drinking their pints and talking. But no one on his own. Markham found him in the room labelled Bridget's Bar, off the main hall. He was the only one in there, sitting at a small round table, a glass of whisky and a small jug of water in front of him.

It had to be Mark Fox. The suit was bespoke, beautifully tailored to fall around his body. He looked to be around forty, and the haircut that trimmed his thick, dark hair hadn't come from the barber on New York Street.

'I'll get them in,' Baker muttered and disappeared.

'Mr Fox?' Markham extended his hand. 'Dan Markham.'

The man smiled, showing white, even teeth.

'Good to meet you finally. Have a seat. Can I get you something?'

'My partner's buying. He'll be through in a second. He's the one who's been dealing with most of this.'

'Very good.' He picked up the glass. Manicured fingernails, Markham noticed. What man in Leeds ever had those?

Baker returned with a pint of bitter, the head thick and white, and a tall glass of ginger ale.

'You two appear to have run into a few snags,' Fox began. There was concern in his voice, but far too little worry.

'Two dead, one very likely a spy,' Baker answered flatly. 'I'd call that more than a few snags.'

'Maybe,' Fox allowed with an easy smile. 'The information's been passed on to the appropriate people.'

Fox wasn't local, Markham decided. He had the long vowels of a Southerner. That seemed curious. Why had he ended up in Leeds?

'There are still two dead men,' he pointed out.

'I had a word with the police before I came out. In both cases there's no hint of anything suspicious,' Fox countered.

'So it's just an unfortunate coincidence?'

'They happen.' Fox shrugged. 'I wanted to set your minds at rest.'

'You'll have to do better than that,' Baker told him. 'I spent a long time on the force. I don't believe in coincidence.'

'That's your choice, of course.' Fox looked at him, speaking slowly and calmly. 'But whichever way you look at it, they've gone, and we'll be keeping a closer eye on those who are still in the country.'

'How many are there?' Markham asked. 'Just the names you've given us?'

'You know I can't tell you that,' Fox answered. 'You spent time in military intelligence. You know the score.'

'Always worth asking.'

'Of course. And I can assure you we'll take the appropriate steps with Mr Blum. That was good work on your part.' Quite elaborately he looked at his watch, showing a pair of gold cufflinks. 'Now if you'll excuse me, I have too many things to do. I hope my answers have helped.' He took an expensive overcoat with an astrakhan collar from the seat and shrugged himself into it with neat, economical movements. 'I'm sure we'll be sending more business your way.'

Then he was gone.

'Ever feel you've been handed a load of flannel?' Baker asked into the silence.

***

The days passed quietly. The police passed on another missing person case, a genuine one this time. That kept Baker busy and out of the office.

'You'd do better if you bought a motor car,' Markham told him.

'It's in hand,' he answered cryptically. 'By the weekend, all being well.'

It was sooner. On Friday morning Baker walked into the office jangling some keys.

'Come on downstairs and take a look.'

It was parked outside, just behind the Anglia. A black Wolseley, two years old, neatly cleaned and waxed. The leather seats were cracked, the walnut of the dashboard a little scarred, but those were minor quibbles.

'Ex-police?' Markham guessed.

'Got it for a good price,' he nodded in triumph. 'Mate of mine down at the police garage. The motor's fine, he says. Souped up, too, do a ton in no time.'

It was a large vehicle. But Baker was a large man. Even at a glance it looked like a police vehicle – the colour and power. Still, Stephen Baker would always look like a copper.

'It'll get you around fast enough.'

'The wife says we can use it for a run out into the Dales and the coast on the weekends. Maybe go and see the children and grandkids.' He sighed.

'How's your case coming along? Found him yet?'

'Got a lead over in York. I'm heading there this afternoon.' He raised his glance to the grey sky. 'Could have asked for better weather. But with a little luck I'll have it wrapped up today, then spend the weekend putting the allotment to bed for the winter.'

'I've got the adultery job on the Duncan divorce later.' He smiled. 'Some jazz tonight.'

'I don't know what you hear in that racket. Give me a good dance band any day. Billy Cotton or Ted Heath, that's the ticket.' He patted the bonnet of the Wolseley. 'Still, this means we can take on more work.'

'Nothing involving Germans, though.'

'I didn't know that when we started,' Baker protested.

They hadn't even discussed it since seeing Mark Fox. There was nothing to talk about, anyway. It was over, out of their hands. The cheque had cleared. Forget about it.

He watched Baker drive proudly away and climbed back up the stairs. He had a few hours before going out to Harehills.

★★★

Buslingthorpe Lane was quiet. Too many of the factories in the area stood empty now, weeds growing from the gutters and the windows smashed. The era of manufacturing was drawing to a close, no matter what the politicians claimed.

Day's Garage was busy, though. The sound of spanners and grunts from inside, a row of motor cars standing outside. He parked and searched for the owner. Martin Day had set up the business after a war spent in the military motor pool. Since then he'd done well for himself, moving to this bigger place five years before. Four mechanics worked for him. He was cheap, good, and quick.

'Can you give it a going over?' Markham asked.

Day took a packet of Woodbine from his overalls and lit one.

'Probably just needs new sparking plugs,' he said, picking a shred of tobacco off his lip.

'You said you could let me have something in the meantime.'

'That one there.' He pointed at an Escort Estate. 'I know it doesn't look much, but it's solid.' He chuckled. 'Won't do much for your image, but …'

'As long as it gets me there and back.'

'It'll do that, right enough. I'll have yours ready by dinner-time on Monday.' In the office he hunted through a drawer and tossed a set of keys across the room. 'Just try not to prang it, Dan.'

He was cautious at first, driving slowly as he got the feel of the vehicle. Up Scott Hall Road, Potternewton Lane, then down Harehills Lane to park a few streets from the small hotel.

Plenty of time to eat. He found a cafe along the parade on Roundhay Road. Eggs and chips with a few slices of bread and butter and a cup of hot, sweet tea. The yolks properly runny, sopped up by the bread.

Mr Duncan was waiting on the corner, perfectly punctual. He looked uncomfortable, but so many of the men did when it came to this.

'Do you still want to go through with it?' Markham asked. A few seconds of silence, then a quick nod.

'I don't have to … you know?'

'Nothing like that,' Markham said, reassuring him. 'You'll just be in the same bed for a few minutes, that's all. You don't even need to touch her.'

Relief seemed to flood through the man's face. He probably had a pair of pyjamas in his briefcase, Markham thought. That was so often the way.

Julie was waiting at the hotel. This was routine for her. Already she looked bored, sitting wrapped in her coat, smoking a cigarette and leafing through a magazine. She barely gave Duncan a glance, smiling at Markham.

'It's not going to take long, is it, love?' she asked. 'Only I have to be in town before five.'

'Just the usual,' he replied. She was a tired-looking bottle blonde in her early thirties. Married during the war and left pregnant when her husband went off to die at D-Day. Now she did what she could to make ends meet and bring up a child, living in a council flat in Belle Isle. She was honest and she knew the drill well enough by now.

The hotel owner signed them in as Mr and Mrs Smith and handed Julie the key.

'Right,' she told Duncan, 'you come with me. We'll be done before you can say Jack Robinson.' His gaze turned to Markham. 'Five minutes, all right?'

A quick cup of weak tea and Markham climbed the stairs, not bothering to knock on the door. The couple were in bed. Julie had the sheet pulled up over her breasts. Duncan appeared awkward and embarrassed, but that would come out just right in the photographs. Caught in the act.

He took ten pictures, six with the flash and four without, before he gave a thumbs up and left. Not even ten past the hour. Another five minutes, paying the owner for the use of the room, and he heard the couple come down again. Ten pounds for Julie, and a quick word with Duncan.

'I'll develop these and get them to your solicitor,' he explained. 'That's it, apart from the court appearances.'

'No one else will see them, will they?'

More than half the men asked that. They needed the appearance of adultery for their divorces but they were embarrassed by it; an odd paradox. The rest of the clients swaggered as if they'd just made a great conquest.

'No,' Markham promised. The negatives and unused images would simply disappear into the file. Down at the corner he asked, 'Can I give you a lift?'

'I'll take the bus,' Duncan muttered and strode quickly away.

***

He'd set up a darkroom of sorts in one of the cellars below his flat. None of the other tenants used the space. Cleaning it out he'd found a strange assortment of items – cigarette cards from the 1920s and '30s, covered in mould, a rotting gasmask from the war, a pair of women's shoes that had probably been fashionable not long after Queen Victoria died.

Developing the film didn't take long. These weren't art shots. All he needed was to be able to see the faces clearly. Three of the photographs worked well, enough for any lawyer. He hung them on a line to dry and took the negatives back upstairs.

Not even five o'clock and the week was over, full darkness outside. Down on Harrogate Road housewives were finishing their shopping. The buses going by were packed with people on their way home. He put on an LP, the new one from Miles Davis, 'Round About Midnight', and let himself sink into the music. The trumpet on the title track brought up images of walking in a night-time city, the light off the street lamps reflected in puddles. It was Monk's tune transmuted for the hours when the pavements were lonely and footsteps provided the rhythm. Music for winter.

***

Georgina was waiting outside Studio 20. Already he could hear the smooth, sensual sound of a tenor sax drifting up from the club as someone worked around 'Body And Soul', a straight copy of the old Coleman Hawkins version, right down to the improvisations.

'Busy at work?' he asked as he kissed her cheek.

'The usual,' she answered. Her eyes were sparkling, and she shivered as a gust of cold wind battered along Briggate. 'Let's go in, it'll be warmer.'

There was faint applause as the number ended. At the bottom of the stairs Markham could see the musicians. Piano, bass and, a basic drum kit behind a red-faced tenor player, a boy of about eighteen, hair cut neat and short. The lad reached into a pocket and wiped the sweat off his forehead. At least he didn't start another tune.

Markham bought two coffees and carried them to a table in the far corner. Georgina had already shrugged off her coat, dressed down in a twinset and burgundy wool skirt. He took out a cigarette and offered it to her. She shook her head. She rarely smoked, looking after her voice.

There was time while the next set of musicians set up. Small talk, bits and pieces of the day. It was idle, easy chat that Bob Barclay interrupted when he dragged over a chair. He owned the club, a jazz fan and musician his whole life.

'Evening, Dan, Georgina. Did you hear about that thing on Briggate? The jazz funeral?'

'I saw it,' Markham told him.

'I wish I had,' Barclay said with a sigh. 'We did something like that years ago with the Yorkshire Jazz Band, you know.'

'No.' Maybe it had happened while he was still in Germany.

'Great fun.' The man's face lit up with pleasure. 'People didn't know what to make of it.' Barclay gave a small cough. 'Georgina luv, I was wondering, would you fancy playing here sometime? I've been hearing good things about your music.'

The question took her by surprise. Markham saw her glance doubtfully at the old upright piano. She was used to a baby grand, the type of instrument in all the nightclubs.

'It would be a real gig,' Barclay continued quickly. 'Two sets. I'd pay you,' he added quickly.

'Yes,' she answered after a moment. She sounded stunned by the offer. It was the first time Barclay had suggested it. And Studio 20 was a real jazz club. The fee might not be as much as other places, but the kudos was much greater. 'Of course. Thank you.' She started to grin.

'Good.' Barclay clapped his large hands together. 'That's settled. I didn't know if you'd want to. It's not the poshest place.' But there was pride in his voice as he said it.

'Really, I'll be glad to.' She still sounded as if she couldn't quite believe it.

Markham sat, drinking coffee and listening to the two of them talk. They hashed out the details quickly. A month away, a Saturday night. He'd put up posters, maybe even an advertisement in the newspaper. By the time he wandered away to his usual place, watching everything from behind a partition, she was beaming with excitement. Georgina reached across the table and took a cigarette from his packet.

'Celebration,' she told him as she flicked the lighter. 'That's a turn up.'

'A good one, though.'

'Yes.' He could see she was already planning. 'There's a club booker from Manchester I've been trying to persuade to see me,' Georgina said thoughtfully. 'Maybe he'd be willing to pop over.'

She was off and running. Music meant even more to her than it did to him. For him it was joy. For her it could become a living.

They stopped talking as the next combo began playing. A trumpeter in his fifties, bald head glistening under the lights, a saxophonist with a sleeveless Fair Isle jumper over a shirt and tie, backed by a young trio. The guitarist with the greasy quiff and denim jeans looked as if he ought to be playing skiffle, but he was a good accompanist, agile and thoughtful, while the bassist and drummer swung things gently through 'On Green Dolphin Street' and five other standards. It was good stuff, better than competent but without the extra something to really lift it.

He glanced at Georgina. Her eyes were fixed on something he couldn't see. She was imagining herself there, he knew.

Four weeks to plan and practice on the battered old piano that filled one whole corner of her tiny bedsit. He was proud of her. Maybe this was the start of the break she needed.

They stayed through the next soloists, a pair of West Indians working with the same rhythm section. Markham had seen them play any number of times in the last three years. They were good. Better than good, they really had something. And they were still working as street cleaners for the council, living in cheap housing off Chapeltown Road. But every time he heard them, the music was full of life, the harmonies and lines spiralling high. By the time they finished he knew they weren't going to hear anything better tonight. Better to leave on a high note.

He'd left the car by the office and they strolled down Briggate arm in arm. The wind tugged briefly at his hat but couldn't dislodge it.

'What's this?' Georgina laughed when she saw the Escort Estate. 'God, Dan, it's hideous. You haven't bought it, have you?'

'The garage let me use it while they work on mine. It's only until Monday.'

Without them discussing it, he drove back to Chapel Allerton, parking behind his flat. Everything was quiet, good people already fast asleep. They made love with soft delight in the darkness, then she curled around and fell asleep.

He had his eyes closed, but his brain wouldn't slow down. The thrill of the music bled into Mark Fox's words and the sense of two dead Germans, then the surprise on Duncan's face when he raised the camera and began clicking the shutter. It took almost an hour by the luminous hands of the clock before his breathing began to steady and he settled.

He stirred to the smell of coffee. Reaching across, the other side of the bed was empty. He blinked, looking at the clock.

Almost nine, the dull light of winter coming through the gap in the curtains.

A few seconds later Georgina entered, wrapped in his dressing gown and holding two mugs.

'Don't get used to this,' she warned as she settled next to him. 'Once in a blue moon. I've been awake for a while thinking about this gig.'

'You'll be fine,' he assured her as he sat up. 'You're good, you know that.'

She gave a tight smile.

'But this, I don't know, it feels different,' she said.

***

She was quiet all through the morning. Long silences filled lunch. When they finished she washed up, then said, 'Would you mind if I went home?'

'Of course not.'

'It's just … you know.'

'Want me to run you there?'

'No, it's fine. I fancy a walk.'

It was a long stroll, at least an hour to her flat in Headingley.

'Are you sure?'

'Yes.' She hugged him. 'I don't know why this gig is making me think so much. I just want to sort it all out. Sure you don't mind?'

'You go,' he said kindly.

***

Alone, he pottered around, tidying the flat, the quicksilver piano playing of Art Tatum pushing him on. He didn't know why playing at Studio 20 worried Georgina so much. To him the place felt almost like a second home; he was as comfortable there as in his flat. Still, he wasn't a musician and the audience knew their jazz. But he had faith in her; she had true talent, one that could shine beyond Leeds one day if she took the risk.

An early evening and a Sunday catching up on domestic things. Cleaning, washing his clothes. The things of everyday that he fitted into the corner of empty time.

It was an evening for crumpets and butter. Just like childhood. Back then they'd gather round the radio, hearing the news on the Home Service as they ate. Sunday suppers were the only meal where they didn't sit at the table, the rules relaxed once a week. He could still recall sitting cross-legged on the floor, his mother reminding him not to drop anything on the rug. For a second he could hear her again. Even the tone of voice she always used. Strange, he thought, the things that stuck in the mind.

He was reading *The Quiet American* when the telephone rang. Without even thinking, he reached over and lifted the receiver, hearing the coins drop into the box when he answered.

'Hello Dan, how are you? It's been a long time.'

CHAPTER SEVEN

The voice was so familiar. He ought to know it ... then she gave a soft, throaty chuckle and he could place her. Carla. She'd walked out of his life three years before, caught up and broken by the case that ruined his fingers. There'd been a final meal when she made her farewell and then she was gone. He'd loved her. It had taken months for him to realise that, even longer before her ghost stopped walking through his dreams.

'I'm doing quite well,' he answered hesitantly. 'What about you? Where are you?'

'I'm down at the station. My train's been delayed. Look, I don't suppose you fancy a drink, do you? I have a couple of hours to kill.'

'Of course.' He didn't even need to think about it.

'Oh good.' She sounded genuinely pleased. 'The Scarborough Hotel in a few minutes?'

'Yes.'

***

He washed quickly and dressed. His good grey suit, white shirt, and a tie in subtle shades of red. God, he felt as nervous as a boy taking a girl out for the first time. His hands were shaky as he drove into town, finding a place to park by the old tram depot.

She was sitting at a table by the window, smoking a cigarette, a glass of something in front of her. He'd never expected to hear from her again. After she left he hoped she'd change her mind. But the silence had continued until he knew there was no hope. And now here she was again.

She hadn't seen him come in; he had the chance to study her. So much the same, but with more polish and poise. More confidence. Wide, draped black slacks and a vivid top in paisley swirls and belled sleeves. Utterly divorced from fashion but someone looking ahead of it. He paid for his ginger ale and sat down across the table from her.

'Well, hello stranger,' she said, and the smile reached up to her eyes. 'Did I take you by surprise?'

'Just a little.' He laughed; he couldn't help it. 'What are you doing here?'

'Oh, train problems on the way back to Durham.' She waved it away. 'Thank you for coming down. You're looking well, Dan.'

'So are you,' he told her, and it was true. 'Still teaching up there?'

'Yes,' she said, 'but I've been down in London. I had a new exhibition that opened yesterday.'

He'd seen her name in the newspapers from time to time, hailed as one of the fresh young things of British art.

'Did it go well?'

Carla shrugged.

'All the appropriate noises. A few pieces sold. Decent reviews in the Sundays. How about you? Still in the detective business?'

'Same as ever.'

'Do you still go to that jazz place? I can't remember its name.'

'Studio 20. And yes, I do. It sounds like your career is taking off.'

She smiled and shook her head.

'I just paint and sometimes people like it.'

The silence held for half a minute. He stubbed out his Craven A in the ashtray and lit another.

'It doesn't look as if Leeds has really changed,' Carla said finally.

'Does it ever?' he asked, then the question that had been nagging him since the phone rang: 'What made you give me a ring?'

'I had some time between trains,' she began, then shook her head again. 'Well no, that's not true. I wanted to see you again. We left everything rather unresolved, didn't we?' Carla frowned. '*I* did, I suppose. Not you.'

'You made your decision to leave. I honestly can't blame you after what happened.' Two years of her work had been ruined. An act of destruction aimed at him.

'It helped, in a way, you know. It changed the way I look at life and what I do.'

He still had a painting she'd given him. A picture of a sooty industrial landscape, the only birthday present she could afford then. It still hung on his wall. The way Carla had become known, it was probably the most valuable thing he owned. But he'd never sell it.

'Do you like Durham?' Markham asked. Small talk was safe, away from the swamp of feelings and history.

'Yes.' Her face brightened and became more mobile. 'I was lucky, I found a place up by the cathedral and the university. Gorgeous old building and my window looks down on the river. Are you still in the same place?'

'I haven't found a reason to move. I still use that espresso pot you brought back from Italy.'

'I'd forgotten all about that!' Her eyes widened. 'Oh God, all the stuff I had in my suitcases.'

The conversation flickered through this and that for half an hour, weaving its way clear of the personal.

Finally she finished her drink.

'Are you seeing anyone?' Carla asked bluntly.

For a second he said nothing, surprised that he was reluctant to give her an honest answer.

'I've been going out with someone for a while,' he admitted finally. 'What about you?'

'I've more or less been a nun,' she said with a mixture of humour and frustration. 'Stupid, isn't it? What's your mystery woman like?'

'She's a singer. Jazz.'

'That should be right up your street.'

'Works at Boots.'

'Is it serious?' The question took him aback.

'Not really. It's …' He searched for the right word. The honest word. 'Convenient. For both of us,' he added.

'I see.' Her eyes moved to the clock over the bar. 'I'd better get a move on or I'll miss the bloody train.' She drained her glass, put on her coat and lifted a small suitcase. He took it from her hand.

'I'll walk over with you.'

In her heels she was almost as tall as him. Close up, he could smell her perfume. Something very subtle, very adult and sophisticated.

'That would be lovely. Thank you.'

He bought a platform ticket and saw her into the carriage. She lowered the window on the door.

'This is all very *Brief Encounter*, isn't it?' she laughed.

'It's been good to see you again.' He meant every word.

'You too, Dan. Really.' She squeezed his hand.

'Do you have a telephone?'

Carla shook her head.

'Never bothered. No telly, either. I'm a terrible Luddite.' She laughed just as the train whistle sounded and a gush of steam surrounded the engine. 'You know, I still listen to jazz because of you. Who's good these days?'

'Monk,' he said and saw her smile. That was the music that had brought them together. 'Miles Davis. And a fellow called Mose Allison.'

'Mose?' Carla asked. 'Really?'

'Really,' he told her. 'Plays piano and sings. He sounds so ...' He searched for the right word. 'Hip.'

'That doesn't sound like a Dan Markham word.'

He could hear the train ready to leave.

'How do I get in touch with you?'

'Write to me at the university.' She leaned forward and kissed him very lightly on the lips. Exactly the way she'd done the last time they'd parted.

'I will,' he promised.

'I hope so.'

Then the train began to move. She didn't lean out and wave, but he still watched until it had vanished from sight.

***

'You look like you lost ten bob and found a tanner,' Baker said when Markham walked into the office next morning. 'You must have had a rough weekend.'

'It was interesting.' He sat behind his desk, still in his overcoat, and tossed his hat on to the windowsill. 'What do we have to do? Did you find that missing person?'

'Camped out in York. Found him in the second place I looked. Had a quiet word and gave him a lift home. Unless he's wandered off again he should be happy in Seacroft. Did you get your snaps?'

'In and out in ten minutes.' In a little while he'd go to the solicitor, deliver them, and pick up a cheque. 'Do we have anything else on the go?'

'Not unless you want me to go and drum something up.'

'There'll be more soon enough.' He slipped the hat back on. 'I'll go and deliver these pictures.'

The wind was bitter, whipping across from the North Sea, scouring the streets as he walked to Park Square. No one was sitting out on the benches today, and the flowerbeds were just dark earth, all the colour gone for winter.

At least the solicitor's office was warm, what had once probably been the dining room of a house, with high, coved ceiling and a view out to the street. He waited as the man read his report and assessed the photographs with silent approval, then wrote out the cheque. All done in ten minutes.

He took his time, stopping at the bank, then at a cafe for a cup of tea. No rush, and he had plenty to think about. His sleep has been fitful, all dreams and thoughts about Carla. Everything had seemed settled and comfortable and then she'd shown up, back in his life like a bad penny. Well, perhaps she was in his life, he didn't know yet. Maybe it really was just a passing visit. Certainly it was the last thing he'd expected; just a few minutes together and she'd turned things upside down.

The telephone was ringing as he climbed the stairs to the office, the insistent urgency of the bell making him run.

'Hello?' he said breathlessly.

'Dan?' A woman's voice. For a fraction of a second he believed it was Carla. Then he recognised the tone – Mrs Fox.

'What can I do for you, Amanda?'

'Could you and your partner come over?' There seemed to be an edge of desperation in her tone. 'Please?'

'He's out, but I'm free. What is it?'

'I'll tell you when you get here,' she answered and then he heard the line go dead. What the hell was going on?

Ten minutes later he was in Woodhouse Square. He pressed the doorbell, waiting for her to buzz him in. Nothing. Markham tried again, then a third time. Still no answer.

Now he was worried.

There was a telephone box on the other side of the square. He dug out some pennies and rang her number. Maybe the bell wasn't working; the explanation could be as simple as that. But no one picked up.

Thinking, he made his way back to Albion Place. Something had gone very wrong, he was certain of that.

Baker was sitting at his card table, munching his way through a cheese and tomato sandwich.

'Do you know how to pick locks?' Markham asked.

'Eh?'

He explained quickly, Baker listening intently as he ate.

'Happen we'd better go and see.' He shook the crumbs from his lap, crumpled the greaseproof wrapping and threw it in the bin. 'It doesn't sound good, does it?'

There was a crunch of gravel as they walked up the short drive to the building. Still no answer when he rang the bell. Baker reached into a pocket in his jacket and brought out a small, flat leather case. Then he leaned over, peering at the lock and selected two flat picks. He moved one around where a key would fit, then used the other, nodding when he felt it click. The door swung open.

'I was joking when I asked if you knew that,' Markham said.

'You don't spend so long in CID without learning a few things.' He was smiling with satisfaction.

He didn't need to work his magic on the Foxes office. The handle turned in Markham's fingers. He pushed the door open, hardly daring to move. But the room was empty.

'And she just rang a short while ago?' Baker asked.

'That's right.'

Baker shook his head.

'Very rum. Best not touch anything, just in case.'

No coat, no handbag. But there was no sign of any struggle, nothing knocked out of place, just the normal jumble of work: folders scattered on the desk, a pen lying on the blotter, a mug with the cold dregs of tea at the bottom.

'It's like the *Mary Celeste*,' Markham said.

Baker was pacing around the room, hands bunched in the pockets of his raincoat.

'It's not normal to leave without locking the office,' he said quietly. 'You came straight over when she rang?'

'Yes. Can't be more than three quarters of an hour ago. Probably less than that.'

'Do you know how to get hold of her husband?'

Markham shook his head. 'I don't even know where they live.'

'It'll be in the directory. We might as well go, there's nothing to see here. But I'll tell you what, I don't think she's popped out to borrow a cup of sugar.'

At the door he carefully wiped the knob with his handkerchief.

They walked quickly, without talking. Baker turned and entered the public library, climbing the wide tiled stairs and leading the way into a hushed room. He searched along a shelf, taking down a bound telephone directory.

'Here we are,' he whispered when he found the entry. 'King Lane. Alwoodley. Do you want to drive or shall I?'

'I will.'

***

The house was hidden away behind a low wall and a series of beech trees. It stood on its own, detached but not too grand, just enough to announce that the owners had money.

'I'll park down the road,' Markham said. 'We'll walk back. Just in case.'

He could see the hinges on the brick wall, but no wrought-iron gates; they'd probably vanished years before to help make Spitfires during the war, and never been replaced.

'Do you see anyone moving inside?' Baker asked.

Markham checked, his gaze moving from window to window. 'No,' he replied finally.

'Let's see who's at home, then.'

Baker shambled along, head down, looking large and harmless. Markham stayed in his wake. The front door had a polished brass knocker in the shape of a wolf's head. But the loud rap brought no answer. He tried again; still no reply.

The garage was empty. The rear of the house had French doors that opened on to a small stone terrace, lawn and flowerbeds beyond. A few seconds with the lock picks and they were inside.

'Remember,' Baker hissed, 'don't touch anything. If you need to open a door, use your handkerchief.'

Markham could feel his heart pounding as they moved from room to room. He hardly dared to breathe. A baby grand stood in the front room, lid raised, the music for a Beethoven sonata open on the stand.

Upstairs, the bathroom, and two guest bedrooms that looked as if they hadn't been used in months. They hesitated at the last door.

'We're going to look like a right pair of Charlies if she just came home for a kip,' Baker whispered.

But the room was empty. They already knew it would be.

The bed was made, all the clothes neatly hung in the wardrobes or folded in a wide chest of drawers.

'What do you make of it, Dan?'

'I wouldn't even like to guess.' He sighed. 'But she wouldn't vanish of her own accord right after asking me to come over.'

'Seems to me that we need to find her husband.'

'Wherever he is.'

'We can't even really tell the force she's missing yet. She's been gone, what, two hours? They'd just laugh at us.'

'Even you?'

91

'Especially me. They'd say I should know better. I don't suppose you still know anyone in the spy business?'

'No.' His only contact had died three years before.

'Looks like it's you and me, then.'

'I'm not sure I want this,' Markham told him. 'But I don't think we have much bloody choice.' He looked around. 'There's nothing more we can do here.'

They left the way they'd entered, making sure the French doors locked behind them.

'We need to think who'd want her out of the way,' Markham said as they returned to town.

'We don't even know if anyone does. We've no idea what else she and her husband were up to,' Baker pointed out.

'It's this bringing people from East Germany thing. It has to be.'

'All we really know is one little piece.'

'Then we'd better find out more.' He had a sinking feeling in his stomach.

★★★

He stopped at the garage on Buslingthorpe Lane to pick up the Anglia. Good for one more year, that was the verdict, and it definitely felt like a different car when he drove it. More responsive, faster. Exactly what he needed.

There was no note from Amanda Fox pushed through the letterbox. The telephone wasn't ringing with her apology and rushed explanation.

'All we can do is wait and see if we hear from her,' he said.

Baker didn't remove his mackintosh.

'I'll pop over to Millgarth and see what they know about her and that husband of hers.' As Markham raised an eyebrow, he added, 'Just some general things. There might be something.'

And right now anything at all was better than the nothing they had.

Time passed with aching slowness. Markham checked his watch, surprised that only two minutes had gone by. It must have been a half hour. He smoked one cigarette after another, cracking the window open to let in some fresh air. When he finally heard footsteps on the stair he dashed to the door. But the heavy tread was definitely male.

'No word from her yet?' Baker asked.

'I wouldn't still be here if I'd heard anything. What did they say at the station?'

'They know the Foxes right enough.' He raised his eyebrows as he spoke. 'Not much time for Mark, he comes across like too much of a toff. But that Amanda, you know what she's like.'

'Plenty of charm.'

'Something like that,' Baker agreed. 'As to what they do …' He shrugged. 'Their paths don't cross much. It's another way of saying they're in the spy game.'

'I'll go over to Woodhouse Square again later. Maybe she'll be back.'

'You don't really believe that, do you, lad?'

'No,' he admitted. 'But do you have any better suggestions?'

***

First, though, he went to the Post Office, carrying the parcel he'd wrapped the night before. Two LPs. *Back Country Suite* by Mose Allison and Miles Davis' *Cookin'*. Addressed to Carla at the Art Department of Durham University. See what reaction that brought.

There was no one in Woodhouse Square and no answer when he rang the bell. It had always been a vain hope. Slowly he trudged back past the Victorian richness of the infirmary and the Town Hall, then up the Headrow.

His mind was roiling. Not about Amanda Fox: there was nothing he could do about that. The return of Carla. He'd gone over and over everything she said, seeking out the clues it held. Had she been dropping hints, or was it truly nothing more than passing an empty hour with someone she used to know?

He still didn't have any answers there, either.

And what about Georgina? Yes, it was casual, no mention of romance or forever, but they did well enough together. At least he didn't have to make any decision yet; perhaps he never would. But every time he looked at her he'd be thinking …

Baker just shook his head as Markham entered, not even raising his head from the newspaper.

***

By five they'd still heard nothing. The telephone hadn't rung once. His head was aching, a pounding that even two aspirin couldn't budge. Baker left with a weary, 'See you in the morning, lad,' and he was left on his own.

He wanted to go home and close his eyes. But he already knew he wasn't about to do that. He was going to try to find Mark Fox if he was still in Leeds.

He started with the places around town – the Victoria on Great George Street where they'd met before, Yates's Wine Lodge, the Horse and Trumpet and the Three Legs on the Headrow, Whitelock's, the Ship, even the Angel Inn. No sign of the man.

There'd be no crowd in the shebeens – the illegal drinking clubs – before closing time at half past ten. Finally he gave up and drove home, too weary to cook, walking round to Nash's on Harrogate Road for fish and chips. Maybe Fox had gone back to Germany.

It was an evening for the balm of silence, more aspirin and the Home Service at a low, soothing volume; a concert of chamber music.

He must have fallen asleep with the lights on. The jarring ring of the telephone made him scramble up, blinking hard.

'Hello?' He rubbed at his eyes with his free hand. For a moment hope pumped through him. Maybe it was Carla. He heard the coins tumble in a phone box.

'Dan?' It was just a whisper. Not Carla. Not Georgina. Amanda Fox.

'Where are you–' he began but she cut him off.

'Can you come and get me? Please.' There was a tone he hadn't heard before. Desperate. Begging. '*Please.*'

CHAPTER EIGHT

Twenty minutes later Markham parked outside the Peacock, across from Elland Road football ground. The pub was dark, the car park empty. He did as he'd promised, flashing the headlamps twice and keeping the motor running.

'If you do that, I'll know it's you,' Amanda had said on the phone.

'What's happened to you?' Markham asked urgently. 'What is it?'

'Just be there as soon as you can. Please,' she had added again, her voice still quiet and on the edge of tears.

He had made good time into town, very little late night traffic on the roads, then moved haltingly through Beeston, unsure of his bearings until he found the spot. The air was damp, a heavy mist clamped low.

Two cars passed, leaving a blurry trail of lights as they vanished into the distance. He looked at his watch, holding it to try and make out the time. He smoked a Craven A, almost finishing it when he heard the sharp click of heels and saw a vague shape emerge from the shadows.

He could see her for a second as she opened the passenger door and climbed in. Her stockings were torn, knee bloody, dirt and bruises on her face.

'Christ, what–?'

'Drive,' she said quickly. 'Make sure no one's behind us.' She leaned back, moving down the seat to be out of sight.

He kept checking his rear-view mirror. Nothing to be seen. But he still took a long, winding route. When he pulled another cigarette from the packet, he passed one to her, watching from the corner of his eye as she sucked down the smoke eagerly.

'Where?' he asked as he drove across Leeds Bridge and started up Briggate.

'Can we go to yours?' She was nervous, hands constantly in motion, pushing the hair back from her face.

'Fine,' he agreed after a moment.

***

Amanda Fox looked around the flat but she wasn't really paying attention. He took her coat and had a closer look at her. No handbag. Someone had hit her, marks on her cheeks and chin. Her hair was tangled, dirt on her hands and fear in her eyes. Her confident shell had been shattered. She looked terrified.

'There's a bathroom through there if you want to clean up a little.' He pointed.

'Thank you,' she answered as if his words had dragged her back from somewhere inside herself.

While she was gone he rummaged in the larder and found a bottle of brandy. She looked as if she needed it.

By the time she reappeared he had a drink waiting for her. Amanda Fox looked a little fresher, but still stunned.

'Sit down,' Markham told her. 'Sip that and tell me all about it. The last I know is when you rang me this morning asking me to come to your office.'

She drank the brandy gratefully, breathing slowly. She'd brushed her hair and scrubbed off much of the dirt. The stockings had gone and the graze on her knee was clean.

'After I talked to you the doorbell rang,' she began hesitantly. 'There were two men.' She stared at him. 'Police. They showed me their warrant cards. They said I needed to go with them.'

'Did you recognise them at all?'

She shook her head.

'I think they must have been Special Branch. They had that … look. You know, very menacing. They had a car outside and they took me over to a house in Beeston.'

Markham stayed quiet for a moment, then asked, 'Why did you ring me? What did you need to talk to me about so urgently?'

'I received a letter from Mark in the second post.' Amanda stared at him. 'He flew over to Germany yesterday. That was what he told me. But in the letter he said he'd been working for the other side and he needed to get out. I didn't know what to do. And you …'

Those two bloody years in military intelligence. Would he ever be able to put them behind him? Still, there was no need to explain who the other side was. The Russians. But he hadn't seen the letter when they searched the office.

'Did the men take the letter?'

'Yes,' she replied quietly.

'Were they the ones who roughed you up?'

'They seemed to think I had to know about Mark. That I was involved. They believed I had to be part of it.'

'And did you know?' he asked baldly.

Amanda stared at him and shook her head.

'No,' she replied firmly. 'I didn't even have an inkling until I received the letter. When you gave me your report I wondered what the hell was going on, but I never imagined Mark had anything to do with it. He'd always seemed so … upright. Loyal.'

'How did you escape?' Had they let her vanish, he wondered, simply to be able to trail her?'

'I was on the ground floor. There was a bed and a bucket for, you know.' She reddened slightly. 'I heard them moving around upstairs. I managed to force the window and climbed out into the garden. After that I just ran. I didn't know where I was.'

'You didn't have any money?'

'They took my handbag.'

'How did you ring me?'

'I spent a lot of time hiding. After I found a place I was too scared to move. I saw one of them go by a few yards away. Once it got dark I moved again. I saw someone walking his dog and asked to borrow threepence from him. I don't even remember what I told him.' Her eyes were gazing into a distance he couldn't see. 'Something, I suppose. I saw Elland Road. I couldn't think of anyone to ring. You were in the telephone book.' She paused. 'Thank you for coming.'

She drained the glass and he poured another. Amanda had regained a little of her poise but he still saw her hands shaking as she took the cigarette he offered. There were plenty of questions to ask, but they could wait a little while. She needed to feel she was safe.

'Do you want to spend the night here? You can have the bed, I'll sleep out here.'

'Are you sure?' The eagerness in her voice gave her away.

'Yes.'

Relief spread across her face.

'I'm scared to go home in case they're waiting for me.'

'You'll be safe enough,' Markham said and hoped it was true. 'We can take care of everything tomorrow.'

'Thank you.' She leaned forwards and took hold of his wrist. A tight grip, as if she was clinging on for life.

★★★

He found her an old, soft shirt at the back of a drawer. The faint hint of her perfume lingered in the bathroom when he washed and brushed his teeth.

Markham settled in the chair and closed his eyes, although he knew sleep wouldn't rush in.

What could they do about Amanda Fox? They couldn't just leave her to Special Branch; that was obvious. He was willing to believe she hadn't known that her husband was working for the Russians – she wouldn't have had them check on the Germans otherwise. But there was something about this affair that smelt wrong. Twisted. For the life of him he couldn't make out what it was, though.

***

Morning arrived too soon. He woke in the chair, stiff and aching, still in his clothes.

Amanda came through while he was making tea, wearing his shirt, long legs bare, bruises like budding flowers on her skin, dark shadows under her eyes. 'I couldn't really sleep.'

He wasn't surprised; it would have been stranger if she'd managed a full night's rest.

'I still can't believe it about Mark.'

'People can be very good at keeping secrets,' Markham told her.

'But we've been married for ten years,' she objected. 'How could he hide it from me? I've been going over it all, trying to see if there were any clues.'

'Were there?' he asked.

She shook her head.

'Was he working for them the whole time?' Her voice drifted away for a moment. 'I was twenty-one when he proposed. I'd just finished at Girton. Mark showed me this whole new world that I didn't know existed. It's a shock. It's like he's ripped my life apart. Right now I don't even know if he ever loved me or if I was some …' She waved her hands helplessly.

'Everything upside down,' he said kindly.

'Yes,' she agreed quickly. 'Inside out. I couldn't believe it. And then those men. I thought they were going to kill me.'

'You survived.'

'Yes,' she replied dully. 'But what if they come back?'

'We'll make sure they don't.'

'How?'

'My partner used to be on the force. Leave that to him.' Markham hoped he was right.

'And Mark? What am I going to do about that?' She seemed lost. He didn't have an answer for tht question.

'I'll switch the immersion on. Take a bath, maybe it'll help.' Not much of a solution, he thought, but all he had for now.

***

With the worst of the wear brushed from her clothes she looked presentable. Markham kept his eyes on the mirrors as he drove, but no one seemed to be following. No large men waiting outside the office on Albion Place or on the stairs.

Baker was already there, eyes widening in astonishment when he saw her.

'We're looking after Mrs Fox for the moment,' Markham told him. 'Special Branch grabbed her yesterday. Took her to a place in Beeston and gave her a going over.'

'What?' The astonishment was plain on his face. 'Why?'

'It seems that Mark Fox has been working for the Russians.'

'I got a letter from him yesterday.' Her voice quavered a little. She took a breath. 'He's defected.'

'I think you'd best tell me all about it,' Baker said.

By the time she finished he was frowning.

'Penny to a pound the Branch didn't tell anyone they were here. I think I'll wander down to Millgarth and let them know. I'm sure they'd like a chat with our colleagues from London.' He turned to Amanda. 'You're certain they were Special Branch?'

'That's what they said.'

He stared at her face and nodded.

'Sounds right from what they did. And they have a place in Beeston?' He rubbed his chin. 'Some people aren't going to be pleased with them. Give it a few hours until they're picked up and I daresay you'll be safe enough.'

'Even at home?' There was a tremor in her voice.

'Even there, luv.' He smiled. 'I daresay you'll still have to talk to MI5 or whoever it is. But they should be fairly civilised.'

'Thank you.' She looked at one of them then the other. 'I don't know what I'd have done …'

'We'll put the bill in the post.' Baker gave a broad wink, put on his mackintosh and left.

***

He was back within an hour, rubbing his hands together and smiling.

'Wait until dinner and you should be fine,' he announced. 'Leeds police picked up two blokes from the Branch loitering outside your office on Woodhouse Square. They were waiting to see if you'd show up. They're not hired for their brains.' Baker shook his head. 'Right now it's just a case of making sure there are no more Branch heavies around, then they'll pack them on the train to London later. They won't be coming back, either.'

'Are you certain?' She sounded as if she didn't believe him.

'Positive. I spoke to the Chief Super myself.' He sat down and lit his pipe, working on it until he was wreathed in smoke and smiling with satisfaction. 'The question is what we do now.'

'Nothing,' Markham said quickly. 'We're in this by accident, that's all.'

'But we *are* in it,' Baker pointed out. 'Can't avoid that.'

A look between them: something to discuss later, when they were alone.

'I'll walk you back over when you're ready,' Markham said to Amanda.

'Thank you.' She looked at Baker. 'Are you sure I'll be safe?' She couldn't keep the fright out of her voice.

'As houses.'

'I still can't believe Mark did it,' she blurted.

'He sent you the letter,' Markham told her.

'I know.' Her voice was bleak. She looked lost, baffled by life. But anyone would. In the last twenty-four hours she'd learned that the man she loved was a traitor, she'd been abducted and beaten by Special Branch, escaped and gone on the run.

Her life had experienced an earthquake. Now she had to pick her way through the rubble of it all and find a way to the future. Whatever that might be.

'Come on,' he said kindly 'You can go home and rest.'

A cup of tea first in the cafe at Schofield's, spinning out the time. It was her suggestion, as if she was reluctant to go and pick up the traces of her life. Finally they reached Woodhouse Square. No men waiting around. Her car was still parked there, a sporty Sunbeam Alpine. As she unlocked the door she looked up at him.

'Your partner, can I believe him?'

'He was a copper for a long time. He knows what he's talking about.'

'I hope you're right.' A sudden thought hit her. 'We had a couple of other small jobs. Nothing related to … would you be willing to take them on? It's very ordinary stuff.'

'Of course,' Markham agreed.

'It's the least I can do after all your help.' Life was falling apart but politeness had to be observed.

He watched her drive away then turned and walked back to the office.

***

'They've been on the blower,' Baker said.

'Who?' He sat at the desk and lit a cigarette.

'Your spy friends.'

Markham glared. 'What did they want?'

'What else? A quiet word about Mark Fox.' He shrugged. 'Par for the course. They'll have someone here in the morning.'

'We don't have much to tell them.'

Baker lit his pipe. The whole ritual of it was a way of taking time to think, Markham realised.

'Of course, you know where all this began, don't you?' he said finally. 'When that Miss Harding came and asked us to look for her missing lodger.'

'De Vries. Vreiten. And it was your pals in the police who sent her here.'

'That's right,' he admitted. 'And he went missing because he was dead. Then another of them died in a car crash. Ask yourself something, Dan: if those two hadn't died, would any of this have come out?'

'Sooner or later.'

'Maybe,' Baker said quietly. 'But it would have been a lot later.' He grimaced. 'Still, it did come out. And we'd already decided they weren't coincidences. You remember?'

'Of course,' he answered. 'And probably not suicide and an accident, either.' It was over. They'd been paid. Nothing to do with them any more. 'So what?'

'Think about it, who could have killed them?'

'Our side or theirs,' Markham said after some thought. 'Who else could it be?'

'Exactly.' He used the pipe stem as a pointer. 'And if it's ours then the spies should know all about it already. True?'

'Yes. So what are you saying?'

'Why did Special Branch nab Mrs Fox?'

'I don't know,' he admitted.

'The spies probably didn't tell them anything.' He snorted. 'But if our side didn't kill those blokes, think about who did.'

'Are you honestly trying to say there's a Russian assassin in Leeds?' Markham asked.

Baker raised his eyebrows. 'Why not? It's possible.'

'Then we're definitely better off out of it. Tomorrow we'll tell them all we know and let them get on with it.' He massaged his useless fingers. 'It's none of our business now.'

'Would you trust them? You were one of them.'

'A long time ago, and at a very low level,' Markham told him.

'Would you trust them?' Baker repeated.

'As far as I can throw them.'

'Well, then.'

'Well what?'

'Seems to me that we should do what we can,' Baker said.

'No,' Markham said and slapped his palm down on the desk. 'This isn't our bloody fight. I keep telling you that. Let them all kill each other if that's what they want.' If they became involved in this they'd be so far out of their depth that they'd drown.

'I don't see how we can avoid it.'

'We can and we will.' He could feel anger rising inside. 'There's nothing happening. I'm going to take the rest of the day off.'

'You're the boss.' Baker smiled.

'That's right,' he said. 'I am.'

***

At first he headed to Boots, hoping to see Georgina for a few minutes. But why? They'd already arranged to meet that evening and his mind was still reeling after Carla's visit.

Instead he wandered around Leeds market. The strong smells of the meat and fish aisles, plenty of fresh vegetables. The second-hand bookstall with its perfume of slightly mouldy paper. A press of women walked around, wrapped in their heavy coats against the November cold, holding their raffia and string bags tightly as they did their shopping.

On Briggate he walked to and fro, looking down into the basement at Woolworth's, then window shopped at the displays in Marks & Spencer and Matthias Robinson.

Stop at the Kardomah for a cup of coffee? He considered it for a moment then returned to Albion Place, unlocked the Anglia and drove home. Chapel Allerton was quiet, just a few housewives moving from shop to shop – Perkin's the baker to the butcher and up to Preston's the grocer.

In the flat he took off his suit, changing into an old pair of trousers and a shirt. The bedroom still smelt of Amanda Fox. The shirt she'd worn was tossed on the bed.

While the tea mashed he put on the Art Tatum and Ben Webster LP. The last thing the pianist recorded before he died. The sound filled the flat, the tenor sax calming him immediately with its lush sensuality. By the time the needle rose at the end of the side he felt better about everything.

Smoke rose from his cigarette in a gentle stream. He stood by the window, staring down at Harrogate Road but not really seeing it. Just letting the world pass by. Finally he stubbed out the butt in the ashtray and went into the bedroom.

Rest. That was what he needed. He'd barely slept during the night.

***

Markham surfaced to the sound of banging, not sure where it was coming from as he opened his eyes. Blinking, he glanced at his wristwatch. Five minutes to four. Almost like night outside.

The noise continued, steady and growing louder. The door. Someone was knocking at his door. He struggled up, body still feeling heavy and moving slowly, dragging on shirt and trousers.

'Hold your bloody horses,' he shouted

Dressed, pushing his fingers through his hair, he turned the lock. There was a man in a trilby, cheap suit, and worn mackintosh, a thin Clark Gable moustache over his upper lip. Next to him a copper in uniform, the point of his helmet almost touching the ceiling.

'Are you Daniel Markham?' the man in plain clothes asked. He was short, probably the bare minimum for a policeman, with an aggressive, bantam expression on his face.

'Yes. Why?'

'I'm Detective Sergeant Anderson, sir. I'd like you to accompany me down to the police station if you'd be so good.' Everything very polite, but the tone brooked no objection.

'Why?' he asked in confusion. 'What's happened?'

'We have reason to believe you might be able to help us in our enquiries.'

'What enquiries?' He put a hand against the jamb. 'If you want me to help you, I want to know with what.'

Anderson glared at him. 'Do you know a man called Morten Blum?'

Markham felt the pit of his stomach sink.

'I know who he is. I've never met him. We were hired to check on him – my partner and I. Why? What's happened?'

'He's dead, sir, and under very suspicious circumstances. If you'd like to get your coat, we can be on our way.'

'Yes, of course.' He slipped on a sports jacket, the overcoat on top, and gloves, then turned out the light and locked the door before following them down the stairs.

Christ, what was going on?

CHAPTER NINE

The smell of disinfectant in the back of the unmarked black Humber Hawk couldn't quite mask the acid stench of vomit. Markham rolled the window down a little; better to be cold than wanting to gag. The leather of the seat was brittle and uncomfortable, scratching against him.

The uniformed bobby drove, Anderson sitting next to him. No conversation, nothing. Just a quiet drive down into town, parking at the back of Millgarth, across the street from the bus station.

In the interview room they brought him a mug of dark, sweet tea and left him with a silent constable at the door. Ten minutes became half an hour. Finally Detective Sergeant Anderson bustled in, accompanied by a younger man in a dark suit, a V-neck jumper over his shirt and tie

No apology for keeping him waiting.

'This is Detective Constable Naylor. We're going to ask you some questions about Morten Blum.'

'That's fine,' Markham said. He settled back on the chair and crossed his arms. 'Before you start, though, what happened to him?'

Anderson paused, looking as though he was unsure whether to answer, then said, 'He was the victim of a driver who hit him and didn't stop. He was dead by the time the ambulance arrived.'

'I see.' Easy enough to prove he wasn't responsible; they only needed to look at his motor car. 'So why do you want to talk to me?'

'His landlady told us you and Mr Baker had searched his room the other day.'

'That's right.'

'Why did you do it?'

'He was one name on a list we'd been asked to check. There were five of them in all.' He waited a moment. 'Blum's the third one to die.' Anderson's head came up sharply and Markham smiled. 'Haven't you talked to Mr Baker yet?' He paused for a second to give emphasis to his words. 'Ex-Detective Sergeant Baker?'

'Not yet. Perhaps you'd better tell me what's going on here.'

He laid it out simply and concisely. Naylor wrote everything in his notebook.

'You've never seen Blum or talked to him?'

'No.'

'And you say you found evidence that this Blum, or whoever he really is, might be a Russian spy?'

'It looks that way. Especially as Mark Fox – the man who brought him over – has defected. You should talk to his wife. She can tell you how Special Branch abducted and hit her.'

Anderson winced and ran a hand through his hair. It was short, sandy, and Brylcreemed to his scalp.

'You've got to understand, this whole story sounds rather unbelievable.'

'Try being inside it,' Markham said wryly and lit another cigarette. Naylor waved the smoke away from his face.

'I took a quick glance at your vehicle,' Anderson said. 'I didn't see any damage.'

'That's because there isn't any.' He was tired, he wanted to be rid of the whole business of Germans and spies and death. 'I don't see why you had to bring me down here to talk.'

'Maybe because murder is very serious, Mr Markham.' His voice was sombre. 'And make no mistake, Morten Blum was murdered.'

'I wish I could help you.' With one more from the list dead, there was something very dark going on. And what he wanted was to stay far away from it.

'We'll talk to Mr Baker and Mrs …'

'Fox,' Naylor said.

'Yes.'

'You might want to ring her first. Otherwise she'll think men from the Branch have come back.'

Anderson ran his tongue inside his cheeks then gave a quick nod.

'One other thing,' Markham continued. 'Someone from MI5 or whoever is going to be here tomorrow. He'll want to talk to everyone, too. Even more so in the light of this.'

'I see.' The detective didn't look happy at the information. He understood that from the next morning he'd be playing second fiddle in any investigation.

Markham glanced at his watch. Almost six. Just enough time to go and meet Georgina outside Lewis's on the hour.

'Is there anything else?' He picked up his hat and stood.

'You're free to go. We might need to speak to you again.'

***

The wind had dropped as he walked along the Headrow. He waited in the doorway of the department store, hands in his pockets, a cigarette burning in his mouth, lost in his thoughts.

Another one gone. His mind drifted back to the conversation with Baker during the morning. Who was murdering these men? And why now?

'You're miles away.'

He turned, seeing Georgina smile at him. She was lovely, talented, a good, sweet person. Yet Carla simply had to reappear, to stroll through the edge of his life again, and he was chasing after her.

'Just work,' Markham said and kissed her cheek. 'Where do you want to eat?'

'I really fancy the Red Lion out in Stanningley,' she told him. They'd gone there during the summer and enjoyed the food.

'Not tonight. I don't have the car.'

'Has it broken down?'

'No, nothing like that,' he replied. Then he had to quickly explain how the police had come, and why, seeing the expression of concern grow on her face.

'How dangerous is all this?' Georgina asked.

'Not a bit. Not for us, anyway,' he assured her. Time to change the subject. 'You'll have to pick somewhere in town.'

In the end they settled on Youngman's. Fish and chips. It was a large restaurant, almost cavernous, and already busy with the evening trade, couples and families hunched over their tables as the waitresses scurried to and fro.

Haddock and good, crisp potatoes. Bread and butter. A large pot of tea. He remembered before the war when a meal like this was a treat. Once a month if they were lucky. And always at home, never going out to eat. He'd be sent down to buy it, carrying the food home, the wonderful smell of it wrapped in newspaper, his hands growing warmer yard by yard until he was running. The time he dropped the package, terrified that the food would spill all over the pavement.

'Dan,' she said after they'd finished, the taste of vinegar in his mouth.

'What?'

'Would you mind very much if I just went home after this? Only it's been a sod of a day.'

'Of course not,' he answered softly, trying not to show the feeling of relief. 'It's fine.'

***

He waited with her for the number 56, then walked back to New Briggate, standing outside the newsagent for the number 2 to take him home to Chapel Allerton. Across the street someone opened the door of Studio 20 and for a minute the sound of trad. jazz drifted on the air. Dixieland. Perhaps it was just as well that Georgina had pulled the plug on the evening; they'd have been back out of there in a minute. That was just noise to him, not the music he loved.

Markham climbed to the top deck and sat at the front, digging out change to pay the conductress when she appeared. So used to driving, this was a different experience, looking down on the streets as they passed with time to savour the view. Through Sheepscar, up Chapeltown Road. Ample time to smoke a cigarette and take in the night. And to try not to think about another death.

The flat was cold. He made tea and put on some Duke Ellington. A big warm sound to fill the place. By the time he was brushing his teeth he was glad the police had come calling earlier.

Everything was official now. The coppers were looking into Blum's killing and they'd examine the other deaths again. The spies were involved. There was nothing at all for a pair of enquiry agents. Thank God. They could go back to divorce and frauds. There might not be any glamour to that but it paid the bills.

***

'Did they have you down to Millgarth yesterday?' he asked Baker.

'Aye, turned up in the middle of my tea.' The big man pursed his lips. 'Told them they'd have to wait until I'd had my pudding.'

Markham laughed.

'Did they?'

'Of course, don't be daft. They're coppers and I used to be one of them. Who talked to you? Was it Anderson?'

'Yes.'

'I feel sorry for the poor sod. He's out of his depth and he knows it.' He packed the pipe with shag tobacco.

'It's his worry now. We can go back to normal.'

'I liked the touch of excitement.' Baker's eyes twinkled and he smiled. 'You did, too. I could see it on your face, Dan.'

'Not really,' he said. 'I'm just glad the circus is over. Amanda Fox said she'd turn over some of their ordinary cases to us, since they're not in business any more.'

'Makes you wonder what's ordinary for them.' Baker glanced at his wristwatch. 'Those spies should be here at ten.'

***

There was only one and he arrived exactly on time. With his bowler hat, overcoat, briefcase and brolly, he looked like the archetypal Whitehall civil servant.

'William Warner.' He introduced himself with a handshake, voice clipped and precise. 'Thank you for seeing me.'

He took out a folder and scanned the contents for a few seconds.

'I gather the local CID has already talked to you about Mr Blum. We had them on the blower last night.' He gave a quick smile. 'I'll pop over to see them later but I just wanted to go over everything with you again.' A quick smile and a nod and he launched into his questions.

A simple rehash. There was no reason not to tell the truth and lay it all out. Finally Warner came around to the heart of the matter – Mark and Amanda Fox.

'Do you think Mrs Fox knew what her husband was up to?' He looked from Markham to Baker.

'No,' Markham answered. 'Why would she have hired us to check on the men if she did?'

'Quite.'

'And she'd have known better than to let Special Branch in.'

'I heard about that. I rather think we owe Mrs Fox an apology.' He crossed one leg over the other, pulling back on the knee of his pinstripe trousers. 'You met Mark Fox once, you said?'

'That's right,' Baker told him. 'Very briefly in a pub.'

'Why there, do you think?'

'It was between here and his office. Made sense. Why?'

He smiled easily.

'Part of my job is to wonder why. You never know when there's a reason.'

A few more questions and he closed the folder once more. He hadn't made any notes. But Warner had remembered every word. Markham was sure of that. There was a quiet, quick intelligence in his eyes.

'He's the type you've got to watch out for,' Baker observed when the man had gone. 'He'll store it all away in his brain and pick up on the slightest thing. Nothing flashy, ordinary as they come, but sharp.'

'All we did was tell him what we know.' He stood. 'Come on, we might as well go and get something to eat.'

'Ten to one he'll be back. They always are, that lot, once they get their hooks in you.' Baker rubbed his stomach. 'You're right. My belly thinks my throat's been slit.'

***

They'd been back for an hour when the telephone rang. This time he knew the voice immediately.

'What can I do for you, Amanda?'

'Those cases I promised you,' she said. She sounded surprisingly cool and controlled, as if the abduction and her terror had never happened. 'If you're free I could bring them by and discuss them.'

'Of course.'

'I'll be there in a few minutes.'

★★★

Skilful makeup hid the bruises. If he didn't know about them he'd never have guessed. She looked elegant, wearing an expensive jacket and skirt, a wide, soft belt emphasising her slim waist. She placed three files on the blotter in front of him.

'It's not much but Mark concentrated on … other things.' Amanda Fox kept her gaze on his face. 'And it's the least I can do after all the trouble.'

'Thank you.'

'They're all quite straightforward. I've rung them to say you'll be in touch.' She started to rise from the chair.

'You saw the police and MI5?'

She settled again and took a cigarette from her handbag.

'Oh yes.' She blew out a long plume of smoke. 'I talked to them both. The same questions over and over. Only to be expected, I suppose.'

'Did they believe you?'

She closed her eyes then opened them again.

'I hope so.' Her voice was weary. 'I really hope so. I was telling them the truth. I didn't know what Mark was doing. I still don't have any idea why he did it. It doesn't make sense. I keep going over and over it.'

'Money?' It was the usual reason; he knew that from his experiences in Germany.

'He had plenty. I thought he did, anyway.' She sighed. 'I haven't had time to check yet.'

'What are you going to do now?' he asked kindly.

'I don't know. It'll take a few days to close up the office. Then I'll go through the house. That chap from London is there now. I told him to look through everything if he wanted, just to show I've got nothing to hide.'

'Are you going to stay in Leeds?' He was curious, nothing more. She cocked her head and pushed her lips together.

'I haven't even thought about it,' she told him emptily. 'I grew up in the south, but my parents are dead and my brother lives in America. My friends are here – if I have any left now, that is. After all, I'm the wife of a traitor. Sooner or later everyone's going to know.' She ground out the cigarette angrily then shrugged. 'But I suppose I have more of a life here than anywhere else. There must be jobs, mustn't there? After all, we've never had it so good.' She made a sour face. 'Sorry, I suppose I'm a little bitter. I'll be fine, don't worry.' She indicated the files. 'Good luck with those.'

She was gone, only the faintest hint of her perfume left in the air. Did he believe her? Yes, he reflected. If the police or secret service had any doubts about her she wouldn't be walking around Leeds now. It sounded as if her husband had betrayed her even more than his country. How did anyone rebuild a life after that?

Markham glanced through the folders. Two possible frauds and one that seemed to involve a man stealing from his mother, slowly stripping away her savings. As she said, straightforward. He pushed them aside.

Baker had left before Amanda Fox arrived. A few errands to run, gone for the day and goodbye.

He sat alone in the office, smoking and staring out of the window at the November gloom. It looked as if a fog was settling in, just in time for going home. It would be bad. The air might be cleaner these days, with fewer smogs, but it would still be thick and sooty. Policemen on point duty wearing white sleeves over their uniforms to direct traffic, the acrid taste in the mouth. People coughing everywhere.

He could ring the new clients and introduce himself, but that could wait for the morning. Better to get a jump on things and home to Chapel Allerton.

Everyone else seemed to have the same idea. It was stop and go heading out of the city centre. Each minute the fog seemed to thicken. Much more and he'd be able to lower the window on the Anglia and stir it.

The farther he went from the city centre, the wispier it became. By the time he reached the flat, the fog was no more than a suggestion, hints in the air that it would arrive later. It was an evening for listening to Monk, for those odd angles of melody and piano to push their way through it all. A night for staying at home with both bars glowing on the electric fire.

At half past seven he glanced out of the window. About one hundred yards' visibility. By eight he couldn't even make out the signs on the shops across Harrogate Road. Tomorrow morning was going to be a mess.

The sound of the telephone bell startled him. Bad news; it usually was when someone called him at home. Another from the list dead? He lifted the receiver cautiously and gave his number.

'You shouldn't have.' For a moment he couldn't breathe and his heart beat heavily. 'But I'm glad you did. That Mose Allison is wonderful.'

'Hello, Carla.' He felt as if he could barely speak the words. God, this was stupid. He had it bad. And that certainly wasn't good.

'He really is hip, isn't he?' The enthusiasm brimmed in her voice. 'That singing just sounds so lazy.'

'Have you played the Miles record yet?' he asked.

'I haven't had time, but if it's as good as Mose …'

'Very different, but yes, it is.'

'Bloody hell, Dan, new music. Do you know how lovely that is? My students all want skiffle or that horrible New Orleans jazz.' She paused for a moment, suddenly horrified. 'Oh God, you don't like that stuff, do you?'

'Can't stand it.' He couldn't help but smile.

'Oh good.' Carla sounded satisfied. 'Thank you for meeting me the other night, too. It was good to see you again.'

'You too.'

There was the smallest hesitation before she spoke again.

'I'll be coming through Leeds again on Friday. I'm going to see Mummy and Daddy for the weekend. I don't suppose I could persuade you out for a meal, could I? Repay you for the drink and the records.'

'I'd like that,' he told her, meaning every word.

'Really?' She seemed surprised. 'Good. How about six at the station? I'll be the one with a carnation in my buttonhole and carrying a rolled-up copy of *The Times*.'

He chuckled. She'd defused the tension growing inside him.

For the rest of the evening he felt as if he was buzzing. In bed his thoughts slid around as he tried to sleep. All she'd done was add to his problems but he didn't really care.

***

One day. Two. They started work on the clients Amanda Fox had passed on to them. Markham took the frauds. He'd worked on cases like this before. Baker had the woman who was being fleeced by her son. He was old enough and bluff enough that she'd open up to him.

The frauds both lacked imagination. Just two hours in and he'd already found the first of them. Now he only had to follow the trail and discover who was responsible. It would take a little time but he'd get there.

Baker pushed himself out of the chair and folded his copy of the *Express*. He still hadn't replaced the card table with a real desk. As he pulled on the mackintosh he said, 'You're looking very dapper today. Meeting the girlfriend?'

'Not tonight.' He was wearing the suit he'd bought at the start of autumn. Pale, subtle grey, a tie shot through with silver thread.

'You'd better hope she doesn't find out, then.'

'I'm seeing an old friend who's passing through.' It was true, as far as it went.

Baker raised an eyebrow conspiratorially and smirked.

'You think she'll believe that, do you, Dan? Let me give you a tip. Nobody puts on his Sunday best just to meet an old friend. You're playing with fire. Better make sure that Georgina doesn't see you.'

'It's all innocent.'

'Aye, and United will win the league this year. I'll see you on Monday unless a woman kills you first.'

He sat, idly massaging the two useless fingers on his left hand as if they might regain some life. He thought about what Baker had said.

It *was* all innocent, he told himself. What they'd once had was history even if he had hoped for more. Carla was too sensible for anything else.

★★★

But he was still waiting eagerly at the end of the platform when the train pulled in with a thick whoosh of steam and the tired screech of brakes. The station was dirty, sweet wrappers and empty cigarette packets blowing across the floor. The thick smell of smoke filled the air but he hardly noticed, watching the people as they alighted.

She was carrying a suitcase, wearing a three-quarter-length coat in bright royal blue, her eyes seeking him out then smiling as she spotted him. A peck on the cheek and the smell of her scent on his skin. He reached for the case.

'I'll take that, if you like.'

'It's light,' she told him, keeping a firm grip on it. 'Do you know where I'd like to eat? Donmar. For old times' sake.'

It had been their place when they were going out. Where they'd had their last meal together and he'd watched her walk out of his life.

'Of course.' He'd tried going back there, alone and with others. But it had never been the same.

There was idle chatter as they walked through town. Carla gazed around, picking out all the changes. The remnants of the fog still clung and people passed with wet, bronchitic coughs. As they opened the door the restaurant felt like an oasis of warmth and light in the gloom.

'It hasn't changed a bit,' she said as they were seated. The same posters on the wall, the same music playing. Even the tablecloths had the bright gingham pattern he remembered.

'Have you been back to Italy?' That final summer she'd gone for a few weeks, in search of history and inspiration for her own art.

'Haven't had the chance.' She sipped a glass of Chianti and lit a cigarette. 'Between students and painting I've been too busy. And the money, of course.'

'You're making a name for yourself.'

'Don't believe everything you read,' she warned.

He was surprised. As they ate the conversation flowed freely and easily. She'd taken off the coat to show a blouse in the bright summer colours she loved. The ones that always seemed so out of place in drab, grey Leeds.

The food tasted better than he remembered, plenty of flavour in the sauce, the spaghetti not too limp. He asked Carla about her work, about Durham. Her questions stayed carefully neutral – business, the way Leeds had altered since she left. Finally, over coffee he made himself ask the question that had been eating at him since they'd sat in the Scarborough Taps last Sunday.

'I was surprised when I heard from you last week. Out of the blue like that.'

She fiddled with the cup. 'I've never forgotten you, you know. It was just the way things were. You remember.'

He nodded, letting her speak.

'I needed to get away from here. And from you. But it all feels like a long time ago.'

Markham smiled. 'Still …'

'I know. I did honestly have some time to kill. But I've sort of kept track of you. I knew you had a telephone. I thought it was time for us to meet again.'

'I'm glad.'

'I thought you might be when you sent the records,' she said wryly. 'And I do love the Miles Davis. That sax player, he's very good, isn't he?'

'Yes.'

'I suppose I wanted to see how we got along now.' She took one of his cigarettes and lit it with slow, deliberate movements. 'Actually, I haven't told you everything,' Carla began. 'I've been back here a few times in the last months. The Art College has offered me a rather good job. Teaching but with plenty of time to paint. I was a bit hesitant about getting in touch with you.'

'That's great news,' he said, and meant it. 'Are you going to take it?'

She nodded her head, thick hair falling around her shoulders.

'I think so. Decent money. I like Durham, the cathedral and the university and the river are beautiful, but I don't know … there's something about Leeds, isn't there?'

'Yes,' Markham agreed. He couldn't imagine living any-where else. The city inhabited him.

'It's not just me, is it?' Carla asked, and he knew she wasn't referring to the place.

'No.' He sighed. For a long time he'd imagined a scene like this. But it had never happened. And now …

He paid the bill and they left. Across New Briggate the Gothic turrets of the Grand Theatre rose up.

'We could go down to Studio 20 if you want,' she suggested.

'Not tonight.' There was the possibility Georgina might be there.

'You know,' she began, voice husky, 'my parents aren't expecting me until tomorrow morning.'

Markham closed his eyes and leaned against the wall, feel-ing the dampness of the fog on the bricks.

'Perhaps you'd better surprise them,' he said eventually. 'I told you I was going out with someone.' If his parents had given him one thing, it was a sense of honour.

'I'm glad you said that,' she told him. 'I like you even more for it.' She gave him a peck on the cheek. 'But I need to ask you again. This thing with her, are you telling the truth that it's not serious?'

'No, it's not. Really. But it wouldn't be fair. Not without me ending things with her first.' He took a deep breath. 'If you come back, would you want us to start going out again?'

'Only if you're free.' She took his hand and squeezed it gently. 'The real question is what you want, Dan.'

'You already know the answer to that.'

'I should tell you, the job's settled. I start in January.' Carla picked up the suitcase and put her free arm through his. 'You don't mind walking me back to the station, do you?'

'Not at all.' He smiled.

'I rather think the ball's in your court now,' she told him.

CHAPTER TEN

It was a weekend on his own. Georgina was working on Saturday then meeting some friends in the evening. Probably for the best, Markham decided; it gave him time to wrestle with the problem.

But it wasn't a problem. Not really. Deep inside he already knew the answer. The only difficult thing was how to let Georgina down gently and carefully. She deserved that, at the very least. They were friends who happened to also be lovers, he told himself again. Even so …

He pottered around the flat, listening to music and reading, only to discover himself staring absently into space, not convinced he hadn't dreamt the fact that Carla still wanted him.

★★★

'You look like a cat that ate the cream and can't decide if it's gone bad.' Markham laughed.

'I didn't know I was that obvious.'

'CID,' Baker told him with a nod. 'Trained observer.'

Rain on Sunday had washed away the last of the fog. There'd been a frost overnight; he'd needed to scrape it off the car windscreen before he could drive to the office.

The office radiator hissed and steamed, and condensation trickled down the window. He'd go back to work on the frauds.

'How are you getting on with that woman?' he asked. 'The one who's being bilked by her son.'

'She just lets things out in dribs and drabs.' Baker sighed. 'I think half of it is that she likes the company.'

'But it's real?'

'Oh aye. I've seen the statements from the bank. I just need a little more from her then I'll go and see him. If he doesn't repay it all then I'll take the information to the police. It's virtually done. Over in a couple of hours.'

'I should have those frauds finished today or tomorrow.'

'This is what it's like, then? Feast and famine?'

'More or less.' He smiled. 'You'll get used to it.'

'I don't mind. I've got my pension.'

They were still talking when the telephone rang. Markham listened for a moment then handed over the receiver.

'For you.' He shrugged. 'Sergeant Anderson.'

He heard Baker's end of the conversation, the one-word replies and frowns.

'You'd better talk to him,' he said finally and passed the handset back. 'About your friend Amanda.'

'When did you last see Mrs Fox?' Anderson asked. He sounded worried.

'Wednesday,' Markham replied. 'She stopped by with folders on three cases she was passing on. Why?'

'Do you know if she was planning on leaving Leeds?'

'No,' Markham replied, feeling a prickle of fear up his spine. 'She said she was staying to sort things out. Why?'

'She's vanished,' Anderson replied with embarrassment.

'Didn't you have someone watching her?'

'Not all the time,' he admitted after a moment. 'We don't have the manpower. No one seems to have seen her since Friday.'

'Are you sure Special Branch hasn't nabbed her again?'

'We made dead certain of that,' he replied darkly.

'What about her car?'

'It's not in her garage or by the office. That's why we think she's gone. I've been in touch with Scotland Yard. She won't get far.' Anderson sounded more hopeful than certain.

If she'd been gone since Friday, she'd had time to leave the country. Maybe they'd all been wrong about Amanda Fox. Perhaps she was cleverer than he'd imagined.

Or maybe someone else had taken her.

'Let me know when you find her, please,' he said. 'Did she take her passport?'

'We found it in her house,' the sergeant said. 'In a drawer in the lounge.'

'What about clothes? Suitcase?'

'Hard to tell, but it doesn't look like she's taken anything. But she wouldn't, it would be too obvious.'

The line went dead.

It was possible. She could have been good enough to fool them all. She could have run. If she really was involved in spying for the Russians she'd almost certainly have a false passport. If no one was following her she could have vanished quite easily.

'She could be in Moscow by now,' Baker said.

It was true. But he wasn't so certain. If she really was working for the Russians she'd have vanished with her husband. When they'd talked she'd seemed completely honest with her feelings and doubts. So uncertain about everything that he'd believed her. She genuinely didn't seem to understand what her husband had done, shocked and taken aback by it. If she'd been acting then she deserved an Oscar.

'Maybe she just needed to get away for a few days.'

'Where? A weekend in Scarborough in November?' Baker snorted. 'Would you?'

'No, but I haven't had everything I know fall apart around me.'

'She fooled us both, that's all there is too it. She's probably in the Kremlin now laughing at everyone here.'

Markham lit a Craven A, drew the smoke deep into his lungs and tried to weigh it all in his mind.

'No,' he said finally. 'I don't buy it. Not if her clothes and her passport are still there. Someone could have her. That Russian assassin you were talking about.'

'It's not our problem, anyway, is it?' Baker said. 'You're the one who's spent the last week or so saying that We're better out of it. Remember?'

'That was before this,' he said. 'If everyone believes she's gone and she hasn't …'

Maybe he felt he owed her a little something. Some trust. Or perhaps he simply needed to know she hadn't played him for a complete idiot.

'And how do we find out?' Baker objected. 'Do you even know where to start? Friends? Family?'

'She said her parents were dead and her brother lives in the States.'

'You don't have any bloody idea where to begin then, do you?'

'I'll give it today,' Markham said. 'If I don't turn anything up I'll let it go.'

***

George Grout. If anyone could point him in the right direction it would be George. He'd be where he always was, sitting in the Market Tavern from opening time onwards, fading away to a house somewhere only when they called time and put the towels over the pumps.

He dressed in bespoke suits, shoes highly polished, hair expensively barbered. George always looked out of place in

127

the den of thieves. It was a rundown pub, at least twenty years past its prime, about fifty yards from Millgarth police station. And filled with more crooks per square foot than anywhere else in Leeds. Odd, with the coppers so close, but there was often no reason to things.

Markham ordered a shandy and a small measure of Teacher's scotch and carried them to a table under a dusty window. Grout was like any number of men he'd met since he became an enquiry agent; his currency was information. From his appearance he did well from it, still with a suntan in the English November. A crisp, folded handkerchief peeked from the breast pocket of his jacket. Dapper, Markham's mother would have called him. On the verge of flash.

'Hello George,' he said as he sat down, pushing the whisky across the table. Grout raised his gaze.

'Morning, Mr Markham.' It was a Leeds voice, but with the roughest edges rubbed away. He raised the glass in a toast. 'Your very good health.' He sipped and gave an approving nod. 'Now, what can I do for you?'

'Mark and Amanda Fox.'

Grout chuckled and said, 'I've heard you've had dealings with them. Before he skipped across the Iron Curtain. And you've done a bit of business with her.'

'True enough,' he admitted with a smile. George always knew what was going on, but he'd say nothing until his palm was crossed with pound notes. 'But I want to know about them before that time.'

'What sort of things?'

'Who knew them, the kind of dealings they had, things like that.' He thought for a moment. 'And whether there might be any Russians in Leeds.'

'Russians?' Grout asked with a worried frown. 'Not heard of any of them.'

'Germans?'

'Always a few.' He shrugged. 'Fox brought some here, but I'm sure you know that. If they've any sense they don't admit they're Jerries, though. Not since the war. I can ask around.'

'Any who've arrived in the last month or so.'

Grout raised an eyebrow, his mind working on connections.

'I'll try to find out. So you need to know about the Foxes. How much do you want to spend?'

'Ten quid?' It was a fair bit of money, but he needed the information.

'That'll get you the basics. Going deep is twenty.'

Markham reached for his wallet, taking out four fivers, and placing them on the table. Grout made no move to pick them up; that would be crass. Later would do.

'You know the enquiry agent stuff they do is just a front,' he said. 'They carry out a few jobs, but it's not enough to keep body and soul together.'

'I know that much.'

'It's all that stuff he did in Germany that paid the bills. And he has money, of course. Had, anyway. I don't suppose they pay much attention to all that in Moscow.'

'Who did they deal with here?'

Grout shook his head.

'Everything's decided down in London '

'But they must have had contacts up here.'

'A few.' But he didn't say more.

'Who are they, George?'

'If I were you I'd want to talk to two people: Tim Hill and John Crews.'

'I don't know them.'

'That's the whole point. They keep a very low profile.'

Markham didn't bother to ask how Grout knew their names. He'd never say, anyway.

'How do I find them?'

'If you want Hill, take a look at Cokely's. Crews works for a company in Hunslet. Farren's.'

'Let me guess: both those companies do defence work.'

'I've heard they maybe do some hush-hush things,' was as far as Grout would commit himself. He adjusted the knot on his tie. 'That's what I know offhand about the Foxes. I'll see what else I can dig up. If there's anything I'll be in touch.'

Back out on the corner, Markham considered what he'd heard. It was a start. De Vries and two of the other Germans had worked at Cokely's. It might be worth another trip out there.

Farren's was closer, just across the River Aire on Hunslet Road. They'd manufactured shells during both wars. God only knew what they were making now. It was walking distance. And he had nothing else to do.

He crossed over Crown Point Bridge. There was very little traffic on the river, half the old warehouses looking derelict, windows broken. Like Leeds, it all seemed to look to a forgotten industrial past rather than the future.

The scent of malt and hops from the huge Tetley brewery filled the air south of the water. It was warm and comforting. But by the time he reached Farren's he barely noticed it any more.

The receptionist was more helpful than he expected, and five minutes later he was escorted down a carpeted corridor, past closed doors, to an office with *Mr Crews* painted on the glass.

John Crews was tall, in his late forties but still in good, powerful shape. He took Markham's business card and tapped it with a nicotine-stained forefinger.

'I don't think we've ever had any enquiry agents in here before.'

'Really? I thought you might have dealt with some others. Mark and Amanda Fox.'

Crews was a poor liar. The truth showed on his face as he said, 'Who? Fox? I've never heard of them.'

'Ah,' Markham said. 'I'm sorry. Someone told me you had.'

'They've been pulling your leg, then. I'm sorry, I can't help you.' A flush of guilt rose up Crews' cheeks.

'I'm sorry for taking up your time.'

A quick handshake and he left. Interesting, Markham thought as he walked back along Dock Street, over Leeds Bridge and up Briggate. Why would the man lie about something like that?

It had been all too easy to read his face. Crews had looked worried from the moment Markham walked in. When the name Fox came up, he'd tried to make his expression blank. But he'd failed spectacularly.

After that he knew that going out to Cokely's would be a waste of time. They'd been turned away the last time; returning with awkward questions would bring the same result.

★★★

'I could ring that bloke at Cokely's,' Baker offered. 'I sound like a copper.'

'Don't say you are one.'

'I'm not daft.' He gave a withering look, picked up the receiver and began to dial.

It didn't take long. Hill was in the other part of the factory, the telephonist told him.

'What other part, luv?'

He was over in the old Avro shadow factory that had once built Lancaster bombers and now looked deserted.

'Don't they have phones over there?' Baker asked.

It took five minutes of waiting. Finally there was a voice on the other end of the line.

'Mr Hill? Hello, it's Baker here from Leeds.' He sound offi-cial, ready to ride roughshod over any objection. 'We have a few questions we'd like you to answer.' He waited, nodding as the man assented. 'About Mr and Mrs Fox.' A pause when the question seemed obvious. 'I said my name's Baker. No, I'm not with the police. I never said I was.'

He waited a moment then lowered the handset.

'Mr Hill didn't want to talk to me. Funny, that, isn't it? As soon as I mentioned the Foxes.'

'We're getting nowhere.' Markham slammed his hand down on the desk in frustration.

'That's not quite true, Dan,' he said slowly. 'We know we're making people uncomfortable. That's something.'

'It still doesn't help us.'

Baker shrugged. 'We'll see.'

★★★

A little more work on the frauds. Markham went to one of the businesses and talked to the owner. An hour of going through the figures and asking questions and he'd identified the thief.

He sat quietly in the corner, hat in his lap, as the owner hauled the man in. The bluster lasted a minute longer than he expected. Then it was admission, guilt, all because he had a wife and family to support.

He was sacked, of course, and lucky not to be reported to the police. Word would spread quickly throughout the busi-ness and discourage others. Markham took the cheque from the grateful owner.

It was already dark, the yellow light of the street lamps picking out the roads back to Chapel Allerton. At least the fog hadn't returned.

He parked behind the flat. On the other side of the fence St Matthew's graveyard was a patch of blackness, filled with the silence of the dead. He locked the Anglia and started across the gravel.

As he reached to unlock the front door a heavy hand came out of the shadows and grabbed his wrist. He was pulled into the gloom.

Leather gloves, a hat, scarf pushed up over the mouth and nose so only small, dark eyes showed. Nothing clear in the darkness, little more than a quick impression.

'You've been poking around.' A gruff voice, muffled by the material. Fraction by fraction the fingers tightened on his wrist.

The training from National Service came like a body memory. Markham lashed out with his free hand, first two fingers extended, aiming for the man's eyes, making him let and back away.

'You like your chances, do you?' It was a taunting voice. He was big, broad, eager for a scrap. The man made a small feint, eyes squinting.

Markham shifted the car key in his fist. It was the only weapon he had. Use it like a knife, slash with it; he'd learned the technique all those years ago. It wasn't much against someone like this, but it was better than nothing.

He tried to make his body loose, ready to react, trying to be aware of every movement while he fixed his gaze on the man's eyes. They were the things that would signal his intent.

A metallic click and, glancing down, he saw a blade extend in the man's right hand. A flick knife. He'd thought this wasn't a simple robbery. Now it looked as if it was going to be more than a beating. This looked deadly.

His mouth was dry. Whoever he was, his opponent was professional. No ducking and weaving, just a slow advance, pace by pace. The knife flashed up and Markham ducked to avoid it. But the man's other fist was already moving, catching him hard on the cheek and making him stagger back.

He was off balance as the man pushed, then a punch in the belly sent him crashing on his back into the dirt, all the air forced out of his lungs.

A kick in the ribs was softened by the heavy overcoat. He saw a foot raised to stamp down on his chest. Markham rolled away before it could land, slashing at the man's Achilles tendon with the car key and connecting. He heard a cry that seemed to come from far away.

The man knelt on Markham's arms, pinning them. Bone dug into muscle. A gloved hand hit his face over and over.

The police station was only twenty yards away, he thought stupidly. If he shouted, would any copper come running?

His hands were trapped, unable to reach anything. He bucked, tried to push his opponent off, but he was too heavy.

The man leaned down, bringing his face close. Sour breath came through the scarf.

It was the only chance.

Markham jerked his head up sharply. A headbutt. His forehead slammed against the man's nose in a quick crack of bone. In a second the weight lifted from him. He scrambled away and heard a clatter as the knife fell to the ground.

Markham kicked it away.

The man looked at him for a second, hate in his gaze, and moved off into the night, half-running, half-stumbling, one hand over his face.

Christ. He leaned against the brick wall and tried to catch his breath. The cigarette packet in his jacket was crushed; it seemed to take an age to pull one out, hands shaking wildly as he tried to light it.

Very carefully, he felt his face. It was tender everywhere, he was going to have a mass of bruises. His arms hurt where the man had pinned him down. The coat had saved him the worst of it. Soon enough he'd start to feel the pain. He was going to ache in the morning.

Very slowly, he finished the cigarette, taking pleasure in grinding it out under his feet. Before he went inside he searched for the flick knife amongst the weeds. He might need it.

CHAPTER ELEVEN

'Dear God,' Baker asked, 'what happened to you?'

'Someone jumped me outside the flat.'

Markham hung up his coat. Each small movement took effort. He'd taken a long bath the night before, and a couple of aspirin before he slept. Two more this morning. But everything still hurt, and his face was badly swollen, covered in deep bruises and cuts.

He explained what had happened. Baker listened intently, drawing on his pipe.

'Who do you think did it?' he asked when Markham finished.

'Special Branch.' He'd thought about it all evening. He hadn't been able to focus on anything else. It had to be them, and a telephone call from Farren's that set them on to him.

'Possible,' Baker agreed with a nod. 'Sounds like their style, right enough.'

Markham pulled the knife from his coat and tossed it on the card table.

'He was going to use that.'

Baker played with the weapon, extending the blade and retracting it.

'Nasty,' he said slowly. 'There's just one problem: the Branch are usually the knuckleduster and heavy boots type.'

'What do you mean?' He turned his head suddenly, feeling the pain as he moved.

'They might do you over or pull you in.' He dropped the knife, blade out again, glittering in the light. 'But they don't use those. Not unless things have changed very recently.'

'Who was it, then?' He felt a chill running down his back.

'Not the spies, either.' Baker smoked silently for a few more seconds. 'Definitely not them. If they wanted you out of the picture they wouldn't do it in public.'

'So – who?'

'I don't know. But we must be ruffling a few feathers.'

'Christ,' Markham said. 'That doesn't make me feel any better.' They were going to have to watch over their shoulders every second. 'Whoever he is, he's a pro.' Then the thought hit him: if it wasn't Special Branch …

'You won. That's something,' Baker continued.

'What if it was the same man who's been killing the Germans?'

For a long while Baker stayed silent.

'The Russian?'

'Yes.' Suddenly Markham felt very cold.

'Why? We're out of it. You said so yourself. And why would we be important?'

'I don't know. Maybe he thinks we're still involved.' Markham raised his head to display his battered face.

Baker puffed on his pipe.

'If it was him, he won't be back.'

'What?'

'He's a professional. We know that.'

'Yes,' Markham agreed.

'For all he knows, you've reported it to the police. He's not going to risk trying again. He's not stupid.'

Baker was right. He knew that. It was the training they gave for everything in military intelligence. You only had one chance to do something. If it didn't work, you abandoned it. That was the only way to stay alive. But it didn't make him feel any safer. He sighed.

'Since we're still in it we'd better find out what's really going on,' he said as he lit a cigarette. 'Maybe it's time we went on the offensive.'

'I think you're right,' Baker agreed. 'We're not going to find anything out by just twiddling our thumbs. Perhaps we can discover a few answers out at Cokely's. We already know they're not going to talk to us. But maybe we can get a look in that shadow factory in Yeadon. It's a good place to keep secrets.'

'How? They're not likely to hand us a key and say "look around."'

'We break in.'

'Break in? You've got to be kidding.'

'I'm deadly serious,' Baker told him. 'We can see what they're up to out there. It has to be something important if they're bringing in East Germans and someone's willing to take a knife to you. They might even have your Amanda Fox somewhere.'

'I thought you were sure she'd run off to join her husband in Russia.'

'That was before last night. You know why I became a copper? Because I like the law. All this is going around it like it doesn't bloody well exist. Or it doesn't matter. So we find out what's happening and do something about it ourselves.'

'It might give us a start,' Markham said quietly. 'God knows we need something.'

'If we don't look we'll never find out, will we?'

'They'll have guards there,' Markham warned.

Baker shook his head. 'Nothing more than a nightwatchman, unless they want attention or gossip. We'll go out tonight for a recce. Go in if we have a chance.'

'Not tonight.'

'Why not?' Baker frowned. 'Meeting someone?'

'I'm not doing it until I can move more easily.' He was meant to see Georgina that evening. But he didn't need her questions all evening on top of everything else.

'All right, fair enough, we'll wait a day or two,' Baker agreed reluctantly. 'Oh,' he added, 'there's something on your desk. Came in the post.'

A small package. A book. He ripped open the brown paper. He hadn't ordered anything. It was odd. *On the Road* by someone called Jack Kerouac. He'd never even heard of the man.

When he turned the front cover a note fell out and he unfolded it. The familiar tiny scrawl. Carla.

I don't know if you've read this. A friend brought it back from America a couple of months ago, apparently it's just been published. It's rather good and the whole thing is just like jazz, like that Monk fellow you like. I thought you might enjoy it.

And remember, let me know when you're ready. If you want to be ready.
Carla.

He set the book aside but inside he was smiling.

'Penny for them,' Baker said quietly.

'You'd get a ha'penny in change.'

'Go home. Get yourself some rest. Read your new book.'

'I want to finish that other fraud.'

'No one's going to thank you for turning up looking like you've gone ten rounds with Sugar Ray Robinson.'

'Does it look that bad?' Markham managed a weak grin.

'Worse.'

Baker was right. He'd been reluctant to admit it when he looked in the mirror that morning, but he knew it was true. He struggled back into his overcoat, every muscle complaining.

'Tomorrow night,' Baker said. 'You'll be feeling better by then. We'll go out to Yeadon. And in the meantime, keep your eyes peeled. Just in case.'

★★★

He felt numb. They were deep in this. Someone had tried to kill him. Might even have succeeded except for luck. All because of a missing person case.

Walking along Briggate, people veered away from him with horrified looks, but he scarcely noticed. The pavement was busy but he had a clear path all the way to Boots. Georgina was behind the counter closest to the door, by the cash register. Her mouth opened wide as she spotted him and saw what had become of his face. She finished serving a customer, had a word with the girl next to her and hurried over.

'My God, Dan, what happened to you?' she whispered. She had fear and concern in her eyes, reaching out and stroking his cheek lightly.

'I lost an argument.' He tried to keep his tone light. 'It looks worse than it really is.'

A white lie. A big one. Her eyes examined his face.

'I hope that's true.'

'Would you mind if we didn't do anything tonight? I don't really want to go out looking like this.'

'No, that's fine,' she agreed quickly. Then she made a decision. 'I tell you what, why don't I come over after I finish here? I can take the bus. Just to talk. I'll pick up some fish and chips from Nash's.'

★★★

At home he checked the locks and bolted the door. The man wouldn't be back, he told himself. If he said it often enough he might convince himself. Knowing it in his head was one thing. Feeling it in his heart was another. He'd stay very wary and alert. At least this time he wasn't in it alone. That was one tiny crumb of comfort, for all it was worth.

Baker was right about that, Markham thought as he settled in the tub. Hot water and bath salts relaxed his muscles. He let himself soak until he began to feel a chill, dried and dressed in his American blue jeans and a heavy jumper and tried to relax with the book.

At first it confused him. It was unlike anything he'd ever read, a rush of words that seemed to career around the page. After a little while he began to understand it. The freedom of the road, the freedom of America. It carried him along in the cars and the changing landscapes.

She was right, it was jazz. Not just the thoughts that came to the narrator at the club in Chicago, but the energy and the wild improvisation. It was bebop on a page, something he'd never imagined before. There was music behind it.

By the time he looked up it was dark outside, too dark to really read. He'd been so caught up in it that he'd lost track of time and let all the bad things slip out of his mind. A welcome relief. Half past four and only the street lamps through the window to bring some light into the flat

He put on some Monk, the only music that could fit after the wild ride of words, and tried to come back to Leeds.

The man looking back at him from the mirror had flesh swollen around his left eye, scrapes on the skin, bruises that were still growing. It would take time for someone familiar to reappear.

Markham held up his two useless fingers, the permanent reminder of what had happened three years earlier. This was heading in the same desperate direction. He'd had angry husbands throw punches at him in divorce cases before, but few of them had ever connected.

Fighting back was a start, he realised. But it would only be over if they won.

And they didn't even really know who the enemy was. All he'd seen was a pair of dark eyes.

Did he have Amanda Fox hidden away somewhere in Leeds? Or perhaps she was already dead, her body hidden somewhere.

He could stare into the mirror as long as he liked. It wasn't going to tell him the things he needed to know.

***

Georgina left the packet wrapped in newspaper in the kitchen as she held him close, arms wrapped around him. He squeezed her gently then pulled away, putting the food on plates as she buttered slices of bread and filled the kettle.

'You took quite a beating,' she told him as they ate. Outside the window a procession of headlights passed along Harrogate Road as people made their way home, the working week over. 'Who did it?'

'I don't know,' he answered and it was perfectly true.

'But why?' She looked confused. 'Was he robbing you?'

'No. It's to do with a case.' He wasn't going to tell her more than that.

Georgina drew in a breath.

'Bloody hell, Dan. What are you involved with?'

'It's messy. Soon be over, though.' Better to leave it at that and change the topic. 'Are you ready for your gig at Studio 20?' Just over three weeks now.

'I'm scared.' She gave a small laugh. 'The people there are going to know their jazz. It's not like a club where everyone's drinking and eating.'

'You'll be fine. You're good.'

'Maybe,' she allowed, then looked at him under her eyelashes. 'Dan …'

'What?'

'After work last Friday I popped over to the Grand Theatre.'

'Did you see anything good?'

She took a breath and continued.

'I went past that restaurant. Donmar.' Suddenly a pit seemed to open up in his stomach as she stared into his face. 'You know what I'm going to say, don't you?'

He'd been there with Carla.

This was the conversation they needed to have.

'I was with a friend. An old girlfriend. She was passing through Leeds.'

'You just happened to run into her, then one of you suggested a meal?'

'She rang me.'

'I see.' She stood, clearing away the empty plates, then pouring another cup of tea from the pot before lighting a cigarette. A very ordinary, domestic scene.

'So?' she asked finally. It was a question that asked everything in a single word.

'I knew her back in '54,' he began. 'We were very close for a while, then she moved away. I never heard from her again until she rang a couple of weeks ago. She was on her way home and her train was delayed here.' Georgina was watching him intently. 'We had a drink, and that was it. Then last Friday.'

'When she just happened to be passing through again?'

'Yes.'

She snorted disbelievingly.

'It was all innocent,' he said.

'No, Dan,' she told him. 'That's something it definitely wasn't.' Before he could speak, she continued, 'It's hardly innocent when you have a meal with an old girlfriend and don't tell the one you're supposed to be going out with now.'

'I–'

'You never said a word about it, did you?' She was angry, but her voice was low and quiet, carefully controlled. 'Not a single bloody word, like it's some secret you have to keep.'

'I didn't sleep with her,' he said.

'Oh God, that's not the bloody point! I know we're not engaged or it's anything special, but I thought neither of us would go out with anyone else. That's what really hurt me. I kept waiting for you to say something.'

'I didn't know how.'

'Of course you did.' Georgina slammed her hand down on the table, making the cups jump. 'All you had to do was come out and say it. For Christ's sake, Dan, we're adults.'

He stayed silent. There was nothing he could give her as an answer. Everything she said was right.

'I saw your eyes when you were talking to her. We're never going to have anything like that, are we?' She waited a moment. 'You're never going to look at me that way, are you?'

'I didn't even know until I heard from her again.'

She stood and paced around the room.

'When were you going to say something? Next week? Christmas? Next year?' He hung his head, silent. 'Don't I deserve something better than that, Dan?' she asked quietly.

'Yes,' he admitted.

Georgina reached for her coat, buttoning it tight around herself. 'I'm going to walk out of here with my head held high. If I see you somewhere, I'll be polite enough. But do me one favour.'

'What's that?'

'Please don't ever come and see me play again. Especially at Studio 20.'

She didn't slam the door. The lock clicked quietly behind her and he was alone again, feeling guilty.

CHAPTER TWELVE

'By God, you still look rough'

'You would too if someone had tried to kill you.' Markham said curtly as he hung up the overcoat. Outside, a chilly drizzle was falling. The aches weren't too bad. Movement was slightly easier. His face still looked like something from a horror film, but it would heal.

He'd spent a sleepless night. It didn't matter what he *knew*, the fear had coursed through him, all the images of what might happen. The sense of panic and helplessness had kept him awake. At least the feelings had receded in the daylight.

Georgina had simply been the icing on the cake. Yes, he'd been thoughtless, a bit of a bastard for not saying anything. But at least it was resolved now. Over.

'Will you be able to manage tonight?' Baker asked.

'Yes,' he answered. 'What time?'

'I thought about half past nine. We'll look like people going home from the pub. I'll come and pick you up.'

'That sounds fine.'

'Do you want some advice?'

'What?' he asked sharply.

'Just keep on moving and try not to dwell on it. It's one time when thinking doesn't help.'

Markham nodded. 'I'm going to crack on and finish this fraud.'

Another hour going through the papers, trying to concentrate, finding one more connection. Then off to the factory, never mind the ugly bruises on his face, checking the wing mirror every few seconds as he drove. People gave him sideways glances. Good, he thought. He wasn't in the mood for chit-chat.

By early afternoon it was all over. A full confession. No begging for any sort of mercy this time. The embezzlement had funded a gambling habit. Markham waited until the police arrived, taking the thief off in handcuffs. On the way home he deposited the cheque in the bank. Alert every single moment.

The alarm woke him at nine. At least he'd been able to sleep. The bedroom looked down on the graveyard. Markham stared out of the window into the darkness as he smoked a cigarette, then dressed. His old army trousers, a snug fit now, the wool scratchy against his skin, but right for this job. Dark shirt and sweater, hiking boots. With a black windcheater he'd be ready.

At half past he was waiting, sheltering from the wind, cupping a cigarette in his palm, the glow of the tip hidden, the way he'd learned when he was still at school. He'd come out with the knife in his hand, checking everywhere to make sure his assailant wasn't waiting to surprise him. When the Wolseley glided over the gravel, he trotted out of the shadows and climbed into the passenger seat.

'How are you going to do this?' Markham asked as they sped out along Otley Road.

'Carefully.' Baker's voice was tight and cautious. 'Did you bring gloves?'

'In my pocket.'

'Torch?'

'Yes, with new batteries.'

'I went out earlier this evening for a recce. There's only one watchman and he doesn't seem too enthusiastic about his rounds. Keep it quiet and we should be fine.' He paused. 'Don't worry, no one's following us. We're safe.'

There wasn't much more to say. It wasn't the time for small talk, just to prepare. If they were caught … he wasn't going to think about that. He lit another cigarette.

Baker turned down a track between two fields, just far enough along to be out of sight of the road. He turned off the headlamps and they were lost in the night.

'Follow this track and we'll come out on the other side of the shadow factory.' He was whispering; noise carried in the darkness. 'Try not to use your torch.'

They moved slowly. Baker took the lead, Markham just a pace behind. Through a small copse with the strong smell of leaf mould. A sliver of moon appeared for a moment, long enough to make out the building two hundred yards away. It was huge, larger than he remembered, dwarfing everything around.

The last fifty yards were bare ground illuminated by floodlights.

'There's a way to get through without being seen,' Baker whispered in his ear. 'See down there to the left? One of those lights has burned out. Go down that way. Close to the factory there's enough shadow to hide us.'

Moving in a crouch, running through the empty space with his heart in his mouth, it was like being back in the training he'd had at Catterick Camp. The only difference being that there was no sergeant screaming at him.

By the time he reached the building he was gasping for breath and his heart was pounding. He waited for Baker. The only sound was the deep thrum of a generator from somewhere inside.

Then Baker was there. He'd moved in silence. Markham could feel breath against his ear and two quiet words: 'Follow me.'

Baker knew what he was doing. He seemed to go on instinct, to disappear as he moved, almost impossible to spot. His footsteps hardly seemed to disturb the ground. Finally he halted.

'There's a door a few yards along. We'll go in there. Give it ten minutes. If the watchman's coming, he should have passed by then.'

'What the hell did you do in the war?'

'Didn't I ever tell you? I was in Number 4 Commando. Now keep your head down and stay shtum.'

The seconds seemed to stretch out endlessly. Markham could feel the sweat rolling down his back and his hands were clammy.

Finally there was a nudge in his ribs and a hand gesture. They crept to the door and Baker handed him a torch.

'Keep that shining on the door whilst I open it.'

The lens was taped so only a pinprick of light showed. He focused the beam on the lock. A few movements and he could hear the tiny click as it freed. The handle turned and he held his breath, praying there was no alarm.

Just silence and they slipped inside. Baker closed the door behind them.

'We can breathe a bit easier now,' he said. He sounded relaxed, almost happy. 'The watchman won't come inside.'

'How do you know?'

'Stands to reason.' He was still whispering but the words seemed to echo away into the vastness. 'If there's something secret in here, they won't want everyone seeing it.' He switched his torch back on, letting the light play around on the far walls. 'This is too big for us to search together. We'll have to split up. You go to the left. Keep your gloves on and the beam covered.' He glanced at his watch. 'Meet back here in half an hour.'

He began. It was nothing more than cavernous, empty space. Even in his hiking boots each footstep felt as loud as a scream. He kept one gloved hand over the torch lens, giving just enough of a glow to direct him.

A door ahead was unlocked and took him into another part of the factory. This had been divided into smaller rooms. He tried every door. All offices, all empty. A row of them that stretched into the distance. How big was this bloody place, he wondered?

The last door stuck. But it wasn't locked. Markham put his shoulder against it and pushed. It gave noisily, scraping against the concrete floor. He held his breath, expecting to hear someone running, alerted by the sound. Nothing. There was only silence.

A camp bed, the type he'd seen so often in barracks. Sheets and blankets neatly folded. In one corner a sink with a towel hanging over the edge. And in the air, something familiar. Just very faint, but definitely there.

The smell of Amanda Fox's perfume.

Markham began to search, opening up the bedding, the towel, looking everywhere for any definite sign she'd been here. On his hands and knees he looked in the corners and along the skirting board. Something glinted under the bed, against the wall. He stretched, fingertips rubbing against it, then pulled it towards him. A gold ring. A wedding ring with some fine engraving and a beautifully set sapphire. He'd seen it before. It had been on her hand the last time she'd come to his office. He slipped it into the side pocket of his battledress trousers, and made sure everything in the room looked the way it had before.

Questions. Too many of them and not enough time. Only fifteen minutes left.

He moved quickly, trying to stay quiet but needing to check everything. Three locked doors; he knocked softly in case she was inside. No answer, only the soft, constant hum of machinery.

He was back at the meeting place on the dot of half an hour.

'I–' Markham began, but Baker cut him off. 'You need to see this.' His voice was sober and chilling. 'Now, Dan.'

He led the way as if he'd memorised it, barely needing the light. The path twisted and turned until he stood in front of a door.

'Open it. Use your torch, it's all right.'

Mystified, he turned the handle and switched on the beam.

The room was as big as a football field, the ceiling high above, lost in the darkness. At first he couldn't make out what filled the space. Then he realised: boxes. Cardboard boxes, folded, waiting to be assembled. Each one about six feet long and two feet wide. Wave after brown wave of them. Thousands of them.

More than that. Hundreds of thousands of them. Maybe millions.

Markham turned.

'What …?'

'They're coffins.' Baker's voice was empty. 'Bloody cardboard coffins.'

'But,' he began and understood he didn't have anything more to say. He let the light play over everything. There were acres of them.

'Everything ready for when they drop that nuclear bomb.' He heard the long sigh. 'I just wanted you to see it. We'd better get out of here.'

Following the corridor back to the door, Markham explained what he'd found.

'She must have left the ring hoping someone would find it.'

'So he's got her. And he's involved with this place somehow.' There was an edge to the man's voice he'd never heard before. Bitterness, disillusion. Baker turned the knob and a rush of cold air hit their faces.

★★★

They were speeding back towards Leeds. Markham smoked one cigarette then lit another from the tip. The Wolseley was on Otley Road before either of them spoke.

'Christ,' he said finally.

'I can't get those coffins out of my mind,' Baker said

'I know.' The picture would stay in his head for a long, long time. Years.

Baker kept looking straight ahead. 'God only knows where that Mrs Fox is now.'

'Seems like we have some work to do.' And he realised that for the last hour he hadn't even thought about a man trying to kill him.

'Aye. It does.'

CHAPTER THIRTEEN

Markham was home in time to fiddle with the dial on the wireless. He'd checked the dark spaces outside and climbed the stairs cautiously, not even realising he'd been holding his breath until he shot the bolts on the door.

Between the crackles and hiss he found Voice of America, the last few minutes of *Jazz Hour* leading up to midnight, Willis Conover talking then the unmistakeable wail of Charlie Parker's alto sax with strings on 'Summertime'.

Outside, a winter rain was falling. Summertime was a long way away.

Markham made a cup of tea, the sound on the radio barely more than a background whisper. He reached into his pocket and brought out the ring, cupping it in his palm before placing it on the table. He'd hold on to the thought of being able to return it to her. But he didn't know how.

And the coffins … he'd never be able to forget them.

★★★

It was almost ten when Markham reached the office. He'd still taken precautions, watched everything carefully but seen nothing. He parked on Albion Street, behind Baker's Wolseley, smoking a cigarette. He didn't want to go in yet. There was too much going through his mind.

Instead he walked down to WHSmith at the top of Cloth Hall Street and bought a picture postcard that showed Leeds in the sunshine. On the back he scrawled *I'm ready* and addressed it to Carla at the Art Department at Durham University. A stamp from his wallet and he popped it in the postbox.

Fighting back, he thought. And now he had a real reason to win.

★★★

'I thought you'd have been here earlier,' Baker said. He folded his newspaper and put it on the green baize of the card table.

'I had something to do first.'

'How did you sleep?'

'Not so well.' His dreams had been filled with corpses climbing out of cardboard coffins, each of them with the dark eyes of the man who'd attacked him, looking for the lives that had been taken from them in a nuclear instant. In the background the giant cloud of a bomb that wouldn't disperse. He'd woken twice, chilled but sweating, and it had taken a long, fearful time before sleep returned. 'What about you?'

'Tossing and turning. I didn't want to tell the wife about it. Don't need her worried, too. She kept asking me what was wrong.' He gave a grim smile. 'I told her it must have been the piccalilli I had with my supper.' Baker paused. 'What are we going to do?'

'Nothing we can do about the coffins.'

'I meant Mrs Fox.'

'If they had her there, then someone at Cokely's knows about it. A few locked doors, but doesn't look as if there's much going on in the old Avro factory besides storage …' He didn't need to say the words. 'It's got to be him. The same one who tried to kill me.'

'Very likely. But the real question is, where is she now? Find that out and maybe we'll have him, too.'

'What about Tim Hill?' Markham suggested. 'He works at Cokely's. You said yourself that he sounded shifty.'

'Good idea.'

'How do we get him to talk, though?'

'You leave that part to me.' Baker tapped the side of his nose.

'What's so important about Amanda Fox?' he wondered after a while. 'Why has he taken her?'

'Happen we'll know once we find her.'

'Yes.' A sudden thought from the night before came to him. 'You said you were in 4 Commando?'

'A long time ago now.' He rubbed his belly. 'I didn't always have this, you know. Came after I was demobbed.'

'I heard about the things your lot did from some troops when I was in Germany.'

'Trust me, Dan,' the man told him, 'you didn't hear the half of it.'

★★★

Baker disappeared, returning a little before four. Full darkness, the buildings all glowing with lights. Markham was sorting through receipts, deciding which to keep for the Inland Revenue, when he heard the heavy footsteps on the stair. He tensed, his hand curled around the flick knife in his pocket.

Baker came in smiling.

'Worthwhile?'

'You forget how many friends you make when you work somewhere for years. Had a few words on the QT and I've got all the gen on Mr Timothy Hill. All off the record, of course.'

'And what?'

'I thought I'd follow him home from work and have a word.'

'I'll come with you.'

Baker hesitated before answering.

'Don't take this the wrong way, Dan, but please, leave this one to me. The way your face looks right now no one's going to open up if they see you.'

He was right, of course. Battered, bruised, beaten, he wasn't likely to put the fear of God into anyone.

'All right,' he agreed after a moment. 'What are you going to do if he rings the police?'

'Trust me, he won't do that,' Baker grinned. 'And if he tries, it's already been taken care of. Don't you worry.'

'Come over to the flat afterwards. Tell me what he says.'

Baker shook his head.

'Tomorrow. I'm already in the doghouse at home for staying out so late last night.'

★★★

He thought he wouldn't be able to settle, that once he was alone all the fear would rise again. But with the comfort of the familiar all around and a hot meal in his stomach he began to relax. He'd never bothered with television. Instead, he listened to the six o'clock news on the Home Service then settled down with Lester Young on the record player. Markham picked up *On the Road* and soon he was lost in the slipstream of Kerouac's words.

★★★

After a while he set the book aside. He needed to think. About the man. About Amanda Fox. Georgina. Carla. About what he'd seen at Cokely's.

Would the man return and try again? Everything in his brain said no. The man was professional. It would be stupid, a dangerous move. But that little bit of terror wouldn't wash away. He was going to stay very, very cautious.

There was nothing he could do about Amanda yet. Not without more information. He hadn't asked Baker how he was going to make Tim Hill talk; from the glint in the man's eyes, he didn't want to know. Tomorrow. They could make their plans then.

He sighed.

He'd hurt Georgina. He would have told her, ended things cleanly and been honest. He'd just wanted to find the right moment, to make it simple.

But maybe nothing in life was that easy. They weren't children any more.

And Carla. She'd stepped back into his life and he couldn't resist her. When she'd gone, three years before, he'd ached with the loss. Time had healed all that; so he believed, anyway. But now it was all back, stronger than before. Maybe this time … She wouldn't be here until the New Year. One way or another everything else would be resolved by then.

***

He needed time to think about the coffins, too, for what he'd seen to percolate through his brain. He read the papers, he knew about the bomb, that it would kill everyone. It was terrifying, but somehow it wasn't real. It just existed out there somewhere, separate from his life.

The coffins had brought it all home. They were where he lived, waiting for him and everyone else in Leeds. The government was behind them, operating quietly and making its plans. All the things they wouldn't tell the people. A way to keep the veneer of civilisation once civilisation had been destroyed. It was the way the future could be. Seeing them there, the cardboard coffins in their hundreds of thousands, made it all very immediate. And it scared him.

***

'You look very pleased with yourself.'

For once he'd been the first in the office, waiting impatiently when Baker entered. The big man hung up his mackintosh and hat, taking his time before sitting with a contented sigh.

'I had an interesting evening,' Baker admitted, taking the pipe from his jacket and lighting it.

'Go on. What did Hill have to say?'

'Not much at first. He didn't want to talk to me. But he changed his mind when I suggested things might go badly if all the things he was doing came out.'

'You took a chance.'

'It worked.' He grinned. 'The bastard's in it up to his neck.'

Markham leaned forward, elbows on the desk.

'Well?'

Hill was a scared man, it seemed. A little man in every way, no more than five feet four. Someone who relished the small power of his position. Some of Cokely's work involved defence. Things covered by the Official Secrets Act. Hill had worked with Mark Fox, first in the Special Operations Executive during the war, and then setting up the jobs for the men brought over from East Germany.

'We're not the only ones doing it,' Hill had told Baker. 'Every company does. The Yanks brought out Nazis to work on rockets, you know that, don't you?'

***

'That all sounds legal,' Markham said.

'As far as it goes,' Baker agreed. 'But when I was doing my checking on him yesterday I turned up a few interesting things. His work means he's still involved with the spies. Fair enough. MI5 doesn't want these men they've brought over working for the Russians.' Markham began to speak but Baker cut him off. 'Turns out that during the summer Hill bought a new house. Moved from Ireland Wood out to Alwoodley. Detached, and you know they don't come cheap.'

'Beyond his salary?' Hill was an executive; he'd receive a monthly salary, not a workman's weekly wage. 'And what would he be making from MI5?'

'It's still a lot more than he can afford. He wasn't too happy that I knew. Kept looking around – we were out in the street, any of the snooty neighbours could have been watching.' He smiled.

'What did he have to say?'

'Once he'd gone through all the bluffing, it was like a gust of wind hitting a house of cards. Someone had come to see him back in June.'

'Someone?' Markham asked sharply.

'That's all he wanted to say at first. A man came to see him and asked about the people from East Germany. Wanted to know the new names they'd been given, where they were living. Put a fat brown envelope on the desk.'

'How much was in it?'

'Two thousand.'

It was a fortune. Certainly enough for a strong down payment on a house in Alwoodley.

'He took it?'

'He opened it and took a look. That was enough. His visitor showed him a little camera and said he'd just been filming him. If he didn't pass on the information the footage would find its way back to MI5. Hill would look like a traitor. He didn't have much choice. At first he thought I was one of the spies, come to arrest him.'

'Did you set him right?'

'I didn't go into details.' Baker stared at him. 'I did get the name of the man who came to see him, though. Simon Harker. It's probably false, but it's something. And a description. Blond, but with dark brown eyes, ordinary looking. About six feet tall, maybe thirty years old.'

Dark eyes. The killer. His attacker. He'd put money on it.

'So Hill's a double agent?' Markham asked.

'Of sorts. A reluctant one.'

'We're treading on dangerous ground now.'

'We always were, Dan. This way we might find a path through. We might even find Mrs Fox alive.'

'If she still is,' he said. 'Would another body really matter?'

'She's English and she's female,' Baker said without emotion. 'All the difference in the world and you know it.'

Maybe. Maybe not. But the man was right about something. They were the best chance Amanda Fox had of survival.

'Right,' Markham agreed firmly. 'Where do we go from here?'

***

Baker called in another favour or two from the police. Surprisingly, soon they had an address for a Simon Harker. Out in Whitkirk, past Temple Newsam.

Markham didn't know the area; he'd only been out there a couple of times in his life. Plenty of newer housing, streets of neat semi-detached houses. The place they wanted was just past St Mary's Church, close to the Brown Cow, an ugly clump of a pub.

'Down that road.' From the passenger seat Baker pointed to a street that ran next to the graveyard.

He parked twenty yards beyond a house that seemed ripe for demolition. The windows and doors were still intact, but the old stone was crumbling and the roof looked as if a strong breath might send it flying away.

'Do you think anyone living here has a couple of thousand to spend?' Markham said as he stared at the place.

'I think anyone living in that place needs their head examining. And I'll bet you we don't find Simon Harker here.'

They didn't; there was no answer. Talking to the neighbours they discovered that no one had lived there since the end of September.

'He was very ordinary,' an older woman told them. As she spoke she kept sucking a set of false teeth into her wrinkled mouth. 'You'd never have even known he was there most of the time.'

'Most of the time?' Markham asked.

'He had a motorbike. He'd work on it Saturday mornings.' She shook his head at the recollection. 'Made a right noise, that thing did. Tried it on a Sunday when he first moved in, but folk complained because it was interrupting the service.' She nodded across to the church.

'Do you know where he went, luv?' Baker asked her with a smile.

She shook her head and sucked on her teeth again. 'Not a clue. Just upped and left.'

'Who owns the place and rents it out?'

'Don Barnes, I suppose.' She scratched at her thin grey hair. 'It's been in his family since the year dot, any road.'

Baker recited the description of Harker that Hill had given him.

'Does that sound like him?'

'I suppose,' she answered slowly. 'Like enough, anyway, although I'd have said his hair was more brown than fair. And he seemed taller.' She laughed. 'But I'm only little.'

'Thank you,' Baker told her and as they walked away he muttered, 'Witnesses. There's not two of them ever bloody agree.'

'Close enough, though.'

'Probably. I can stop in at Millgarth and track down this Barnes character and see what I can find on the motorbike Harker owns. Just as well we're an agency with good police contacts, eh?' He chuckled and winked. 'They'll be thinking I still work there.'

'As long as you don't run out of goodwill.'

'I'm safe enough. They'll be happy to leave this with us for now. They don't want to get their teeth into something just to be warned off by the spies again. Can you blame them?'

'And no sign of MI5.'

'I know. So it's up to us, lad. Every hour we take is another hour this Harker has Amanda Fox. Best remember that.'

***

He stopped and bought a cheese sandwich and wandered down to the Central Library, looking at the reflections in shop windows to make sure no one was following him.

At least it felt like they were doing something and making some progress. Maybe one small step closer to finding Amanda.

And after they found her? He didn't care. Let the spies from both countries go hunting each other.

In the reference section he did a little research on 4 Commando. It seemed they'd paid a heavy price in the war. Lofoten Island, Dieppe, holding the flank at D-Day with fifty per cent casualties, then on to Walcheren. It was hard to reconcile the Stephen Baker he knew with someone who'd gone through all that.

Finally Markham made his way up the Headrow and down Lands Lane back to Albion Place. Baker was a tough man, no doubt about it, and he'd seen his share of death. Add to that his stretch as a copper and he had a fuller picture of the man.

The phone started to ring as he unlocked the door. He sprang for it, automatically reciting, 'Markham and Baker.'

'Are you sure you're ready?'

No hello, no how are you. No name, but he knew exactly who it was. Carla being Carla. He took a deep breath.

'Yes,' he answered and realised he was smiling as if nothing terrible had happened.

'I'm glad, Dan. I really am.' She paused for a moment. 'Look, I need to come down this weekend and start looking for a flat.'

'I can drive you around,' he offered. As long as the case didn't intrude.

'That would be wonderful.' He could hear the relief in her voice. 'Are you sure you wouldn't mind?'

'As long as you don't need me to look at places with you. I took a bit of a beating a few days ago. I'm not exactly a pretty sight at the moment.'

'My God, are you all right?'

'It's just surface, that's all. I'm healing, it's nothing too bad.'

He knew all the bad memories would be flooding back to her. All the pain and the fear. 'Are you sure?'

'Positive,' he assured her. 'Honestly.'

'Promise?'

'Yes.' And he prayed he was right.

'Good, then,' she said. There was a brief hesitation. 'Can I stay at your place? Would you mind?'

'You know there's only one bed.'

'I remember.' The words were half-invitation, half-hope. 'But if we're really going to do this, Dan, we might as well do it properly.'

'Yes,' he agreed. 'We should.'

'I'll ring you once I know when I'm arriving on Friday.'

'OK.'

'And look after yourself. Please.'

He didn't know if Carla simplified his life or made it more complicated. Maybe it didn't matter. All he knew was that seeing her, hearing her, had rekindled that fire inside him, the one that had never died completely. He had a chance and he was going to take it.

Markham was staring out of the window and smoking another cigarette when Baker returned, his face set.

'Get your coat on. We going to see Simon Harker.'

'Where?'

'Harehills. Gathorne Terrace. I'll drive.'

The Wolseley's powerful engine ate up the ground along North Street, through Sheepscar and past the grimy, tired buildings that lined the bottom end of Roundhay Road. He indicated the left turn on to Gathorne Terrace and slowed.

It still teetered on the edge of respectability. The bricks of the houses were black with years of soot from all the factories, but the windows were clean, net curtains hiding the families inside. Baker parked outside number fifty-three.

'Harker lives at number twenty-seven. Looks like he's home, there's a motorbike outside.' An old BSA M20 motorcycle was the only other vehicle on the street. 'You go to the ginnel round the back in case he tries to run.'

Markham counted down from the end of the block and stood just outside the tall back gate. The stone wall was his height, impossible to see over. He fitted leather gloves tightly over his hands. This time he was going to be ready for the man.

It only took a minute until he heard the back door fly open and footsteps run across the flagstones in the yard. By the time the gate was thrown back he was waiting, ready, fists clenched.

For a short moment the man looked surprised. He was somewhere between the descriptions they had: large, sandy hair, broad shoulders, wearing a sleeveless V-neck jumper over a white shirt with an open neck, baggy trousers and a pair of brown brogues. The dark, empty eyes he remembered from the night outside his flat. The face, ugly from the bruising it had received, broken nose still swollen.

Markham stepped forward.

Harker raised his hand. He was holding a pistol, an automatic. *Jesus*, he thought. He'd got Carla back and now he was going to die in a ginnel in Harehills. Markham started to back away, raising his arms.

But Harker didn't shoot. He gestured, moving Markham away until there was almost ten feet between them. Then he began to run, the pounding of his soles echoing off the walls and the cobbles.

Markham didn't give chase. He didn't even move until Harker had turned the corner and vanished into a tangle of streets. At the other end of the ginnel he saw Baker. The man was panting and red-faced.

'Why didn't you bloody stop him?'

'He had a gun.' That was enough to silence the big man. 'I thought he was going to pull the trigger. Did you see his nose?'

'Broken.'

'It's him. I remember the eyes.' He shook the memory from his head. 'We'd better get back to the car. He'll have circled the block and started his bike.'

'No he won't.' Baker smiled and brought a hand from his pocket. He was holding a rubber-coated wire. 'That thing won't be going anywhere. But there's no sense going after someone who's tooled-up.'

'Ring the police?'

Baker shook his head and tipped the brim of his hat back.

'They'll spend four hours asking us questions before they even start to look for him.'

Markham glanced thoughtfully at the house.

'I think we've earned the right to look inside, don't you?'

They entered through the back door, into the scullery. A wash was drying on the clothes airer hanging near the ceiling – shirts, underwear, socks. A loaf in the bread bin, cans, vegetables, and jars in the larder. Pots, pans, plates, cutlery. Everything very ordinary.

The parlour held a worn three-piece suite, everything facing a television in the corner. A small bookcase with some battered hardbacks and a few Penguin paperbacks. Markham rifled through them, looking for telltale pinpricks to indicate a code pad. Nothing.

He could hear Baker moving heavily around upstairs, shifting furniture. They spent a full hour searching, checking the floorboards and the skirting boards, taking up the rugs and going through the clothes in the wardrobe.

In the end all they found was a British passport in the name of Simon Terence Harker and a passbook for the Post Office Savings Bank with twenty-two pounds, eleven shillings and ninepence in the account. Not a fortune. Ordinary, like everything else, at least on the surface. Not someone likely to have two thousand pounds to hand out.

'Not much, is it?' Baker asked. 'There's got to be more.'

Markham stood for a moment. A lesson from his training came back.

'Did you look in the cistern?'

'No.'

The house was new enough to have indoor plumbing. He stripped off his coat and jacket and rolled up his sleeves before standing on the toilet lid.

The cistern was high on the wall, flushed by a chain that hung down. Markham lowered his arm into the cold water, moving it around slowly, fingers spread. At first he thought there was nothing to find, then he touched something.

He grabbed at it, lifting quickly. In the bathroom he looked at it as he towelled himself dry. A package, small, square, wrapped in oilcloth and carefully sealed. He carried it downstairs.

'Shall we wait until we're back at the office?' Baker raised an eyebrow.

Markham nodded. 'We'll take everything else, too. See how well he survives without it all.'

'There's one good thing.'

'What?' He couldn't think of any.

'If he didn't kill you there, you're probably safe enough for now.'

Maybe. But he wasn't ready to stake his life on it.

CHAPTER FOURTEEN

Markham placed the package on the card table and took out his penknife. One slice with the sharp blade, then a second and he peeled back the oilcloth. Inside was an automatic pistol with an extra clip of ammunition, a knife in a sheath, and an address book.

'Is that a Walther?' Baker asked.

'Yes. A PPK.' Like the James Bond character had in the books, but that was just fiction. This was all too real. He'd seen enough of these during his National Service to know where they belonged. Back then, when he was in Germany, everyone who owned a weapon was trying to sell it for a packet of cigarettes or some scraps of food.

Still wearing his gloves, he picked up the weapon carefully. It was small enough to fit comfortably in his hand. This one looked brand new.

Baker looked at the pistol and the blade then started going through the address book.

'There are only two names in here and I know one of them.'

'Who?'

'Gus Howard. I tried to have him up for murder more than once when I was on the force. I know he did them, but no one would talk and there wasn't enough evidence. It doesn't look good. Not if Harker's dealing with him.'

'Why would Harker need someone like that if he kills people himself?'

'I don't know. But it worries me.'

'Who's the other name?'

'Someone called Trevor Peel.'

'Clever Trevor?' Markham asked in astonishment. 'Are you sure?'

'That's what it says here. Why, do you know him?'

'It can't be him. Trevor wouldn't hurt anyone. He doesn't have the brawn, never mind the brains.'

'Maybe it's a different one, then.' Baker stared at him. 'Who is he?'

'Just a lad who works at Cokely's.' Even as he said the name of the company he knew it had to be more than coincidence.

'Cokely's eh?'

'It looks like we have a couple of visits to make,' Markham said.

Baker picked up the knife and slid it in his pocket.

'If we're going to see Gus Howard I'm taking this.' His smile was dark. 'Always did prefer a knife to a gun, anyway. Silent.' He paused. 'I'd grab that gun if I were you.'

'I don't like them.'

'Good. I'd wonder about you if you did. But I'll worry about you less if you pick the bloody thing up. When we run into Harker again it'll even things up.'

Reluctantly, he did, feeling the hard plastic of the grip and the cold metal of the barrel, then slipping it into his overcoat pocket. He felt as if it made a bulge, something everyone would see.

'Let's go and see Trevor first,' Markham decided. 'What's his address?'

Baker opened the address book. 'Kirkstall.'

***

It was in sight of the old abbey. But no one was walking in the grounds around the ruins. The sky was grey, the wind whipping through the tall trees and making the river flow fast in the distance.

They walked up a street of back-to-back houses, the weary remnants of an industrial age.

'I'll handle this one,' Markham said.

The door must have just been painted that summer, the finish still glossy, the colour bright. He waited and heard footsteps shuffling inside.

The woman wore a scarf around her head and a long tabard apron.

'Hello, Mrs Peel, I'm looking for Trevor. Is he at home?'

'No, luv, he's at work.' She looked from Markham to Baker. 'What are you, coppers?'

'Nothing like that,' he assured her quickly. 'Does Trevor still work at Cokely's?'

She leaned against the doorjamb, assessing them as she brought a battered packet of Woodbines from her apron and lit one.

'That's right.'

'I met him down at Studio 20.'

The woman shook her head in disgust. 'Always got that racket going on in his bedroom. Radio Luxembourg. Just noise, if you ask me. You don't look like the type to enjoy that.'

'I'm not. I like jazz,' Markham told her and she snorted. 'Do you know when he'll he home?'

'It'd better be by six or his tea'll be cold. Same for his dad. They know the rules.'

'Thank you.' Markham began to turn away then stopped. 'Has he ever mentioned someone called Simon Harker?'

She pursed her lips then shook her head. 'Doesn't ring a bell. Why?'

'I'm looking for him, I thought Trevor might be able to help. Never mind.' He smiled and raised his hat in farewell.

'What's your name?' Mrs Peel asked.

'Dan Markham,' he replied. 'Can you ask him to get in touch with me?'

'Aye, if you like.'

★★★

'I'll go back later,' Markham said as he settled behind the steering wheel of the Anglia. 'Where now?'

'Off Burley Road.' Baker didn't even need to look at the address book.

It wasn't far, just a little closer to the city centre. More back-to-back houses, more poverty.

'Up Cardigan Road, then turn on Burley Lodge Road. Might as well park in front of the place. It won't matter to Gus.'

Baker banged hard on the door. No one came to answer it. He bent, lifting the flap of the letterbox.

'Come on, Gus. I know you're in there. You might as well open up.'

He straightened again, smiling. Half a minute later they heard a lock turn and the door snicked open an inch.

'What do you want?'

'A word, Gus.' Baker paused. 'Two words. Simon Harker.'

'Piss off.'

It happened quickly. Baker raised a foot and bought the thick sole of his shoe crashing down on the wood. Gus Howard toppled backwards as the door fell open.

'Nice of him to ask us in like that.'

Howard was still on his back, shaking his head to try and clear it. He was a big man, thickly muscled, the shirt tight across his chest.

The way the knife appeared in Baker's hand seemed like magic. He grabbed the other man's shirt and pulled him to his feet. 'I've been wanting to do this for a long, long time.'

Markham closed the door. This wasn't his show. He simply stood, one hand in his pocket, holding the pistol, ready.

Baker's face was flushed through with anger as he rammed Howard against a wall, hard enough to shake the house.

'Harker,' he said again.

'Don't know him.' The wind had been knocked from the man and the words came out with effort. Baker moved his hand against Howard's neck.

'I'm not here to play any bloody games.' He brought the knife up and laid the flat of the blade against the man's cheek, the tip close to the corner of his eye.

'You don't want to do this,' Howard warned.

'Bit late now, isn't it? I'm doing it.' He waited. 'Well, are you going to tell me?' His hand clamped tighter on Howard's windpipe. 'I'll count to three. One … two …'

The man held up a hand. Baker eased his grip, grabbing Howard's hair as he started to topple, then dragged him to the scullery at the end of the hall before pushing him into one of the chairs gathered around a table.

It was a neat, spare room. No washing up waiting to be done, everything tidy and in its place.

'Harker.' It was an order. The knife glistened in the light through the window.

'He got in touch two months ago.' Howard rubbed his throat. His voice was a raw, dry rasp. 'I need some water.'

'When you're done,' Baker told him coldly. 'What did he want?'

'Gave me fifty quid to make myself available.' He shrugged.

'Available for what?'

'I didn't ask.'

Baker tightened his grip on Howard's hair, drawing his head back and placing the knife against his throat.

'I said I'm not messing about, Gus. For what?'

'Any jobs he needed. Said he'd heard about me.'

'And what have you done for him?' A single bead of blood trickled slowly down to Howard's collar.

'Nothing.' There was pleading in his voice. 'Really. He came back every month and gave me more money. Said the same thing.'

'What have you done for him?' Baker repeated.

'Nothing. I told you.' Howard's eyes were open wide. 'He never asked me to do anything.'

'There are three people dead so far. Maybe four. You kill people, Gus. It's what you do.'

Another drop of blood made its way along his neck.

'Honest.'

'I don't believe you.'

'I just took his money.'

Baker stared into the man's eyes for a long time. The knife didn't move. Markham stayed silent in the doorway, watching, his hand tense around the butt of the Walther. Finally Baker took the blade away and let go of Howard's hair.

'If he comes back, you don't answer the door,' he said. 'If you see him, you turn around and run the other way. You understand me?'

The man nodded. He brought a handkerchief from his trousers and dabbed at the blood.

'And I wouldn't bother reporting this to the police, Gus. Most of them think that killing you would warrant a medal.'

He walked out, pushing Markham out of the way.

'Find a pub,' he said when they were in the car. 'I need to take the taste of him out of my mouth.'

He settled on the Fenton, just down from the university. A table of students enjoyed an afternoon pint instead of their lectures. Markham bought a whisky for Baker and a shandy for himself.

Baker had his pipe lit, the smoke like a cloud around his head. For two minutes they stayed silent.

'I thought you were going to murder him.'

'I was tempted, believe you me,' he said. 'He's got away with it too often. Mostly I wanted him terrified enough to tell me the truth. What did you think? Did you believe him?'

Markham took a sip of his drink.

'Yes. I did.'

'So did I.' Baker sighed. 'Looks like it's all down to this Trevor if we're going to get anywhere.'

'I'll find him later.'

The students left noisily and the landlord put a towel over the taps, calling, 'Three o'clock. Time, gentlemen, please.'

Baker downed the Scotch in a single gulp.

'Howard's had that coming for years.' He shook his head and laughed. 'Still, better I didn't. The wife would have killed me before they could hang me.'

Outside, Leeds was spread before them, chimneys belching smoke into a sky the colour of worn lead.

'Harker's probably long gone now,' Markham said. It was what all the field operatives were taught: have a bolthole and don't tell anyone where it is. They'd never find him in the city.

He parked on Albion Place.

'You go in. I've a few things to do. I'll catch up with Trevor later.'

'Let's hope you can make him talk.'

He knew, Clever Trevor was all they had if they were going to find Amanda Fox.

***

He didn't have any pressing errands; he simply wanted time to think. He'd seen a different side of Baker and it disturbed him. Right on the edge of violence, so close to going over. And what could he have done to stop it? Nothing.

Did he really want someone like that as a partner? The man had always seemed straightforward enough. This was like opening a door and finding someone familiar but completely unknown.

Markham sat in the flat, a Billie Holiday LP spinning quietly on the record player. If it hadn't been for Baker they'd never have had the missing person case that drew them into this maze.

Harker. Since the confrontation in the ginnel his fears had started to recede. The man couldn't have missed at that range but he hadn't pulled the trigger.

Maybe he was safe. For now, at least.

His mind turned to Amanda Fox.

Every day that passed made it more likely that she was dead. He knew that. But someone had her, and until a body was discovered it was still worth searching. He ground out another cigarette in the ashtray.

They'd find her. They'd find her alive. Then perhaps he'd sit and have a long talk with Stephen Baker.

CHAPTER FIFTEEN

It was seven o'clock when Markham parked in Kirkstall. Time enough for Trevor to have eaten his tea and be watching television. But his mother just shook her head when she opened the door.

'He rang down to the corner shop, they have a telephone there. Left a message that he was meeting some of his mates and he'd be home later. I'm sorry, luv, you've had a wasted journey.'

'It doesn't matter.' He raised his hat.

'You've got good manners, you do,' she told him approvingly. 'Your mam brought you up right.'

★★★

He could guess where Trevor would be. This was a skiffle night at Studio 20. They started early and finished early for the kids still at school or on apprenticeships who had to be up in the morning. Afterwards the jazz players would slide in and keep things going well into the small hours.

Markham waited until eight, walking along New Briggate and smoking, stopping outside the Grand Theatre to read the playbill, before walking down the lino-covered stairs at Studio 20.

There was a crowd. A few had seats, but most were standing. A small space was clear for dancing, couples swinging round.

Bob Barclay, the owner, sat in his booth, raising an eyebrow and rubbing his fingers together in a money gesture. Markham grinned.

The music was nothing much. A pair of acoustic guitars, one of the players singing, tea chest bass, and someone rubbing the washboard far too loudly. But the audience ate it up.

He peered through the crowd, looking for Trevor Peel. He was over in a corner with a small group of friends, all of them dressed in black leather jackets and carrying motorcycle helmets.

Markham edged between people who paid him no attention, faces focused on the music, until Trevor noticed him approach. The lad said something to his friends and moved closer, raising an arm in greeting.

'Hello, Mr Markham.' He was smiling, happy. He nodded at the band. 'What do you think?'

'Not quite my taste,' he replied with a shrug. 'I was looking for you.'

'Me?' Trevor seemed astonished.

Markham smiled. 'I thought you might be able to help me.'

Peel looked at him uncertainly. 'How?'

'I heard your name somewhere.'

Now the lad was worried. 'Who was talking about me?'

'It was in an address book.' He watched Peel bouncing slightly from foot to foot, as if he was ready to flee. 'Don't run,' he said quietly. 'I've got a gun. It belonged to the man who had your name. Do you know who I'm talking about?'

Trevor nodded, defeat on his face.

'How do you know Simon Harker?' Markham asked.

Trevor's eyes slid around, seeking a way out, then glancing back at his friends.

'Well?' Markham repeated. 'Come on, Trev, I'm not asking for the fun of it.'

Suddenly he was surrounded by young men with hard faces.

They bumped against him, trying to bounce him between them. Their jackets had the smell of new leather, hair shining with Brylcreem. He reached out and grabbed Trevor's wrist; he wasn't going to let him vanish.

Markham stood his ground, saying nothing, just staring at Peel. Then Barclay was there, pushing the lads away.

'I'm not having any trouble in here,' he said loudly. 'If you want that, you can get out right now. You,' he told one of them, 'you're banned now. The rest of you want the same?'

Reluctantly, they moved back, turning their heads to glare. It was over as quickly as it had begun. But Markham kept a tight grip on Trevor before the lad could vanish with the others.

'Are you all right, Dan?' Barclay asked.

'Fine,' he answered. 'Thanks.'

'Bloody kids,' he muttered and made his way back to his booth.

'I still want some answers,' Markham warned Trevor. 'Proper answers.'

'He came up to me at the bus stop,' Peel said finally, 'I'd just got off on my way home from work. Asked if I worked at Cokely's.'

'Go on.'

'We went down the pub and had a couple of drinks.' He looked down at the scuffed floor.

'What did he want?'

'Information.'

'About what?'

'The shadow factory. I told him I didn't know much about it. I hadn't been there long.'

But Harker had picked him out as not too bright, easily flattered and persuaded. And tempted.

'Did you find out?'

'Some of it,' Peel admitted after a moment. 'They have some rooms in there. They're doing defence stuff. Secret things.'

'Did you tell him? How much did he pay you?'

'Fifty quid.' He reddened, the spots standing out angrily on his cheeks.

'There was more, though, wasn't there?' He felt sure of it. His name wouldn't have been in the address book just for that. Trevor nodded.

'He got me to steal a key for one of the doors at the shadow factory. They're just in a drawer.' He raised his head hopefully. 'Don't shop me, Mr Markham. It's a good job. It's got a future.'

'How much did he pay you for the key?' He was going to learn as much as he could.

'Two hundred. I bought my bike with it.'

'And did he say why he wanted the key?'

'I didn't ask,' Trevor answered quietly.

Markham leaned close enough to smell the man's fear.

'You're going to tell me everything you know about him. What he wants, what he's doing. If you're good and do it right, no one else needs to know. You understand?'

The group had finished and were packing away their instruments. The crowd was thinning as people vanished up the stairs.

'Can you keep an eye on the place, Dan?' Barclay asked him. 'You know how it is. I won't be long.'

'Of course.' Markham didn't even glance over his shoulder. He and Trevor were the only ones left in the place. A thin cloud of cigarette smoke hovered below the ceiling. 'We might as well sit down. Make ourselves comfortable.'

Trevor perched on the chair but he didn't look relaxed.

He'd given Harker the key, he said slowly, and thought that was it. A week later the man was back, wanting to know more. He'd forced Trevor to meet him there one night and take him through the shadow factory, to explain what was going on there.

'I'd been over there a few times, you see,' he explained. 'Just delivering stuff, like. But I'd learnt my way around. He said he'd tell the bosses if I didn't help him. I didn't have much choice, did I?'

'That wasn't all, was it?'

'There are places in there that they keep well locked. It's where the boffins work.' It must have been in an area he and Baker hadn't explored. 'He wanted to get in there. I told him I couldn't get a key. He kept pressing me.' Trevor was quiet for a moment. 'Threatening me.'

'Did you get him the keys?'

'Just for one evening. I managed to borrow them. I told him I'd need to put them back the next morning.'

'What was in there?'

'I didn't go in. I didn't want to know. I was too scared.'

A thought struck Markham.

'Was this before the two men who worked at Cokely's died?'

'Yeah.' Trevor looked quizzical. 'Why? One of them was an accident, wasn't it? And the other killed himself. That's what everyone said.'

'That's right.' There was no need to burden the lad. 'What else?'

'That's it. I haven't seen him in a few weeks. Don't want to, neither. Is that it, Mr Markham? Please?'

'Do you know where Harker lives?'

'No,' Peel answered, and he believed him.

'Go on,' he said, and heard Trevor dash away up the stairs as if he was escaping.

***

He sat for a few minutes, going through all he'd been told. Harker was smart. He'd used Trevor Peel in a very clever way, forcing more and more from him until he'd taken all he could. But none of this was going to help him find Amanda Fox, and that was what he needed to do. All the rest of it, the spying, any state secrets, that didn't matter. That was abstract and theoretical. He couldn't do anything about it. If someone dropped the bloody bomb, it wouldn't matter anyway.

Where did he go from here …?

Markham turned at the footsteps. Three people coming down the stairs. Someone struggling behind a bass drum and behind him, a pair of West Indians with battered saxophone cases. They played here regularly, he'd seen them a week or two before; they were always good, letting the music curl and glow, playing like each note meant something vital, that it had something important to say. Worth staying to hear.

'Hi, man.' One of them nodded a greeting. 'What happened to your fingers?'

He hadn't thought about the useless fingers for a while.

'I had an accident a few years ago.'

'Maybe you should take up guitar.' The man laughed. 'You could be the new Django.'

***

They were sitting in the cafe on the balcony at the market, looking down at the shoppers wandering and the traders opening their stalls. There was a sharp sizzle as the cook took bacon from the grill and put it on a plate. Condensation ran down the windows. The place was a small oasis of heat.

'So we're still no further on,' Baker said after Markham finished recounting everything Trevor had said. He put another spoonful of sugar in his tea and stirred it absently.

'Not really.' Markham was warm in the overcoat, acutely aware of the gun in his pocket; he wasn't about to take it off. 'The only way we're going to find Amanda is to shake things up a bit.'

'Someone knows Harker. Someone has to.'

Markham shook his head. 'He probably has another identity by now. He'll have all the papers for a spare one in his bolthole. And money, too.'

'There has to be a way,' Baker said. 'Doesn't there?'

They left, crossing Vicar Lane and walking up King Edward Street. Baker nodded at people he knew; after decades on the force hundreds of folk around Leeds were familiar with his face.

The office felt stuffy, the radiator burning to the touch. Feast or famine, cold or boiling; it could never just be comfortably warm.

They had no ideas just when they desperately needed a few. For an hour they tossed thoughts back and forth. Nothing useful. Not a damned thing. They were still discussing it when the second post arrived. Markham sorted through it. An income tax reminder in its buff envelope, a note from a solicitor about some possible work, and another envelope.

The address was printed in capitals. He tore it open. Inside there was a lock of hair. The same shade as Amanda Fox's hair. He held it up.

'He's saying she's still alive.'

'Where was it posted?'

The mark was too blurred to read clearly. Holbeck? Holt Park? It was impossible to be sure. And it probably didn't matter. Harker wasn't stupid enough to drop it in a post box close to his hideaway.

But they had a sign. That was something. And it was a goad. He was still thinking when the telephone rang and he heard the tumble of coins into the slot.

'I think your postman has been, Mr Markham.'

He sat up straight.

'That's right, Mr Harker.' He looked across at Baker. 'It was just delivered.'

Markham raised his eyebrows. With a brisk nod, Baker left quietly. If the man knew they had the envelope, he was somewhere close. There were telephone boxes at either end of Albion Place.

'I'm sorry we didn't have time to chat yesterday.' Harker chuckled. 'You caught me just as I was leaving.'

'Then perhaps we can meet somewhere.'

'You're very droll. I'm sure we can find a more … anonymous way to do business. I think you'd like to see Mrs Fox again.'

'I'd like to see her alive.'

'She is. For the moment.'

'I don't know why you took her. Her husband was working for your lot.' He wanted to keep Harker talking, to give Baker a chance to spot him.

'But she wasn't. And whilst she might not realise it, she knows a few things. I just need a little time to make sure her knowledge is unimportant.'

I, Markham noted; the man was definitely operating alone.

'Why should I believe you?'

'Why not? This was your trade once, I believe. *Können Sie noch Deutsch sprechen?*'

'*Nur ein Bisschen,*' he replied. A bit, yes, but his German was rusty now. Harker knew about his National Service. That was no surprise, really. 'When will you release her?' He wasn't going to ask if the man would kill her.

'When it's time,' Harker said coolly. 'But it would be safer for her if you weren't looking for me. Do I make myself quite clear on that?'

'I understand what you're saying.' He tried to pick out any background noise, if there was anything that might pinpoint the location.

'If you back away, no harm will come to her.'

'So you say.'

'That's a promise. Now you know how we stand, Mr Markham. The choice is yours.'

Then just a click as Harker replaced the receiver.

***

He waited for Baker to return, pacing around the small office and smoking. What was Harker doing? Did he just want to taunt them? No, the man was a professional. But a phone call like that, sending the lock of hair, that didn't fit with everything else.

There had to be something more. What was it?

Baker didn't return. Maybe he'd found Harker. Maybe.

The seconds ticked past with no footsteps on the stairs. He finished his second cigarette and lit a third. When the telephone bell shrilled again he leapt for it.

'Pick me up at Millgarth in quarter of an hour,' Baker told him.

'Did you find him?'

But the line was already dead.

Markham threw on his overcoat and gathered up his hat and gloves. He was pulling out his keys to lock the office when the phone rang once more.

'Dan?'

'Hello.' His voice softened. Carla.

'Are you in the middle of something?'

'Sort of,' he admitted.

'I'll be quick, then. My train arrives at half past five tomorrow. Can you meet me?'

'I'll be there,' he promised.

'Good.' A small hesitation. 'I've missed you.'

For a second he couldn't say anything.

'I've missed you, too.' He had. A lot.

CHAPTER SIXTEEN

Markham kept the engine running as he parked outside Millgarth police station. In less than thirty seconds Baker was grunting into the passenger seat. His face was flushed.

'Drive out to Morley,' he instructed.

'Morley?' He put the car into gear and eased out into traffic. 'Why?'

'I thought Harker wouldn't use the telephone boxes so close to us,' Baker explained. 'But he knew that the postman had come. So I looked a little further away.'

'You found him?'

'Down on Commercial Street.' He dug out his pipe, lit a match and started to smoke. 'He had a car parked right there. I took down the number plate and went to Millgarth.'

'Well?' he asked impatiently.

'It's registered to someone called David Thorp on Gillroyd Parade in Morley. A Ford Prefect, two years old. Bought it three months ago.'

'Did he see you?'

'I don't think so,' Baker told him. 'Maybe he wasn't as clever as he thought.'

Maybe. But they wouldn't let someone who made such basic mistakes operate abroad. There was something more behind this.

'We should just let the police take care of it now,' Markham said.

Baker sighed.

'Tell me something, Dan. What do you think of Leeds Police? Be honest now.'

'Not much,' he replied.

'Aye, much as it hurts me to say it, you're probably right. In this, anyway. I've talked to them, they don't have a clue. And I was one of them for years. They'd go in mob-handed and balls it all up. The only way we're going to take care of this is to do it ourselves.'

They drove in silence along Elland Road, past the football ground. On the waste ground close by, the team was training, playing a five-a-side match. When they reached the turning for Churwell, Markham accelerated up the hill.

'He wants us to find him,' he said finally. He'd reasoned it out.

'Don't be daft.' Baker turned in his seat. 'What are you talking about?'

'He has Amanda Fox, agreed?'

'We already know that from the hair and the phone call.'

'If we find her, he has us all together.'

'There are two of us and only one of him.'

'And he's a professional, he's trained. How many people here know about him?'

'Mrs Fox. You, me. Tim Hill, Gus Howard, and that Peel lad.'

'How many men has he managed to get rid of so far?'

'Three. And he tried for you.'

'You think he'd stop at that? He has a job to do.'

'That's too twisted for me,' Baker sighed.

'He could have gone once Mark Fox disappeared,' Markham insisted. 'I think there's one thing he said that's true – Amanda Fox probably knows something important. Maybe he's right and she doesn't even realise it. He has to take care of that. And we've become dangerous so he's decided we have to go, too.' He turned off the main road, down into Morley. 'Now, where's Gillroyd Parade?'

The Ford Prefect was parked on a patch of waste ground five minutes' walk from the street. The bonnet was still warm. As Markham peered in the windows on the driver's side, Baker squatted.

'What are you doing?'

'Letting down two of the tyres. He won't be going anywhere in a hurry.'

Number twenty-one was halfway along the block. A through terrace of blackened brick, like all its neighbours. There was a small yard at the back that opened on to a ginnel, the same as the house where they'd found Harker in Harehills.

'How are we going in?' Markham asked.

'If we try to kick in the front door, Morley police will be along before you can swat a fly,' Baker said. 'We have to be quick and fast. Make it the back door. Did they teach you to do that when you were a spy?'

'No.'

'Follow me, then. And keep that gun ready.'

They kept low, moving along the ginnel in a crouch below the high walls, counting the houses as they passed. A thin drizzle began to fall, chilly on the skin.

'This one,' Baker whispered. Very quietly he unlatched the gate, then moved with surprising grace and speed over the flagstones and up the stone steps to the back door. He brought his foot down hard on the lock. It gave on the first kick and he shouldered his way in, knife in hand.

Markham followed, pulling out the gun. Throughout the house the curtains were closed, leaving the place in gloom and shadow. The scullery was empty. The same in the front room. Baker gestured to the stairs and Markham led the way, staring up, scarcely daring to breathe, weapon ready to fire.

No one in either of the bedrooms. Only one looked lived-in, a small dent in the pillow where someone's head had been.

He bent to examine it and saw a couple of dark blond hairs. Harker. The wardrobe had been cleaned out, no suitcase on the floor or under the bed.

'Cellar,' Baker said quietly. 'You stay up here in case he's around.'

He waited, constantly glancing round, nervous, as Baker descended the steps. The electric light didn't work and Baker took a small torch from his mackintosh.

'She's here,' he called up after a moment. 'Alive.'

Markham felt relief surge through him. But he was worried. This was far too easy. Harker had almost led them here. It had to be a trap of some kind. He stood where he could see both the front and back doors, alert for the slightest sound and on edge. His hand was sweaty as he gripped the Walther.

It felt like the better part of five minutes before Baker was gently urging Amanda Fox up the stairs. She came out, blinking in the light. Bedraggled, terrified, dirt on her face and clothes, her hair a tangle. But nothing damaged that he could see. Tears were streaming down her face. Her wrists were red and raw where she'd been tied.

As soon as she saw Markham, she hugged him, clinging tightly, making a low, moaning sound.

'Let's get her out of here,' Markham said. 'You take the gun and I'll look after her.'

He felt nervous going out of the back door and along the ginnel. They were exposed, vulnerable. Amanda Fox clung to him. Here they made easy targets. But nothing had happened by the time they reach the Anglia, and he settled her until she was lying along the back seat. Baker kept watch, shaking his head as Markham started the car.

'No sign of anyone.' The Ford Prefect was still there, leaning drunkenly to one side. 'Maybe he's decided to cut his losses and scarpered.'

'Perhaps.' But he didn't really believe it. The man was too professional for that.

***

He headed back towards Leeds a different way, down Gelderd Road. The city was spread out below him. The top of the Town Hall, the tower of the Parkinson Building at the university. Low cloud and smoke hung over Leeds; so much for cleaner air.

Traffic was light; it was easy for Markham to keep an eye on the mirror. Harker must have another vehicle, he reasoned. But no cars seemed to be following them. A dirty white Commer van came up from behind. Over the speed limit, like so many tradesmen.

At first he paid it no mind. Another builder or plasterer.

It was just thirty yards away when he could make out the driver's face. Harker.

'Better hold on,' he warned.

He stamped down on the brake pedal for a second, hearing the screech, then jammed his foot on the accelerator, feeling the Anglia jump, grateful for a good mechanic. But the van had power, closing the gap between them as they sped down the long hill.

There were places to turn, he thought frantically, but all that would do was trap him somewhere. He needed to be *in* Leeds to be safe. His gaze moved constantly between the mirrors and the road ahead. Hands so tight on the wheel that his knuckles were white. And still the van was getting closer. It was going to ram them.

Markham tried to swallow. His throat was dry. Off to the side, past the pavement, was rutted scrubland and piles of bricks. The factory that had once stood here had been hit in a German raid. If he could judge it perfectly …

He let up on the speed, just a fraction, enough to make the car more controllable.

'Hang on,' he warned through clenched teeth.

The van was very close. He could see every feature on Harker's face. No expression, only hard concentration.

As soon as he felt the first small thump of contact, he tore the wheel to the left, bouncing over the kerb, feet on the brake and clutch, gearing down into second, then first as he heard the engine whine in complaint.

From the corner of his eye he registered the van speeding past, going too fast to stop. Markham tried to steer away from the rubble. But there was too much of it, too close. The Anglia crashed, sending him forward, the breath squeezed out of him by the steering wheel. His head cracked against the windscreen, but the hat saved his skin. The engine died with a sharp judder.

He was dazed, but nothing broken or damaged. In the passenger seat Baker looked grim. He had a split lip, blood on his chin. Nothing more.

He turned his head. His neck hurt. Amanda Fox had tumbled on to the floor, but she glanced up.

'I'm all right,' she said in a small, cracked voice.

'Let's get out of here,' Markham ordered.

The front doors worked, but they had to tug and force the back open until the three of them were standing on the waste ground, the drizzle feeling fresh on their faces.

'Looks like a write-off, Dan,' Baker said as he shook his head. 'But you did well there.'

Markham didn't speak. It wasn't the ruined car. It was how close he'd come. He breathed deeply for a few seconds then reached for his packet of cigarettes.

'Can I …?' Amanda asked. He gave her one, his hand shaking wildly as he lit them. She drew down the smoke, keeping it in her lungs for a long time before blowing it out again, staring down at the broken ground.

'There's a telephone box down the road.' Baker pointed into the distance. 'Do you want me to go?'

'I'll do it.' Markham passed over the gun and started to walk, glancing all around with every step. One chance, he told himself. Harker had taken it and failed. He wouldn't dare circle back. Not in such a public place.

For the first few paces he stumbled; his legs felt weak, as if they couldn't support him properly. But by the time he was ringing the garage on Buslingthorpe Lane he was starting to feel himself again.

As he waited, then pushed the coins in the slot, he kept his eyes on the road for the white Commer van. But there was no sign of it. One chance. Maybe. Markham wasn't going to relax just yet.

Martin Day answered the phone himself.

'You can't have a problem with the Anglia, Dan,' he laughed. 'I worked on it myself. A Swiss watch couldn't tick over better than that thing.'

'It's a write-off. Someone pushed me off the road.'

'Bloody hell.' He could hear the man exhale slowly. 'What do you need?'

'Can you send someone out to tow it?'

'Yes.' Day spoke slowly, the sound of a man making quick calculations. 'I've got a mate who does that.'

'I'm going to need a car, too. Until I try to claim on my insurance.'

'There's that Escort Estate you had before.' He paused. 'I did get something in on Monday. Bigger than the Anglia, but it might be up your street. A Riley Pathfinder. You can borrow that, if you like. Runs really well. I'm going to be selling it.'

The Pathfinder was big, with a powerful motor. Larger than anything he'd ever driven.

'Are you sure?'

'If you like it, we can work something out once your insurance pays you, Dan. How about that?'

'Very fair.'

★★★

Now all they had to do was wait. Smoking, on edge, still constantly looking around.

'What do you reckon?' Baker asked finally.

'I think we're safe enough for now. He hasn't given up yet, though. I'm sure of that. At least we found her.'

Amanda Fox sat quietly on a pile of bricks. This was the second time he'd rescued her. But he didn't feel like a knight in shining armour. They had her, but what could they do with her now? How could they keep her safe?

'I'll take care of her,' Baker offered. 'We have a spare room and the wife will see she's looked after.'

'What if Harker tries something?'

Baker snorted.

'My Nancy would have scared Hitler. A Russian spy isn't going to worry her. I can run up and get some clothes from her house. She'll be safe enough.'

★★★

At first the Riley scared him. It was so bloody big. But as soon as he was used to it, he loved the car.

'It's had a couple of dents,' Day told him breezily, 'but they're easily knocked out. A quick respray and it'll look like new. And don't worry about the miles on the clock, it runs perfectly. I had it up to ninety yesterday.' He smiled.

It was speedy, commanding and sturdy. If he'd been driving this then Harker would never have caught him. By the time he parked at the flat he was convinced. All he needed was to scrape up the money to buy it. It wouldn't be cheap to run, not with petrol at five shillings a gallon, but he'd feel safe; the car was built like a tank.

***

Markham's neck ached a little and he had a couple of bruises on his chest after yesterday's crash. But at least his face had almost healed; he wouldn't look like Frankenstein when Carla saw him.

He was washing the breakfast pots when he heard the metal clack of the letterbox. Only one thing, a thin cardboard box, with something rattling around inside. Standing by the window, watching people queueing at the bus, he ripped it open and felt inside.

He froze.

Very gently he drew the item from the box. A bullet, the metal cold against his fingertips. He rested it on the sill and look at the package. The same printing as the envelope with the lock of Amanda Fox's hair. Harker.

It was his message.

When he left, the box and bullet were in a jacket pocket, and the gun in his overcoat. Just in case.

***

'That Riley downstairs, is that yours?' Baker asked as he walked in and dropped his newspaper on the card table.

'Yes,' Markham replied. 'How is she?'

'Still sleeping when I left.' He hung up the mackintosh and hat and sat with a contented sigh. 'Twelve hours and counting. I went out to her place last night and picked up a few bits and pieces. The wife thinks she needs feeding up.'

Did you get anything in the post this morning?'

'Just bills,' Baker answered. 'Why?'

'This came for me.' He placed the box on the green baize. Baker looked at him for a moment, glanced inside, then at the address.

'A reminder. He's not subtle, is he?'

'It scared the hell out of me.'

'That's what he wants. You're the one he sees as a threat. I'm just the fat old bloke. He's not worried about me.'

A threat? How? All he'd wanted was to find Amanda Fox. She was safe; it was done. The rest of it didn't interest him. For all he cared, Harker could bugger off back to Russia.

'Me?'

Baker shrugged. 'Don't ask me why, but he must.'

'I know; I haven't forgotten.' Markham's reply was icy.

'And you don't give up. It's one of the things I like about you. You're like a bloody terrier.'

'But it's done. We've got her back.'

'Not to him, it's not.' Baker weighed the bullet in his large palm. 'That looks like it'll fit your Walther. You'd better carry it. Always better to have one spare.'

CHAPTER SEVENTEEN

Markham arrived ten minutes early and waited outside the ticket barrier. Leeds station was drab and dull, the night already closed around it. Steam filled the air as a wind blew down the platforms, scattering ticket stubs and sweet wrappers.

He smoked a cigarette, more anxious that he'd imagined. There was a screech of brakes as the train pulled in, slowly juddering to a halt just before the buffers. Smoke poured up to the dirty glass ceiling, making the lights appear hazy and distant. And then a push of people leaving the carriages. He held his breath as he tried to spot Carla.

Then suddenly she was there. A brilliant daub of colour in a bright red coat and scarlet beret, standing out against the greys and browns and boring blues, peering ahead intently then beaming as she saw him.

He held her tight. For a moment it was as if the last three years had never happened, that they'd always been like this. She felt so natural in his arms, so right. Markham closed his eyes, only opening them again as she moved and her lips found his.

'Well hello, Dan.' She smiled. People parted around them as if they were an island.

'Ready for this?' he asked.

'Oh yes. Very.'

She had two suitcases. He lifted one, surprised by the weight inside.

'I thought you were just coming for the weekend.' He raised an eyebrow.

'I am. But I thought I'd bring a few things down and leave them here. Less to move later. You don't mind, do you?'

'No.' He laughed. It was so typical of her, the way she'd always been. And he had the room. 'Do you want to eat first or just go home?'

There was seduction in her eyes.

'That had better not be a serious question, Dan. Not after all this time.'

★★★

It was half past eight before he slid out of bed and dressed in shirt and trousers. Carla was dozing, curled up under the covers. Barefoot, he tiptoed around the tangle of clothes she'd left on the floor and into the living room.

The record was still spinning on the turntable, the needle clicking in the final groove. He replaced it with *The Amazing Bud Powell, Volume Two*, piano, bass, and drums like a soft undercurrent in the flat.

He peeled and diced potatoes, putting them on to boil, and lit a cigarette as he gazed down at the street. For tonight, the world could go away. It was just him and Carla, locked and bolted safely in this place.

He'd forgotten what it was like to be so eager for someone, to feel how they were moving, for everything to become so urgent that nothing else existed. But that was how it had been, just like the old days. With Georgina it had been fun, but without that fiery edge of passion.

★★★

Corned beef hash. The only rationing dish he'd ever enjoyed. Simple, quick. He turned over the LP and went back into the bedroom, rubbing her shoulder gently.

'I've made something to eat.'

'God, you're a lifesaver. I'm famished.'

She stood and stretched, not self-conscious about her body, pulling on a turquoise Chinese-style dress from one of the suitcases before turning her back to him.

'Can you zip me up?'

Everything felt natural. The small talk over the food, the shift in musical mood as he replaced Powell with the concentrated intensity of Mingus' *East Coasting*. Carla raised her head as the trumpet came in on 'Memories of You'.

'Is that more by the chap you sent me?'

'No. That was Miles Davis.'

'That's right. This is good, though.' She listened for a few seconds more. 'It's like these splashes of prime colours peering through a very delicate background.'

Markham grinned. That was exactly what it was like. And of course she'd see it like a painting.

'Tell me about your work,' he said. 'What you've been doing.'

'I can show you, if you like.' She padded to the other side of the room and pulled a small packet from her large handbag. 'One of the blokes in the art department loves photography. He wanted to take a few snaps. They actually came out quite well.'

He'd worked in colour, not the black-and-white of holiday pictures developed at the chemist. Markham went through them slowly. There were ideas he remembered from the things she'd done when they'd known each other before. But she'd developed it in startling ways.

Some of them were abstracts, but containing the ghost of something real, as if it had only just departed. Others took objects but changed them, transformed them.

'Wonderful,' he said when he eventually pushed the pile back towards her.

'Do you really think so?'

'I do.' He meant it. He might not understand what she was doing, but it touched him. What was inside her that she could look at the world and see things that way? He spooned coffee into the pot she'd brought back from her trip to Italy three years before, added water, and put it on the gas.

'What about you, Dan?' Carla reached across and stroked his face. 'It's not as bad as you said.'

'Better than a few days ago.'

'How did it happen?'

He told her about Amanda Fox, the dead Germans, Simon Harker, even the bullet, watching her mouth turn down into a deep, concerned frown. He couldn't blame her; she'd suffered once because of him. Why would she want that again? But he needed to be honest with her. He wanted her aware.

'God,' she said when he finished.

He stared at her.

'After last time I want you to know everything. If you don't want to get involved, I'll understand.' He swallowed hard, wanting the answer but fearful of it. She took a cigarette from his packet and lit it. Carla stayed silent until she finally ground it out in the ashtray.

'How long before it's all over?' she asked.

'Soon,' Markham told her. 'Very soon. Long before you move.'

'I hope so, Dan,' she sighed and put her hand over his. 'I really bloody hope so.'

***

On Saturday they trailed around Headingley and Hyde Park. Postcards in the windows of newsagents' shops showed flats for rent. Some she dismissed without even going inside. Others needed inspection but didn't satisfy.

Finally, about three o'clock, she spent a good half hour in one of the flats. He sat in the Riley, reading the newspaper. Today was good. This was normal life. Real life. Made up of mundane little tasks and favours. Right now, at least, it made him happy. But he'd still kept his eyes open and checked the mirror regularly when they were driving.

By the time Carla emerged, smiling triumphantly, he'd finished the paper and set it down on the passenger seat.

'You like it?'

'I've taken it,' she announced excitedly. 'Do you want to come and see?'

It was the top floor of a small, detached Edwardian house, with stairs up to an empty attic. Four rooms, including a small kitchen and a bathroom.

'Look at this,' Carla said once they were in the attic. 'Windows at each end. There's plenty of light. It'll be perfect.' He hugged her. She seemed to be buzzing and glowing with pleasure. 'There's a garden at the back. I'll be able to sit outside in the summer. And it's cheap. It's perfect, Dan.'

The plans gushed out of her. She was going to learn to drive and buy a car. Travel more.

'We need to celebrate,' he said when she slowly wound down. Her face was flushed with excitement for the future.

'My treat,' she said firmly. Before he could object, she added, 'My work sells reasonably well these days. I can afford it.'

'I'm happy for you.' He was smiling. 'I am, really.'

★★★

A meal at Donmar. They didn't even need to discuss it, it couldn't be anywhere else. It had been their place before, now it would be again. She wore a dress with vivid slashes of burgundy and blue, bright against the tired grey of a Leeds winter night.

She talked about the things she'd do with the flat. The living room was large; she'd break it up with a Chinese screen from a junk shop. Find an old velvet settee.

He listened happily, sipping at a glass of Chianti, then a cup of the strong coffee once they'd finished eating. It was still only ten. Carla took hold of his hand and started to pull him playfully down the street. He looked around; no one was watching them.

'Studio 20,' she insisted. 'Come on, Dan, we have to.'

Just a few yards from the restaurant he could hear the sound coming from the club. A tenor sax built on a melody, then trumpet took over, the player trying hard to sound like Miles Davis. But who could ever really pull off a trick like that, Markham thought? Good, but not good enough, and not original enough.

The noise grew as they went down the stairs. He nodded to Bob Barclay and they found a pair of chairs back against the wall. The rhythm section of the band was cooking – double bass, a drummer careful with brushes on the snare and cymbal. And a guitarist he'd seen earlier in the week, leading the skiffle band. This time, though, he was concentrating hard and holding his own.

There was a poster on the wall advertising Georgina's appearance. Georgina Taylor. Coming very soon. He'd have liked to see her win over the crowd. But stay away, that was what she'd told him, and he'd do it. She deserved that. It would be her night, her triumph. He didn't want to ruin it.

Then the door to the stairs opened and she appeared, as if he'd just summoned her out of thin air. Georgina glanced around and saw him. For a moment they stared at each other. Then she turned quickly on her heel and left again.

Carla watched it happen, glancing from one face to the other. She leaned close to him and under the music said, 'That was her, wasn't it?' All he could do was nod. She put her hand over his. 'We can leave if you'd rather.'

'No.' He gave her a sad smile. 'It's fine.'

'She's rather lovely.'

How could he begin to answer that?

They stayed for an hour. After a few minutes the music reeled him in. Not perfect, but there was passion behind it as well as thought. The guitarist took a solo, gaining confidence halfway through the first chorus then letting rip as if he'd spent a long time listening to Charlie Christian's playing. Nothing like his work with the skiffle group. By the time he handed off to the trumpet he'd let the music spiral up to a climax that deserved the applause it received. He smiled bashfully, taking a moment to push back his quiff.

Hand in hand they walked back to the car. After eleven but the Saturday night people were still moving around. Drunks wandering home from the pubs, couples who'd been to the pictures or the theatre, a few haunted stragglers who seemed to have nowhere to go. No Harker.

Chapel Allerton was silent. Just the hoot of an owl drifting down from the park a quarter of a mile away. In the flat, Carla flicked on the two-bar electric fire to warm herself and poured a last glass from a bottle of wine. Over the rim she stared at him with mischief in her eyes.

★★★

'It doesn't matter, you know.'

Tea in bed, the light through the window like slate.

'What doesn't?'

'Me seeing her. It was bound to happen sooner or later.'

She was right. Leeds might be a big city but it was also a very small town. Little groups of people always ran into each other, going to the same places, running with similar crowds.

'It's not as if I expected you to pine away to nothing, hoping for me,' Carla added. 'It's the past now. Isn't it?'

'Very much.' He leaned across and kissed her. Markham thought of asking her about the lovers she'd had. But he didn't want to know, not really. It was safer to leave that cave unexplored. 'What do you want to do today?'

'Spend a lazy morning. Maybe we could take a walk later. And I don't want to be too late back to Durham. I still have to prepare some materials for a class tomorrow.'

★★★

Carla had her wish. They ate and sat around with the *News of the World* and the *Observer* as he played records she wouldn't have heard. Sandwiches and fruit for dinner, then down to Gledhow Valley Woods in overcoats and gloves. The Walther in his pocket. Back by three.

She packed her suitcases and stacked them in a corner of the bedroom.

'Are you sure you don't mind me leaving them here?'

'Not at all.' It was a guarantee that she'd return. He liked that. In the living room she stood with her arms around his neck.

'How would you feel about me coming back in a fortnight?'

'I'd like that a lot.' He grinned.

'Maybe you could come up to Durham, too. It's a beautiful place.'

'And transport more of your stuff down?'

'Well …'

★★★

'How's Amanda?' Markham asked as soon as Baker entered the office on Monday morning.

'Improving.' He sat heavily, unbuttoning his suit jacket to show a grey cardigan over his shirt and tie. 'The wife's feeding her up and she's sleeping normally.' He pulled out the pipe and began to fill it. 'You look happy today. Good weekend?'

'It was, as it happens. Have you had a word with her yet?'

'Last night.' He settled with a sigh. 'She's still very scared.'

'You can't blame her.' Markham lit a cigarette.

'I told her she could stay with us as long as she needed. She'll be sick of our Nancy soon enough. The woman's clucking round like a mother hen.'

'Did Amanda have anything useful to say?'

'Not much. He had her out at Yeadon, then hauled her over to Morley.'

'What does he think she knows? Why did he kidnap her?'

Baker shook his head.

'She hasn't a clue. To hear her tell it, he asked her all kinds of things, didn't seem to focus on one thing.'

'Strange.'

'He did mention the Leeds War Room.'

'The what?'

'Region Two Leeds War Room.' He reeled off the official title. 'Doesn't mean anything?'

'No.' Markham had never heard of it. The place sounded horrific, final.

'They keep it pretty quiet. It's up on Otley Road, not far from Lawnswood cemetery. Glance to your right when you drive up and you'll see the radio mast.'

'How do you know about it?'

'Part of being a copper.' Baker shrugged. 'Anyway, they don't use it much these days.'

'Why not?'

'Something to do with the change from atomic bomb to nuclear. It doesn't give the right protection, they reckon. Seems to me that whatever it is it'll kill us all anyway.'

They were both thinking of the thousands of cardboard coffins stored at the old Arvo shadow factory; Markham could see it in the man's eyes.

'With luck Harker's gone by now,' he said.

'If he has any sense,' Baker agreed. 'But that bullet you got in the post makes me wonder.'

'I haven't seen any sign of him.'

'Not seen anyone hanging around near us, either. Maybe your package is his goodbye and he really has scarpered.'

'Maybe. I've been trying to work out what this is all about.'

'Go on.' Baker filled his pipe.

Markham held up a finger

'First of all, we know at least one of those Germans was a spy, right?'

'Yes.'

A second finger.

'And we know Mark Fox was quietly working for the Russians.'

'True enough. But—'

'Let me finish. It's reasonable to assume one or both the other dead Germans were spying, too.'

'We didn't find any evidence in their rooms,' Baker objected.

'We weren't really looking, remember? And that first death looked like suicide. Reasonable enough at the time.' He saw the older man nod. 'Even the second one, that car crash, was plausible.'

'What are you driving at?'

'What if someone had turned these spies, got them working for our side and sending false information back to the Reds?' Markham said. 'They found out and started to eliminate the double agents.'

When he was in Military Intelligence he'd done it himself with a Russian agent, managed to have him working for both sides. All very convoluted, but spying was like that. Yes, it was possible.

'Who turned them, though?' Baker asked. 'It has to be someone local to keep an eye on them.'

'I'd put my money on Tim Hill, that chap from Cokely's. He's in the perfect place.'

'That would all fit,' Baker admitted eventually. 'It even makes sense.'

'Did Harker ask Amanda about Hill?'

'Yes. She'd talked to Hill a few times, that's it. Doesn't really know him.'

'It doesn't matter now, anyway,' Markham said. 'We got her back. It's over, we won.'

'The question is, does Harker believe we've won, too?'

Markham leaned back and closed his eyes.

'We need to find him, don't we?'

'It looks that way.' Baker sighed.

'Did Amanda give you any hints?'

'No. But we can talk to her again. Why don't you come over for your tea? We can chat after.'

'All right.' He'd never been to Baker's house, never met his wife. That could be interesting.

'We eat at quarter to six on the dot. Just get yourself there by then or our Nancy won't be happy.' He rose from his seat. 'I'm going out to talk to a few people. You never know what I'll stir up.'

'Be careful,' Markham warned.

'You too, Dan,' Baker said seriously. 'I'm not the one who was sent the bullet. Remember that.'

CHAPTER EIGHTEEN

As Markham left the office he could feel the weight of the pistol in his pocket. Baker's words were ringing in his head. He'd spent half an hour sitting there, going through everything, trying to convince himself that Harker had gone, that the bullet was just a vicious farewell.

But he hadn't succeeded.

The man was out there, biding his time. Watching. Waiting.

The Riley purred sweetly to life. Markham drove out past the university, then through Headingley and along the Otley Road. There it was, the radio mast of the War Room, poking above the bare treetops. Real, and another reminder of how powerless they really were. All someone had to do was press a button and it would be over. Cold comfort on a winter's day.

Ilkley felt frigid, the wind off the Pennines bitter against his skin. It was a postcard village, close enough to Leeds for the rich to commute, yet distant enough to feel removed. The shops and restaurants all looked like money.

He hadn't been out here in three years, but he'd rung the man he wanted to see.

Ted Smith had aged since his last visit. The lines were deeper on his face, his shoulders more stooped and his old clothes hung loose on his body now. But there was still plenty of vitality in his eyes and his voice was strong.

'It was a pleasant surprise to hear from you, Dan,' he said with a smile. 'Come on in, it's perishing out there.'

The kitchen was warm enough to take off his coat as Smith fussed around the cooker, making a pot of tea. The man had made a fortune with aviation inventions. They'd met when Smith hired him to find evidence of his wife's adultery. Then, later, he'd been helpful in a case Markham worked on. He felt guilty about not keeping in touch. But Smith had good contacts, and he needed help.

A few minutes of small talk and the man stared at him.

'You're not here for chit-chat, and you're not here for your health. So you must want something.' But there was no rancour in his voice.

Markham grinned.

'I'm in a bit of a spot. Do you know anyone in MI5 or the War Office?'

Smith frowned as he thought. The hands cupping his mug were covered in dark liver spots.

'Not so many these days. The ones I knew are mostly pensioned off or dead. I can ask around.'

'I'd appreciate it.'

'But,' he said with a smile, 'there's a price. You've got to tell me what's going on.'

Cut to the nub, it made a short tale.

'Blimey, Dan,' Smith said when he'd finished, 'you get yourself in some things, don't you?'

'It's not by choice.' He winced at the idea.

'Life likes its surprises.' Smith pursed his lips. 'Take me. I'm thinking of getting wed again.'

'Who's the lucky woman?' It was the only response he could give. Smith was well into his seventies. But maybe you were never too old for love.

'A widow in the next street. She moved here last year. From Watford, but you can't have everything.'

'I wish you luck.'

'I've not popped the question yet. Holding my horses a bit, but …'

He looked happy. Content. Ted Smith was a wealthy man, far more than his house and wardrobe showed. But he'd earned every penny.

They talked for a while, Smith pouring another cup of tea and finding some digestive biscuits. Finally Markham stood.

'I need to get going, Ted.'

'I'll have someone ring you this afternoon. How about that?'

'Perfect. Thank you.' If he could make that promise, Smith's name still made people in London drop everything at his request. 'And invite me to the wedding.'

'If it happens. She might say no.' He laughed. 'Or maybe not.' His eyes twinkled. 'Would you be escorting someone?'

'Yes,' Markham answered with pride.

'Next time you'll have to tell me all about her.'

'I will,' he promised.

★★★

On the way back to Leeds he stopped at the Black Bull in Otley for a sandwich. As he ate he read a sign behind the bar: during the Civil War, Cromwell's troops had drunk the pub dry before the Battle of Marston Moor.

Three hundred years ago, and still fresh in the memory. An attraction.

He cleaned the office, emptying the bins, wiping down the desks and the filing cabinets. Make work, his mother used to say. Something to keep busy while he waited for the telephone to ring.

Finally, not long after half past three, the sound of the bell filled the office, jarring him out of a doze.

'Is this Mr Markham?' The clipped, condescending tones of Received Pronunciation.

'Yes.'

'My name's Turnbull. I believe you want to talk to me.'

'Yes,' he answered slowly, 'I do.' He tried to imagine the man in his office on Curzon Street in London. He'd had to report there once while he was still in uniform. A maze of corridors and closed doors, and barely a working-class accent to be heard. 'Does the name Simon Harker mean anything to you?'

'Should it?' Turnbull sounded amused.

'How about Tim Hill?'

'I assume you have a reason for your questions, Mr Markham.'

'You've had enough time to have someone research me, and a couple of telephone calls will have told you what I've been working on and that a chap of yours named Warner has already asked me some questions. So yes, I have a reason.'

'You were a chum of Ged Jones, weren't you?'

'I was.' Ged, shot to death in this chair, his body quietly disappeared by the service. The past that could never quite lose its grip. 'And I saw Mark Fox before he defected. But I'm sure you know that already. I explained it all to your man.'

'There's a very limited amount I can tell you,' Turnbull said after a long pause. 'Most of it requires clearance you and your partner will never have.'

Was that supposed to wound, he wondered?

'Then tell me what you can.'

'You mentioned a man called Hill. Who do you think he is?' Markham took a chance and hoped he was right.

'One of yours.'

'I can't comment on that.' Fine, he thought; it was as good as an admission.

'Simon Harker.'

'That's not his real name. But I'm sure you've realised that. Let me ask, have you ever been to Leipzig, Mr Markham?'

So he was originally from East Germany.

'Is he still in the country?'

He had the sense of a hand covering the receiver, cutting off all the background sounds. A few seconds later Turnbull was back.

'We have no record of him leaving.'

'Are you looking for him?' The man had killed three people. A foreign assassin on the loose in England. They had to be searching.

'Please, Mr Markham,' Turnbull said patiently, 'do you think I'd be willing to tell you that? Now, was there anything else?'

'Amanda Fox.'

'What about her?' He sounded unruffled.

'Is she one of yours?'

'If she were, I couldn't tell you. But I can categorically say she's never worked for Her Majesty's government.'

'Or any other government?'

'Indeed. And now I've said all I'm going to say. Goodbye, Mr Markham.'

The line went dead.

Had it been worth pulling in a favour to learn that? Yes. At least now he knew exactly where he stood.

★★★

Baker's house was a 1930s semi on a quiet street that lay between Burley, Kirkstall, and Headingley. The Wolseley was parked in the drive, next to a neat square of lawn surrounded by the bare branches of rose bushes.

Markham had taken care that no one followed him, but as he knocked on the door he looked around anyway. Not a soul in sight, just the fleeting glimpse of a nosy neighbour behind the net curtains of a box room.

Baker nodded as he stood aside and stared at the street for a moment. His hand was wrapped around a pint glass, still wearing a tie, the cardigan fully buttoned.

'Come on in, lad.' He checked his watch. 'Five minutes to spare. You timed it well.'

Nancy Baker was a short woman, as round as her husband, greeting him with a smile as she bustled between the kitchen and the table in the lounge.

'Where's Amanda?' Markham asked.

'Still upstairs.' Baker nodded at the ceiling. 'I'll give her a shout when it's ready.'

'Did you find anything today?'

They were standing by the window, gazing out at the back garden. Neat borders around a lawn, leading down to an old wartime Anderson shelter.

'Nothing. I didn't expect much, but it was worth a shot. How about you?'

'I had a chat with someone from MI5.'

He enjoyed the surprise on Baker's face.

'How did you manage that?'

But before he could answer, Nancy appeared and placed a steaming dish of cottage pie on the table.

'Get yourselves sat down,' she told them, and it was an order, not a request.

He studied Amanda Fox as she entered. The sleekness had gone from her appearance. Her hair was still glossy, her makeup still careful and understated, but she seemed to have shrunk into herself a little, as if she didn't want to be noticed.

She greeted him with a small, shy smile then settled down to her food, eyes down and looking at the plate as she ate.

'How are you?' Markham asked. Amanda glanced at him then looked away.

'I'm fine.' Her voice was soft, without the confidence it had held when they first met.

The food was filling, enough left for a small second helping. Nancy Baker cleared away the dishes, then came back with jam roly-poly and a beaker of custard.

He hadn't eaten like this since his mother died; there never seemed to be a point in cooking big dishes for himself. It brought back memories, some good, a few bad.

'That was lovely,' he said as he pushed the empty dish away. And it was true. It had satisfied something within him. 'Thank you.'

'I'll bring in a pot of tea and leave you to talk.' She stood and smoothed down the front of her apron.

'That was grand, luv,' Baker said.

'All you care about is having your belly full,' Nancy chided him, but she was smiling; there was love behind her words.

***

'You're safe here,' Markham told Amanda. They were still sitting around the table. The cloth had gone. The smell of waxed wood filled the air. He offered her a cigarette, watching as she bent to the flame of the lighter.

'I'm scared to go home,' Amanda said in a small voice.

'You don't have to,' Baker assured her. 'Not until it's over.'

She looked at his face. 'When will that be?'

'Soon,' Markham said. 'Soon. We know you weren't involved in anything.' He saw Baker shoot him a glance. 'And Harker will be out of the way.'

'How?' She turned to him.

'He'll have to run very soon. He doesn't have any choice.'

'But he's still here, isn't he?' She couldn't hide her fear.

'Probably. For now, anyway,' he admitted. After a short pause, he continued, 'I need to know, when he was questioning you, what names did he ask you about?'

'Too many. I didn't know them.'

'Tim Hill?'

'Yes.' She raised her head. 'We worked with him at Cokely's.'

'John Crews?

Amanda nodded. 'He's with Farren's in Hunslet. We worked with him, too.'

'Who else?' Markham asked. He needed to press her, but gently. 'Who do you remember?'

'Mike someone,' she answered after a little thought.

'What was his surname?'

'I don't know.' There was an edge of panic in her voice. 'Graham, something like that. And there was Teddy Post. I remember that, his name just seemed so odd.' She stared at him hopefully. 'Does that help?'

'Yes,' he told her. 'It does.'

'I really didn't know what Mark was doing … for the other side. Do you believe that?'

'I do.' He'd seen her reaction after she'd received her husband's letter detailing the truth.

'Thank you. Harker, or whatever his name is, he didn't. He didn't think it was possible.'

'I'm sure you're telling the truth.'

'Thank you,' she said. She took a breath. 'I don't have anything else to tell you. All I want to do is forget it. I'm sorry.' She stood quickly. 'Excuse me.'

When she'd gone, Markham looked at Baker and raised an eyebrow.

'Has she been like that since you brought her here?'

'More or less. She's a bag of nerves. It's going to take a while for that to go. And as long as Harker's still on the loose …'

'He is. And MI5 won't say if they have someone looking for him.'

'They must have,' Baker snorted.

'Let's hope so.'

'How did you end up getting anything from one of their muckety-mucks, anyway?'

'With the help of a friend.'

'What else did they say?'

He recounted the conversation.

'So you're reading a lot into a bunch of non-committal answers?' Baker asked doubtfully.

'Because there was a lot in them.'

'Perhaps.'

'What about those names? Has she mentioned them before?'

'Not to me. Mike Graham doesn't mean owt, but I've come across Teddy Post.'

'Who is he?'

'I can see his face in my mind, but nothing more than that.' He shrugged. 'I'll find out in the morning. Do you want to ask around about Graham?'

'Yes.'

Before he left, Markham ducked into the kitchen to thank Nancy Baker for the meal. The room was spotless, the back burner glistening with black lead, the lino mopped. She was standing and reading a copy of *Woman's Own* while Billy Cotton's dance band played quietly on the wireless.

'I'm glad you could finally come,' she said with a smile. 'I've been after Stephen to invite you. He's always talking about you.'

'Don't believe half of it.' He laughed.

'Oh no. He sings your praises. Now you've been here you'd better not be a stranger in future.'

Baker singing his praises, Markham wondered as he unlocked the car? The world was becoming a strange place.

★★★

Mike Graham.

He could start looking tomorrow or begin tonight. Why put it off?

It was a little after eleven when he parked on Chapeltown Road. He'd pottered at home, reading a little, listening to music. There was no sense going to the Tempest Club before the pubs shut; no one would be there.

This early in the week it was quiet. The real business came on the weekend, when people wanted to wring every drop of pleasure from the hours. There was no sign outside the place. If you didn't know about it, you weren't welcome.

It was in the cellar of a house, the bar made of plywood, a few tables and chairs around, low-wattage bulbs casting shadows. There was a scattering of drinkers, one or two familiar faces.

Markham thought about some of the people he'd known in clubs like this. Brian, who drank to forget all he'd seen in the war. He'd finally found release twelve months ago, throwing himself out of a third-storey window while going through the DTs. Others who'd faded away to nothingness.

There was precious little joy in these shebeens, just a constant sense of desperation, of men holding on to life with their fingertips. He ordered a Scotch then carried it over to a table where a man sat, eyes half-closed. He wore an old army greatcoat, the Royal Signals insignia still on the sleeves. But there was nothing military about the rest of him. Hair long and greasy, hanging on his collar, face in need of a shave. A packet of tobacco and papers on the table in front of him. And an empty glass.

'You look like you could use that, Carl.'

The man looked up and nodded his appreciation.

'I won't say no, Dan. It'd only go to waste with a teetotaller like you.' He downed it in a single gulp. 'Haven't seen you for a while.'

No one knew much about Carl's past. He'd appeared from nowhere two years before, dressed much the same as he was now, without a surname to weight him down. But he was a listener, a man who remembered what he'd heard. Another lost soul.

'I've been busy,' Markham replied. 'Does the name Mike Graham mean anything to you?'

Carl pursed his lips. 'Can't say that it does.'

'It might be something like Graham.'

'There's Mike Grant. But he's in his sixties. Why?'

'I'm just trying to track someone, that's all. Can you ask around?' He took out a half crown and his business card. 'Let me know if you hear anything.'

'I will,' Carl promised, and he hoped he could believe the man.

***

In the morning he started early, going around the cafes where men sat staring into their cups of stewed tea, trying to face the morning after a long night. Half of them still stank of booze as it came out of their pores.

He paid for a round of toast or a chocolate wafer here and there, but no one had much to tell him. Shaking heads to match the shaking hands. Nobody seemed to know Mike Graham until he sat down with Harry Pearson in a cafe on New York Street.

'Mike Grant, that's who you mean,' Pearson said as he stirred a third spoonful of sugar into his coffee. 'It has to be. I've never heard of anyone called Mike Graham.'

Pearson had a grizzled face split by a pale, jagged scar that extended down one cheek all the way to his jaw; the rumour was that he'd received it in a razor fight before the war. Whatever the truth, it made people keep their distance. He scuffled a living as a debt collector. Along with his big frame, his face was his fortune in the job. People paid up before the threat of a second visit.

'Who is he?' Markham lit a cigarette. The same name Carl had given him.

'Did you ever hear of Pat Shea?'

'No.'

'Before your time, maybe. He died back in '48. Mike Grant started out working for him.'

'What did he do?'

'Nosying around, this and that.' Pearson took a cigarette from Markham's packet, lit it and blew out a long stream of smoke. 'Then he found he had a talent for getting in and out of places. Keeps it very quiet, mind. The coppers have never had a sniff of him.'

A burglar. That might fit with Harker.

'What's he up to now?'

'I see him here and there. Mostly at the Hyde Park pub, he probably lives round there somewhere.'

'Do you know how I can get hold of him?'

Pearson shrugged and narrowed his eyes. 'I can ask. What do you need him for?'

'A couple of questions.' He handed over another business card, two pound notes wrapped around it.

'I'll pass the word.' It disappeared into Pearson's pocket. 'You'll hear if he wants to be in touch.'

★★★

Baker was already in the office, writing in a notebook. It was a police habit, keeping everything straight, everything documented. He looked up as Markham entered.

'Did you find Graham?'

'Mike Grant. That's the name I've heard. A burglar.'

Baker shook his head.

'They're pulling your leg. I'd have heard the name.'

'The word is that the police don't know about him. What about Teddy Post?'

The big man leaned back in his chair and stretched.

'Didn't take long. He's been inside for the last six months. Got caught breaking into a house.'

'Another burglar?'

'Yes. Nothing to do with Harker, though. Not unless he's tunnelling out to help him. He's not due for release until 1959.'

Interesting, Markham thought. A pair of burglars. That didn't sound like coincidence. The telephone rang. Without thinking, he picked up the receiver.

'Mr Markham,' a terrified voice said, 'it's Trevor Peel. You've got to help me.'

CHAPTER NINETEEN

'What is it?' Markham asked urgently.

'That man. He came back this morning.'

'Harker?' He saw Baker's head jerk up.

'Yes. He wants me to get him into one of those special rooms again. Steal the key for him.' Peel was whispering the words. Straining, Markham could hear a dull babble of conversation in the background and the tinny sound of a radio. 'If I don't, he said he'd tell them what I've done.'

'Where did he find you?'

'Outside the house. I was just getting on the bike. What can I do, Mr Markham?'

He was trying to think quickly.

'Tell the management you're poorly and you need to go home. Meet me in an hour.'

'Where?' Trevor sounded desperate.

'The cafe at the market.'

'OK.' He rang off quickly.

'Harker's pressing Peel,' Markham told Baker. 'He's scared.'

'It must be something important if he's still hanging around. I was sure he'd have skipped the country by now.'

'I'll get Trevor to leave Leeds for a while. That should keep him safe.'

'Do you want me to come with you?'

Markham shook his head.

'No. He knows me.'

'All right.' He paused. 'I still don't believe you about that Grant bloke. The coppers would be on to him.'

'I only know what I was told.' He shrugged. 'If we're lucky he might ring.'

He did, a little later, as Markham was preparing to leave.

'You've been looking for me.' No hello, no preamble. Just his name and straight into it.

'Yes, Mr Grant, I have.' He settled back in his chair, keeping an eye on his watch. He didn't want to be late to the cafe; Peel was frightened enough as it was. 'What do you know about Simon Harker?'

There was the slightest flicker of hesitation before Grant asked, 'Why?'

'I'm looking for him.'

'What for?' Full of suspicion.

'Do you know what he does?'

'Don't care.' An abrupt, simple answer.

'I need to get in touch with him,' Markham said.

'What's in it for me?' Grant asked.

'Maybe some protection. He's a Russian spy.'

'Is that right?' He sounded amused. 'No one can connect me to him.'

'Yet. If MI5 start looking ...' He let the idea hang.

'I'll have a think.'

'Make it quick. There's not too much time.'

'I'll be in touch.'

***

The cafe was full of people eating dinner. The clatter of knives and forks and the smell of gravy. Markham waited until a table came free and sat down, ordering a lamb casserole and tea.

Exactly an hour since Peel had called. No sign of him yet. He ate, glancing around, looking at his watch every few seconds. Trevor still hadn't arrived when he'd finished the food. He lit a cigarette, eking out the moments while he drank the tea. Twenty minutes past and he still hadn't shown.

Something had happened. Could Peel have run? Had Harker caught up with him first?

Finally he had to admit it. Trevor wasn't going to show. Out on Vicar Lane he stared around, hoping against hope that the lad was simply late. But there was no familiar face pushing through the crowd on the pavement.

Markham trudged back to the office. Baker had gone somewhere. Alone, he sat and worried. Should he wait and hope that Trevor rang or arrived? Go to the lad's house and see if his mother knew anything?

He'd give it a few more minutes. He chain-smoked through the time. Finally he stubbed out his fourth cigarette, picked up his hat and locked the door behind him. Driving out along Kirkstall Road he kept an eye on the mirror for any vehicle following him, holding his breath hopefully as a motorbike came up quickly. But it zipped past and vanished into the distance. Not Trevor.

The lad's mother knew nothing. Surprise filled her face when Markham asked if she'd heard from him.

'Not since he left this morning, luv,' she answered. 'Why? What's wrong?'

'I was going to meet him at dinnertime and he never came.'

'Wasn't he at work?' She frowned, wrapping a tea towel around her hand.

'He wasn't feeling too well when he rang me.' It was a white lie but better than the truth.

'Why didn't he just come home if he was poorly?' The worry was growing in her voice.

'There was something he needed to tell me, he said.'

'I don't know.' She stared at him. 'You'd better not be lying to me.'

'Can you ask him to ring me when he comes back?'

'After I've had a word with him myself.' Mrs Peel straightened her back. 'Whatever's going on, I want to get to the bottom of it.'

No you don't, Markham thought, but he kept his mouth closed.

***

Back to the office, stirring at the slightest noise on the stairs and willing the phone to ring.

Nothing.

Eventually Baker returned.

'Well?' he asked.

'He didn't turn up.'

'That doesn't sound too good.'

'I went to his house, his mother doesn't know anything. Where were you, anyway?'

'This and that. I followed you down to the market and back.'

Markham was startled.

'Why?'

'In case Harker was setting a trap,' Baker said flatly.

'Any sign?'

'Not a dicky bird. I did some checking on that Mike Grant afterwards. You're right; the police don't know him at all.' He grinned. 'They'll be keeping an eye on him now, though.'

'Not until I've heard from him, I hope.'

'If he sets a foot wrong they'll be all over him. You did a good service there.' He looked at his watch. 'I'd better get going. We're due at the brother-in-law's tonight.' He rolled his eyes. 'It's their anniversary.'

***

By five there was still no word from Peel. And nothing they could do. Markham had no idea where to start looking. With a sigh he put on his overcoat and hat. As he took the office keys from his pocket the telephone bell shrilled and he lunged for it.

'Hello?'

'I talked to our mutual friend.' It was Grant, curt and to the point.

'What did he say?'

'He said he'll see you when he's good and ready.' Markham felt a chill move down his spine.

'Anything else?'

There was the sound of a match being struck and someone inhaling.

'He said you should have a look off the Otley Road. Not far from the crematorium. There's a radio mast. Take a hunt around.'

'Why?' he asked. 'What—'

But Grant had gone.

By the War Room bunker. That had to mean something. It wasn't a spot chosen at random.

He tried ringing Baker: no one answered.

Markham saw his reflection in the window. Outside it was pitch dark. If he went there alone he'd just be blundering around, not even knowing what he was looking for. He'd have to wait until tomorrow. They'd go out there then. In the light.

And Trevor? Maybe he'd go home tonight and save his mother all that pain, he thought. But inside Markham knew that wasn't about to happen.

★★★

By nine he knew he wasn't going to settle easily. There was only one answer: Studio 20. But it was still quiet there, some-one doodling on the piano as a bassist attempted to play along.

Bob Barclay sat in his booth, adding up columns of figures as he worked on the books.

'If you're hoping for magic you're probably out of luck tonight, Dan,' he said wryly. 'I'll tell you what, though, we've sold quite a few tickets for Georgina's show. It might be a winner.'

'I hope it is. She deserves it.'

'Shame you two are on the outs. That lass you were with the other night, she looked vaguely familiar.'

'An old friend.'

Barclay nodded. He wasn't likely to ask more.

Ten o'clock passed and the music didn't improve. Probably some others would drift in later but he was too restless to stay. As he climbed the stairs to the cold of New Briggate, Markham wrapped his hand around the pistol in his overcoat pocket.

But no one was waiting to take him by surprise. The drive home was uneventful, no one around on the November streets. He was still cautious as he parked. The bruises might have faded but the memory was strong.

In the flat he rang Baker again. Still no one there. He put on a Nat King Cole album. It was light, a confection that was more pop music than jazz. But the voice was like silk, and when the man decided to play, his piano work had a delicate, easy beauty.

By eleven he'd had enough. The locks were secure on the door and he was ready for bed. Yet Trevor Peel kept gnawing at his mind, the guilt chewing at him.

What he needed was sleep, he thought. He stirred from the chair and the telephone bell filled the silence.

'Hello?' he answered tentatively, feeling his heart beating faster as he heard the coins drop in the slot.

'I'm not ringing too late, am I, Dan?' It was Carla, and her voice calmed his fears.

'Not at all.'

'I just wanted to hear your voice, that's all,' she said softly. 'Rather silly, isn't it?'

'I'm glad you did.' He lit a cigarette, ready to settle into the conversation.

'It's only quick, I don't have much change. But I miss you.'

He looked around, imagining he could see her shadow disappearing into the bedroom.

'You'll be living down here soon.'

'I know … why don't you come up this weekend?'

'I'd enjoy that. It all depends on if this case is done, though.'

'Of course,' Carla answered quickly. 'If you can, though … bugger, the pips are going.'

'If I can, I will,' he promised before the empty dial tone took over.

★★★

Baker drove, guiding the Wolseley out through Headingley while Markham stared out of the window.

'Out by the radio mast, he said?'

'That's right.'

'The War Room's been empty for a year or two now. They'll probably knock it down soon.'

'It could be a wild goose chase.'

'Maybe.' He yawned. 'I didn't get home while almost one last night. Bloody Terry likes nattering on and on.'

'What did you do with Amanda?'

'As far as I know she never even came out of the spare room.'

'Is she any calmer?'

'Just the same as when you saw her. The wife's keeping a close eye on her.' He shrugged inside his mackintosh. 'I don't know. Maybe it's what she needs.'

'While Harker's around, at least.'

Beyond Leeds Modern School and the ring road he slowed, searching for the spot, and turned on to a small paved road.

'It's back in here,' Baker said. 'Do you have the gun?'

Markham pulled it from his pocket.

'Right here.'

The War Room was ugly concrete, hidden from the road by a stand of trees and surrounded by a wire fence. They walked around until they discovered a place where it had been cut. Off in the distance, tyres hummed softly along Otley Road. Back here, though, everything was quiet, only the cawing of crows as they moved from branch to branch or swooped down on something in the nearby field.

Thick steel doors, heavy air vents set deep in the walls. If the Russians had dropped the atomic bomb, all of Yorkshire would have been run from here, he thought. From this tiny place, no more than thirty feet by thirty. Christ.

And now there was the threat of nuclear war always hanging like a sword. Somewhere another, better place had been built to withstand things and try to keep things functioning. Why? What would even be left?

'Over here,' Baker called.

Out of sight, in a scrubby patch of gorse that had grown up behind the building. A motorbike, on its side, abandoned, half-hidden. Petrol had leaked from the tank and into the dirt.

'Doesn't your friend Peel ride a bike?'

'Yes.' He didn't know what make, but this was a Norton, the familiar line of the name painted on the fuel tank. It could have been Trevor's; he'd have come along Otley Road on his way home from Cokely's. But it definitely wasn't the same machine they'd seen outside Harker's house; that had been an old BSA M20 motorcycle. 'This must be what Harker wanted us to find. He has Trevor.'

'Or he could have just nicked a bike somewhere and be pulling a fast one on us.'

'You don't believe that any more than I do,' Markham told him. 'Check the number plate with your police mates.'

'I will once we're back in town.' Baker eyed the building. 'We should have a look inside.'

'Why?'

'If he's really taken Peel, this would be a good place to keep him. Safe enough.'

'Can you get in?' Markham asked doubtfully. 'It looks secure.'

'I'll try. Can you get the torches from the car?'

By the time he returned, the thick metal door was a few inches open. Markham flicked on the beam and entered.

It was a dark, claustrophobic world of cramped rooms. Inside, everything had been stripped, just leaving a shell. Here and there the concrete had begun to crumble, leaving chips and powder on the floor. The air was old and thick, the stench of years gathered inside.

They played the lights around, moving slowly from doorway to doorway. Finally, in a small space by the far wall they saw a camp bed, a blanket tossed on the top. Baker crouched and began to search around it as Markham explored more of the place.

There was nothing else in there. Empty of everything. He made his way back to Baker, following the flashes of light through the doorways.

'Anything?' he asked.

'Someone was here recently.' He lifted up a newspaper. 'Yesterday's edition. Can't tell who it was, though. Could have been your friend or it could have been Harker.' He thought for a second. 'It would be a good place to hide out. No one would think of looking here. Could have been his bolthole.'

'If it was, he has another one now.'

Even the pale November light seemed bright after the War Room. He blinked a few times. Another dead end. And they still had no idea where to find Peel or Harker.

CHAPTER TWENTY

'Is this Mr Markham?' A woman's voice, speaking loudly, as if she wasn't used to the phone. He'd heard the coins fall; she was calling from a telephone box.

'It is.'

'This is Mrs Peel, luv.'

'Has Trevor come home?' he asked, hopes rising.

'No. Not even a message.' She was trying to press down the fear; he could hear it under her words. 'Have you found him?' It came out like an accusation.

'Not yet.'

'I'm going to the police,' she told him firmly. 'This isn't like him.'

'It's probably the best idea,' Markham agreed. 'They can do more than me.'

'All right.' She seemed surprised, taken aback at his honesty.

'And I hope he shows up very soon.' He daren't tell her what he believed.

'So do I, luv,' Mrs Peel said bleakly. 'I didn't sleep a wink last night. I just hope to God nowt's happened to him.'

★★★

'What now?' Markham asked.

'I'm thinking.' Baker had rung a friend on the force and given the number plate of the motorbike. It belonged to Trevor Peel.

'Fair to say that Harker has him.'

'Yes.' He thought about the lad's mother and what she must be going through. 'But how do we find him?'

'I don't know, Dan,' Baker said quietly. 'I don't bloody know. Harker's the one calling the shots on this. I'd keep that gun close, though. I've feeling we're going to need it before all this is over.'

***

Markham sat upstairs at the Kardomah, taking his time over a cup of coffee and looking blankly down at Briggate.

Nothing. They had absolutely nothing. No way to find Harker. Nowhere to even begin.

The man was in charge; they were trotting along behind and hoping.

He'd ground out the cigarette when a movement below caught his eye. Hurriedly, constantly glancing out of the window, he counted out change before dashing out of the cafe.

The figure was about seventy yards ahead, strolling and taking his time, as if he didn't have a care in the world, carrying a small brown-paper parcel under his arm. Markham stayed back, just close enough to keep him in view, exactly the way he'd been taught in the service. He ducked his head, taking off the hat and crushing it into his pocket. A quick change of appearance in case the man was watching in shop windows.

There were plenty of pedestrians around. And up ahead, in the middle of the throng, was Simon Harker, moving carelessly along Briggate towards the Headrow. Across from the Odeon he turned, heading down the hill. Markham hurried up to the corner, holding his breath that the man was still in sight.

Harker was walking faster now, weaving through the people, and there were fewer of them around. If he tried to keep up, he'd stand out. Markham quickened his pace a hair, not too much, straining his neck to keep his quarry in sight.

At Vicar Lane Harker had to wait for the traffic lights to change, gazing around. Markham stayed behind a knot of women out shopping together. He took out the hat and placed it back on his head. Anything that might mean the man didn't spot him.

Then Harker crossed Eastgate through a gap in the traffic and disappeared down the steps by the Gas Board showroom. Markham waited for an opening and darted across the road. At the bottom of the stairs he paused. They were a short cut through to Lady Lane and the West Yorkshire bus station.

He counted to five then pushed his head around the corner of the building. Harker was already far down the street. No other pedestrians; he daren't follow. All Markham could do was watch as the man turned left on to Bridge Street, then try to cover the distance to the corner rapidly and quietly.

Harker had vanished.

It couldn't have taken more than twenty seconds. But he was nowhere in sight. Bridge Street stretched out ahead. There were buildings, other roads that ran off it. He must have taken one of those.

Cautiously, Markham walked, his hand around the butt of the Walther in his pocket. Harker could have spotted him and be waiting, ready to pounce. He walked two hundred yards, through the tunnel under the bridge, engines roaring above him, glancing up the side streets as he passed, then coming back again to Lady Lane.

Nothing.

So bloody close and he'd come away empty-handed. As he stood and lit a cigarette he could feel his heart pounding, all the fire roaring through his body.

Christ.

He strode back to the office. They had an area to search now. A start. But it was a place filled with small businesses and the last remains of slum housing. Too many possibilities.

'You took your time,' Baker said when he walked in. 'I thought you'd hopped on a charabanc to Scarborough or something.'

'I saw Harker,' Markham said.

'Where?'

He went through it all from the moment he'd run out of the Kardomah. When he finished, Baker said, 'Let me get something from the car.' He returned within a minute, unfolding a map of Leeds on the card table and pointing with a stubby finger.

'You lost him on Bridge Street. But he only had a thirty-second start, is that right?'

'Less.'

'And no sign of him at all when you walked along?'

'Nothing at all.'

'We know he couldn't have gone too far in that time.' He traced a small circle on the paper. 'Nothing beyond that.' He smiled, a feral grin showing tobacco-stained teeth. 'We might just be closing in on him.'

'There's still plenty to go through. And he might have known I was behind him. He could have led me down there and ducked off somewhere else.'

'Do you think he did? In your gut?'

'No,' Markham told him. He felt certain of it. 'I'm sure he never saw me.'

'That's good enough for me.' He rubbed his hands together. 'Let's make a start.'

***

There were more businesses and doorways than he'd imagined. They'd split up; it was the only way to cover the ground.

'It's like when I was a detective constable and we did house-to-house questioning,' Baker said. 'It's boring, but it can work. Just give them a very quick description and ask if they've seen anyone like that in the last day or so.'

★★★

By five o'clock his knuckles felt raw from knocking on doors and his voice was hoarse from saying the same words over and over. Two people thought they might have seen Harker, but neither remembered exactly where; he was no more than a faint impression.

The day had turned colder. At five he gave up. All the small business had closed for the day and the streets were empty. There was still plenty left for tomorrow. His feet ached as he walked back to the office on Albion Place.

Markham felt a hard knot of frustration. He should have just run and confronted Harker, taken his chances. Instead he'd tried to be clever and ended up losing him.

He sat at his desk, smoking and trying to warm up. The chill hadn't left his bones before Baker arrived, raising his eyebrows in a question. Markham shook his head.

'Never mind. We'll see the rest of them in the morning. Someone down there will know him.'

'If we're lucky.'

'Then hope that we are.' He adjusted his hat. 'I'm off for the night.'

★★★

He listened to the six o'clock news. Productivity was up, wages were rising. But there was always something going on somewhere to leave the world an unsafe place. The faint shadow of nuclear war always on the horizon. Markham switched off the wireless and selected a Basie LP. It was full of life and joy. The kind of music to dispel gloom. Just what he needed right now.

★★★

'Back to it,' Baker said. 'We'll find something today, don't you worry.'

They marched over to Bridge Street side by side.

'When I started out on the beat, all the Leylands round here were still full of people. They've knocked most of the houses down now. Good job, too, if you ask me. You wouldn't have wished them on a cat.'

'Bad?'

'They were packed inside. No indoor plumbing, outside privies down the block. You can say what you like about the past, but it wasn't pretty. All this renewal, it's the best thing. Give people somewhere decent to live like Quarry Hill Flats.' He gestured to the huge estate on the other side of Regent Street. It looked grey, forbidding, secretive, the main archway like a gate into some dark place. 'We were not long wed and moved in there in '38, when it opened. Everything new and modern. It was like paradise. You thought you'd walked into another world.'

He was just filling time, and they both knew it. A distraction before the grim work.

'We'll meet back at the office at twelve,' Markham said.

★★★

After an hour a thin drizzle began to fall and then passed. The sky lowered as more clouds rolled in. By afternoon they'd probably have another fog. Not good weather for hunting someone.

Trevor Peel was still missing. He'd heard nothing more from the boy's mother. He'd half-expected the police to come calling with questions, but there'd been no word from them. Maybe she hadn't reported it, after all. Like so many people, the family probably kept their distance from the law. From some, the avoidance was natural, drummed into them over generations. Ringing the coppers would be a desperate resort.

More knocking on doors, more going into offices, small warehouses and factories. He kept at it doggedly until quarter to twelve. Not even a hint of Harker. Finally he gave up and strolled back to Albion Place.

Already there were the first wisps of mist in the air and he could hear people starting to cough, walking with scarves held over their noses and mouths.

Baker was scribbling a note.

'You just missed a telephone call,' he said. 'Someone wants you to ring them back sharpish.' He handed Markham the scrap of paper with a number.

'Who is it?'

'Said his name was Turnbull.'

The man who'd rung from MI5. Ted Smith's favour.

'Did you find anything?'

'Not a sausage. How about you?'

'The same.'

He settled at his desk and began to dial the number. What did the man want? Maybe they'd found Harker. Maybe it was all over. Maybe.

He was shuffled through two layers of secretaries before Turnbull picked up the phone.

'I'm glad you rang me back.' That confident, patrician accent.

'What can I do for you, Mr Turnbull?'

'There's something you ought to know. It won't be in the newspapers or on the news. You mentioned a chap called Tim Hill when we talked.'

'That's right.' The secret service's contact at Cokely's. The one who'd turned the Germans into double agents.

'Did you know him at all?'

'I never met him. My partner talked to him.'

'Then perhaps you can remember him in your prayers.'

Dead? Hill was dead?

'I'm sorry to hear that,' Markham said. He turned the scrap of paper over, scrawled *Hill's dead* on the back and pushed it over to Baker. The man read it and raised his eyes in alarm. 'How did it happen?' Markham continued.

Turnbull was slow to answer

'It wasn't natural causes. My people are looking into it.'

MI5 had taken over the murder investigation from the police. That was what he meant.

'I see.'

'That other chap you mentioned. Our Deutscher friend.'

'Harker.'

'We're very eager to talk to him,' Turnbull said.

'So are we,' Markham told him.

'Ah.' A long pause and then, reluctantly, 'Perhaps we should join forces.'

'What did you have in mind?'

'We have two people on their way. They should be in Leeds by three. I've instructed them to come to your office.'

Not a request for help. A command.

'Go on.'

'I already have Warner there. He's looking into the matter with Mr Hill.' So bloody circumspect. He knew it came from years of caution, but no one was going to be tapping this line.

'We've met.'

'Very good. I'm sure I don't need to tell you that the country would be grateful for you doing your duty.'

'We'll talk to your men,' Markham said.

'Very good. Expect Mr Davidson and Mr Molloy.' Turnbull put down the receiver. Not even a thank you.

'It seems we're assisting MI5.'

'From what I've seen of them in the past, someone needs to,' Baker said. 'If we're going to have to put up with them later, we'd better get some dinner now.'

***

Davidson and Molloy looked more like clerks. The same as Warner, Markham thought. Bowler hats, dark suits and overcoats, eyes slightly glazed from the long train journey, mouths pursed in disdain at being sent north.

They asked their questions, not bothering to take notes. But Markham expected that. They were recruited for their minds. They might look bored, but they'd be thinking. He hoped so, anyway.

'We're going to need local knowledge,' Davidson said. He was a lanky man in his forties with jowls already developing. 'We'll co-ordinate with our chap who's here already and find out the state of play.' He glanced at his watch. 'You say you can't find Harker but you know where you lost him.' He made it sound like Markham's failure.

'That's right.'

'We'll start with that in the morning,' Davidson said briskly as he picked up his briefcase. He stood, his companion following quickly. 'Nine o'clock?'

'They make me feel like one of those native guides you see in the pictures,' Baker said after the footsteps faded on the stairs.

'Not very friendly, are they?' They'd been supercilious, acting as if everything would be fine now that the professionals had arrived. And he didn't believe a word of it. They were just two more blunderers in the dark. 'I saw some like that in West Germany.'

'How good were they?'

'A few did well,' Markham answered after a little thought. 'Most of them were a waste of time.'

'Well, I don't want to play second fiddle to a pair of spies. No "yes sir, no sir, three bags full" whilst they balls it all up.' He curled his hand into a fist. 'We know what we're doing, don't we?'

'As much as they do.'

'Then let's handle it ourselves. The way we were before their bloke Hill got himself killed.'

'And what do we do if we find Harker?' he asked soberly.

'We'll cross that bridge when we come to it.' But Markham knew what it meant. No mercy, no hauling him off to stand trial.

***

An evening of singers. Ella, Sarah, Billie. He loved the way they twisted themselves into the words, the way that Holiday could show the depth of emotion simply by slurring a word. There was beauty in it all, and it swung like the devil.

But always the sense of time passing. Running out. A clock relentlessly ticking.

He had strange dreams, Harker breaking into the flat and destroying his record collection, taking pleasure in smashing the records one by one. Even while it was happening he knew it wasn't real, but he was unable to move or stop it happening. All he could do was sit and watch it, the tears streaming down his cheeks.

Markham woke with a start, gulping for breath. The tendrils of the dream clung to him. He had to get up and smoke a cigarette before his mind cleared. The records were still there, neatly filed in alphabetical order.

He'd never expected to feel so much for music, that it could move him. But he'd grown up on the sound of the radio. The polite, reserved dance bands and the classical music of the Home Service. Music that seemed to peer down from a height.

Jazz invited him in. It spoke to him. There was freedom in it, that sense of exploration. It didn't have limits or boundaries. Markham ran his hand over the top of the LP covers, finished the cigarette and went back to sleep.

***

In the morning he felt the broken night. It took him a little while to wake up. His toast tasted like cardboard. Only after a second cup of tea was he ready to face the world.

Davidson and Molloy were waiting outside the office door, dressed in exactly the same manner as the day before. No small talk, they just sat and waited in silence for Baker to arrive. But he didn't. Nine o'clock. Half past and his seat was still empty.

'Perhaps he's poorly,' Markham said.

'Then why doesn't he ring?' Molloy sniffed. 'We have work to do and he knows that.'

But this was his protest. Markham understood that. Quietly and firmly withdrawing his labour. He knew exactly where the man would be.

Molloy and Davidson stayed until quarter to ten. They finally asked a few questions and Markham answered them honestly. He even explained about the house to house and saw them glancing at each other with contempt. But he doubted they could come up with anything better.

Finally they'd had enough.

'We'll note your unwillingness to help in the file,' Davidson said stiffly.

'I've told you what we know.'

'We expect *active* help, Mr Markham, not just words.'

Once they'd gone he hurried over to Bridge Street. He didn't bother to look over his shoulder. If they wanted to follow, that was fine; it wasn't a secret. But men like that would get short shrift around here. The superior attitudes would only get peoples' back up.

It only took ten minutes of searching before he found Baker leaving a small welding shop.

'Have they buggered off yet?'

'They weren't too happy.'

'Sod them.' He began to walk briskly up Templar Street.

'Where are we going?' Markham asked.

'The Olympic Cafe. I want to show you something.'

CHAPTER TWENTY-ONE

The coffee was tasteless, weak as dishwater. Markham pushed the cup aside.

Baker lit his pipe and was sitting back, smoking contentedly.

'Well?' Markham asked. 'What is it?'

With a smile, the man brought a large, folded piece of paper from his pocket and placed it on the table, shaking his head as Markham began to reach for it.

'I told you we used to live in Quarry Hill Flats,' he began.

'I remember,' Markham answered impatiently. Every minute in here was one they could use searching.

'My Nancy stayed there after I joined up in 1940. Last night I was telling her how we're looking for Harker and she reminded me about something.'

'What?'

'There are tunnels under the area, all round the market. They used them as air-raid shelters. Half the people from the flats would go into them when the sirens sounded. I was gone so I was never down there.'

Markham glanced at the paper. 'You got a map of them.'

'I went down to the Civic Hall first thing this morning.' He grinned. 'They marked them on a map of Leeds. Turns out they've been around a while. Built in 1910, the lass at the council told me. There's a whole bloody warren of them down there but they haven't been used since the war.'

Carefully he unfolded the paper, weighting down the corners with the sugar bowl, salt and pepper shakers, and his saucer. Lines ran across the map in red pencil.

'Are those the tunnels?'

'They are,' Baker said with satisfaction. 'You see what I mean? There were plenty of them.' A mile or more just around the market, as best as he could judge. 'But it gets even better. One of the entrances is on Bridge Street.'

'What? Where?' He couldn't believe it.

'Under the bridge for the road. There's a steel door in the wall. We've been walking right past it for the last two days and never even noticed.' He jabbed at the map. 'There.'

'It explains how Harker could disappear like that and why we haven't found him. But how would he even know about them?'

Baker shrugged.

'It doesn't matter. It makes sense, though. And it would be a perfect place to keep Peel.'

'If he's still alive,' Markham pointed out. He hadn't forgotten about the lad. 'After all, Harker's killed Tim Hill.'

'Only one way to find out. We'll go down there and look.'

Markham stared at the map. The tunnels were long, veering off from each other and heading all the way over to Kirkgate.

'What about the door?' he asked. 'It must be locked.'

'If Harker picked it, I can too. Don't you worry about that.'

Markham thought for a moment.

'We're going to need good torches.' He looked down at his suit. 'Different clothes, too. Wellington boots?'

'It's not a sewer, it's dry down there.' Baker looked at his watch. 'Let's meet back in the office in an hour; that'll give us both time to change. And make sure you're armed.'

★★★

Walking boots and thick socks, his khaki army trousers with the side pockets, a heavy sweater and a thick jacket. He slid the Walther into the pocket and checked the torch. With fresh batteries, the light was strong. A final look around the flat and he locked the door behind him.

It was a completely different Baker that he saw. A black windbreaker over a heavy polo-neck jumper, trousers that seemed to have a dozen pockets. Like Markham, he was wearing his walking boots, but his had the scuffed look of hundreds of miles of tramping across country.

'Ready?' he asked. Baker brought a Luger from the jacket. 'War souvenir. Better safe than sorry.'

People looked at them as they walked up Briggate. No more than passing glances, but enough to leave him self-conscious. In a world of shirts and ties, they looked out of place. Memorable.

On Bridge Street their footsteps echoed off the buildings. The door was there, exactly as promised, in the concrete wall of the bridge. How many times had he passed it in the last couple of days and never noticed? Eastgate was just around the corner, the bustle of Vicar Lane just up the hill. But a world away.

Baker shone his torch on the lock, bending to examine it. Then he drew out the flat wallet with his tools, selecting two. A first attempt. He stood back, switching one of the picks for another. A few more seconds, his face reddening as he applied some pressure, and the door swung open a couple of inches.

'Let's see if our friend is down here.'

He led the way, moving with soft confidence along a short passageway then down a metal ladder. Markham followed, the beam from his torch playing on the walls. The tunnel arched above him, ten feet high, the brick surprisingly clean and dry.

There was plenty of dust and small pieces of debris all along the concrete floor. In his head he tried to picture the map. But down here there was no sense of direction. And right now, no choice. Just follow the tunnel. Every hundred yards or so there were pinpricks of daylight from grates set into the ceiling.

Somewhere in the distance he could hear the gentle sound of water.

'Lady Beck,' Baker whispered. His voice still rang along the tunnel. Their boots crunched over things as they walked; it was impossible to be silent.

Markham tried to slow his breathing. He had the torch in one hand, the pistol in the other. The safety was off. He was sweating, ears pricked for any sound.

They seemed to be moving in slow motion. Each step felt as if it lasted a minute or more. Something skittered up ahead. He moved the beam and caught sight of a rat disappearing into the darkness.

His eyes had to adjust to the gloom before he could pick out details. Heavy black cables ran along both sides of the tunnel, lying on the base of the passageway. An old metal pipe was attached to the wall, stretching off into the distance. It was another quiet down here. Apart. Unknown. The liquid sound grew louder, the air damper.

Baker held up a hand and leaned close enough for Markham to smell his sour breath.

'This is where it joins up with the other tunnel. Off to the left it goes to an office building on the other side of Regent Street.'

'What about the other way?'

'That passes under Appleyard's garage in the roundabout, the bus station and all the way to Kirkgate.'

Half a mile, he calculated. Certainly no more than that.

'We've found no sign of Harker so far. Let's go that way.'

They edged around a cavernous space where the dome of bricks seemed to soar as high as a church. The dark water of

Lady Beck ran through the middle in a stone culvert, disappearing somewhere on the far side of the wall.

Baker kept playing his torch along the ground, stooping to examine the things he saw – old cigarette ends, wrappers. After a few seconds he'd toss them aside again.

There was a vibration overhead and more powdered mortar underfoot. They must have reached the roundabout. There was nowhere to hide down here. No alcoves that offered protection, just the lines of brick and concrete.

Fifty yards further and the tunnel seemed to widen a little. Wooden benches had been attached to both walls, covered with dirt and spiders' webs. From somewhere above came the deep note of an engine.

'This is what they used as a shelter during the war,' Baker told him softly. 'The door was in the ladies' waiting room in the bus station.'

Facts, fragments of history. But it didn't bring them any closer to Trevor Peel or Harker.

Markham felt tense, throat dry as sand. His palm was slick and sweaty on the plastic grip of the Walther. Baker had the Luger drawn. The man was moving more cautiously now, as if he sensed some danger ahead.

But the only sign that anyone had been here was a small collection of fag ends.

'These are recent,' Baker said after examining them. 'Woodbines. What does your friend Trevor smoke?'

Markham shrugged. He had no idea; he'd never paid attention.

They followed the tunnel all the way to a set of iron steps. Beyond them, a door that opened on to Kirkgate.

'Let me check something.' Baker ran up the steps with surprising speed. 'That lock's been picked,' he said when he returned. 'No more than a few days ago, either, the scratches on the metal are still shiny. Harker's been down here, Dan. I know it.'

He was right. Markham could feel the man's presence.

Could he have moved on? He knew the rules: when you're hunted, never stay too long in one place. But somewhere like this was safe. Hardly anyone knew the tunnels even existed. Unless Harker was incredibly disciplined, the temptation to return here would be strong. It was dry, out of the weather. Perfect.

They made their way back; it seemed like no time at all before they were standing under the dome again, Lady Beck shining like a black mirror in the torchlight.

'There's one place we haven't searched yet.' Baker played the torch into the far darkness. 'The other spur that leads to the office building.'

'You take that. I'll look around the edges in here. It's big enough, there could be something.'

It was simple enough; just follow the wall around the circle. Crossing the beck took no more than a large stride. But still no hint that Harker was still here. He'd almost given up when the beam caught something. A black tarpaulin, carefully folded and pushed against the join of wall and floor. Unless someone was searching closely they'd probably miss it.

Wrapped inside was a sleeping bag and some tins of food. Baked beans, tomato soup, fruit cocktail. A tin opener and a spoon.

Markham could feel the pulse in his neck. The man was close. He rummaged a little more and his fingers brushed against something. In the torchlight he saw a photograph of a young woman, the kind of picture that could have been taken anywhere. He stared at the face for a second. Keeping that, carrying it, made Harker seem more human.

But a human who killed.

He rewrapped everything, trying to leave it exactly the way he'd found it. A low whistle made him raise his head and tighten his grip on the pistol. Creeping along, he followed the sound.

It was a short length of tunnel, just fifty yards and then a wall of rock with a metal ladder that rose to a trapdoor.

Baker was kneeling over a wrapped bundle. Another black tarpaulin. He'd used the large knife to rip it open.

'Better take a look at this, Dan.'

He approached warily, suspecting what he'd find, not wanting to see it. The light from the torch told him all he needed to know.

'That's Trevor.'

CHAPTER TWENTY-TWO

He'd been dead at least a day, his limbs stiff, his skin waxy and hard. Baker slit the rest of the tarpaulin and they pulled it off him.

Markham could feel the bile rising in his throat. He had to move away, close his eyes and breathe with his mouth for a moment until the feeling passed.

'They're never pretty,' Baker told him. 'And you never get used to it, no matter how many you see.'

Finally the body was free. Trevor's eyes were staring at something he'd never see. There was no blood on the front of the body, nothing to show how he'd died.

'You grab that side,' Baker said matter-of-factly. 'We'll turn him over. It must be on his back.'

It was, a small, deep wound at the base of the neck that buzzed with flies, a small swarm rising up when they were disturbed.

'It must have been quick,' Markham said as he examined it.

'Ice pick, by the look of it. The Russians have a history with that. It's how they did for Lenin. But yes, it was fast. He wouldn't have known a thing.'

'We should get out and tell the police.' He rose and started to turn away. Baker put a hand on his arm.

'Not yet.'

'Why? For God's sake, his family–'

'If we do that, this place will be crawling with coppers and those MI5 people. We'll lose any chance we have of catching Harker.'

'Then let him go. For God's sake, Trevor wasn't the brightest but he deserves better than just being left down here to rot.'

'It won't be forever.' Baker kept his voice low and reasonable. 'Just until we get Harker. We'll take care of him and then tell them. They can clean it all up.'

'But …'

'But what? You and I can get the job done.' He was still staring down, the torch shining on Peel's dead body. 'Did you find anything?'

'A sleeping bag and some food, hidden away.'

'He'll be back, then. We just have to be ready for him.'

Markham turned away. He didn't want to see Trevor's face this way. Better to think of him alive and full of all his plans.

'How?'

'We keep watch. And once he's back we'll corner him down here.'

'He can still get out at the other end and vanish on Kirkgate.'

'No he won't,' Baker said. 'I'm going to make sure of that.'

★★★

He was going to use the picks to jam the door at the Kirkgate end of the tunnel.

'After that we've got him trapped.' Baker clapped his hands together. The sound echoed off the bricks.

'We'll still need to keep watch on this entrance.'

'There's a place further down Bridge Street where we can park.' He hesitated before the next question.

'What are we going to do once we have him?'

'Let the people who are paid to do it make that decision.'

'Not kill him?' He glanced at Baker's Luger.

'Not unless we have to.'

Markham nodded. Baker pointed down at Peel's corpse.

'Just remember, though, Harker did that in cold blood. He probably didn't even think twice about it. And killing us wouldn't keep him awake at night.'

He strode away, guided by the torchlight, back towards the entrance.

The sky was dull, the threat of sleet in the air when they came back out on to the street. But it seemed as bright as high summer after the gloom and blackness underground. They both had to blink and stand for a few seconds, getting used to the light.

There was no one around as Baker locked the door behind him. A couple of quick movements and it was done.

'You go and get the car,' he said. 'Bring the Wolseley, it has a good heater. We might need it.' He passed over the keys. 'I'll wait out of sight until you're back.'

***

He found a place to park on Bridge Street. Far enough from the metal doorway not to look suspicious but still close enough to see anyone approaching the door.

Baker came out of the shadows, hands in the pockets of his windbreaker.

'I'll pop over to Kirkgate. It'll only take a moment to jam the door.'

He watched the big man walk away with the rolling stride all policemen seemed to acquire. Markham settled back in the seat, smoking. Nothing to see. Thursday afternoon and Bridge Street was deserted. An occasional car passed. Sleet began to fall. He turned on the heater.

Before it had time to work, though, he switched off the engine. He didn't want to risk anyone seeing fumes from the exhaust. A figure was moving along the pavement, coming from Eastgate, pausing often to glance back.

He could make out the man's sandy hair. Markham slumped down in the seat, eyes just above the dashboard. A moment later Harker stood by the door in the wall. A quick look each way, a few deft movements, then he was inside.

Markham locked the car and walked along the pavement, one hand on the Walther, his eyes fixed on the door. He could wait for Baker – the man would be back soon. Or he could go into the tunnel after Harker.

The torch weighed heavy in his left hand as he gripped it. He reached out and tried the door handle. It gave easily and silently; it had been oiled.

Five minutes, he thought. That should be ample time for Baker to return.

But five minutes became ten and still no sign of the man. Sixty seconds more. He'd give it that long, watching the hand move across the watch face. Come on, Stephen. He felt like his brain was screaming the words. Where the bloody hell are you?

The hand swept past twelve. He took a deep breath and went through the door, pulling it to behind him.

Absolute darkness. For a few seconds he simply stood, until the blackness seemed to take on slightly different shades. Up above, every hundred yards, the pale glimpses of daylight through the grates and air shafts.

He could hear the faint scuffling of footsteps in the distance, but no beam from a torch. Markham took short, careful steps, making as little noise as possible. Harker would think he was safe down here. He wouldn't be listening for anything.

It seemed to take forever to reach the ladder down, although he knew it couldn't be more than twenty yards. He lowered himself, hardly daring to put weight on the metal rungs, using his arms to take the strain.

At the bottom he paused, breathing gently, then walked on as lightly as possible, alert for any noise. He tried to remember how far until the tunnel opened up into the dome. One hundred and fifty yards? Something like that. The only way to keep track of the distance was by counting his paces. He tried to work it out in his head. Each long pace was about a yard; that was what they'd taught him at school.

He knew he was close when he could hear the soft echo as the soles of his boots came down on the concrete. Markham crouched, extending his hand until he touched brick. He slid to the side, then round and into the dome.

Nothing. Just emptiness. His pulse was loud in his ears, beating fast. He tightened his grip on the pistol, checking again that the safety was off.

Where was Harker? Over by his camp? Or had he sensed something was wrong and vanished to try and escape through the door into Kirkgate? The only thing Markham could do was stand and listen, hoping for some clue.

A few seconds dissolved into a minute. He waited, as still as if he'd been on parade, ear cocked for the slightest thing. Then he heard a metallic click. Without even thinking, Markham fell to the floor just as a shot was fired, whining harmlessly down the tunnel to his left.

He'd seen the muzzle flash, aimed his pistol and fired once, then rolled over to his right, away from where he'd been. He heard his bullet strike brick, the echoes of the ricochet reverberating around the large room.

Harker's second shot was closer, where Markham had been when he fired. It hit the wall less than three feet away, raising chips of stone. One struck his cheek and he could feel the warm trickle of blood on his skin.

Harker was good. Markham gritted his teeth. He'd never been a great shot and he hadn't pulled a trigger in years.

Where the hell was Baker? He should have been back before this. He must have heard the shots.

Markham tried to think, to come up with a plan. If he stayed here, Harker was trapped. There was only one way out now. To reach it the man would have to kill him. And he planned to make that as hard as possible.

Seven rounds in the clip. Six left now. Each one needed to count. Once they were gone he'd be defenceless.

He wiped the sweat away from his forehead, eyes straight ahead, trying to make out something, anything in the distance. But there was only blankness. Darkness. Silence.

Sound would carry and reverberate. He felt around on the ground until he found what he needed. A piece of mortar about the size of his thumb. Standing, he drew his arm back, aiming towards the tunnel that led to Kirkgate.

For something small it made a lot of noise, bouncing off the brick and concrete. Enough to make Harker fire off two shots in quick succession. It didn't look as though he'd moved. The reverberations rolled around the dome like thunder.

It gave Markham the opportunity to move to the other side of the Bridge Street tunnel. He could confuse the man, at least. The gunfire still filled his ears. It was hard to believe that people outside couldn't hear it. But they were deep under Leeds, everything muffled and hidden.

He had to be careful. To make sure every decision was the right one.

His life depended on it.

And he daren't move too far. That would just give Harker a fighting chance of reaching the tunnel and escaping.

Christ, where was Baker?

His throat was coated with dust. There were decades of it gathered down here. He wiped his face for a second time.

Harker wasn't going to fall for the stone trick again. Markham needed something that would keep the man on edge. Something to wrong foot him. An advantage. It was the only way he might come out of this alive.

He rubbed his palm on his jacket, getting rid of the sweat. When the opportunity arrived he had to be ready.

Something caught his ear. One step, a sole coming down on the concrete, then another and another. Slow, insistent. *Jesus.* Harker was walking towards him. Daring him to shoot, to stop him. The man was gambling with his own life.

He didn't have a choice.

He raised the pistol, trying to aim it out towards the nothing, to gauge the direction of the sound among the echoes. Gentle pressure on the trigger. He remembered the instructor's voice. Squeeze it, slow and steady.

One shot and he was spinning away to his right, back into the tunnel.

No answering fire, just another footstep. Then another.

Think. Why wasn't Harker going the other way, towards Kirkgate? Only one answer: he knew there wasn't a way out for him there. While Markham was still outside he must have gone and checked.

He felt the panic rising inside, the fear making his body start to shake and shiver. That's what he's banking on, he told himself. That you'll be so scared you'll do something stupid.

Two more footsteps, the second just a fraction longer. Harker must have crossed the beck. Too close. Markham had five bullets left. And there was only one way to be certain he aimed in the right place.

He hefted the torch, finger over the switch. In his right hand the gun was ready. As soon as he flicked on the beam and saw Harker, he'd shoot. No hesitation. And then the light straight off again.

A small breath. He stood exactly the way the weapons instructor had taught him in military intelligence. Feet apart for balance, the wrist of his gun hand tucked against his belly.

One. Two. He heard another step but he didn't rush. Three. Four.

The light hit Harker, blinding him. The man couldn't help himself, he had to close his eyes . In the split second before he turned off the torch, Markham fired twice.

One bullet missed, a high whine as it careened into the far wall. But the second one hit the target.

He heard the grunt of pain. Yet even as he was listening Markham was moving. Don't bloody stay there. The words had been drummed in. Don't give them the chance to aim at you.

A half-second pause that seemed to hang forever. Then something heavy and metallic fell and suddenly the feet were stumbling away, shuffling as they tried to escape. He waited, letting the echo ring around then moved softly forward.

Harker had been right in front of him. Fifteen feet, no further than that. Close enough to make out the features on his face. The mouth in a rictus grin. The glint on the metal in his hand.

His hand was trembling. He'd never shot anyone before. Harker was still alive, but where had he gone? He needed to risk the torch again.

The gun lay on the concrete. He bent and put it in his pocket. A small pool of blood glistened close by, a thick trail of it leading away. He'd done some real damage.

Markham let the light play over the blood. The dots of it leading over into the distance. Not towards Harker's pack. Not towards the tunnel to Kirkgate. They seemed to be going to the tunnel where the man had put Peel's body. Why? It was a dead end, only an unused trapdoor as a way out. With all the blood Harker looked to be losing he'd be in no state to force his way out there.

He began to walk, softly and gently, letting the torch guide him. Harker didn't have a gun; he was wounded and losing blood quickly. Markham could still hear the raw explosion of the gun blasting against his eardrums and the thick recoil in his belly.

The drops of blood made dark, tiny pools spattered across the concrete. Markham kept following them, glancing ahead, looking for Harker. But he must have hidden in the shadows along the tunnel.

One step after another, always the soft crunch of mortar under the soles of his boots. He breathed shallowly, gripping the gun, aware and ready.

He stopped at the entrance to the tunnel. The torch picked out Harker. He was slumped next to Peel's body, his back against the wall, eyes open, staring back at Markham. There was still some fire in his face, some hatred.

'I didn't think you'd fire.' Harker's voice was a tired croak. 'All the records said you hated guns.'

So the Russians knew all about his past.

'You were going to kill me. Just like Trevor Peel.'

Harker shrugged and gave a sad smile.

'I've tried twice before. I thought maybe third time lucky.'

'Perhaps you should have learned from the first two.'

'I didn't have much choice, I like living. I have a wife who'll be glad to see me.'

'It's a pity she won't, then,' he said. 'You need to be in hospital.'

'And then jail?' He shook his head. 'They'll never let me go. They'll execute me.'

'That's the price. You're not exactly an innocent.' Markham moved three steps closer and looked down at the man. His face was drawn, trying to hide the pain. 'Can you move?'

'I don't know. Maybe with help.'

Where was Baker? What had happened to him?

'We'll get you to the hospital.'

'Why?' Harker was suspicious.

'Isn't it better than dying?'

'A secret trial and a quiet hanging? That's not much of a bargain, Mr Markham. Or would you prefer Dan?'

His accent was good. No trace of Germany or Russia or wherever he was from. He even pronounced his words like a Yorkshireman.

'Maybe they'll swap you for one of ours.'

Harker winced and moved the hand covering the wound in his side.

'I'm not important enough. I'm a soldier. They trained me and sent me out to kill.'

'We'll see. Come on, let's see if we can get you out of here.'

He moved closer, watching the man's eyes.

There was a sudden, sharp pain in his leg. For a moment he didn't understand what had happened. Then he couldn't stand, his leg gave way under him and he fell to the ground. The Walther jarred out of his grasp.

Harker was smiling. He had a knife in his hand, dripping with blood.

'You ought to know better,' he said. 'You're too trusting.'

Markham's hand scrambled for the pistol.

'Don't,' Harker said. 'I can kill you before you'll reach it.'

He could feel the blood flowing softly from the wound. At least it wasn't an artery. If he managed to get out of here he'd be fine. Where the hell was Baker?

'You'd better hope I die soon so you can go,' Harker continued, no emotion in his voice. 'Or maybe I'll kill you first. Who knows? Your fat friend, too, if he appears.'

'What's the sense in that?' Markham swallowed. He felt dizzy, trying to force his thoughts into focus. Shock.

'It rounds things off.'

'Amanda Fox.' The name came into his head.

'Of course,' Harker said with satisfaction. 'She knows everything.'

'Then why didn't you kill her when you kidnapped her?'

'You don't understand, do you?' The man chuckled.

'Understand what?'

'She's my contact here. I never took her. She left with me. We just made it look that way.'

'But …' He tried to make sense of it all, but he couldn't concentrate properly. 'Why didn't she leave with her husband?'

'Because someone had to tie up the loose ends. That was her job.' Harker sighed. 'All we need now is your friend and everything will be complete.'

'He's already here.'

Baker came out of the shadows at the far end of the tunnel. His face was set and hard. The knife blade shone in his hand.

Christ, Markham wondered. Where had he come from? How had he got down here?

The big man moved with surprising speed. With a short, graceful kick he sent Harker's blade flying off into the darkness.

'The lad here might have some compassion. I don't.'

'Then you win.' Harker sounded resigned. Markham pressed down on the vein above his wound, trying to staunch the thin flow of blood. All he wanted to do was close his eyes and go to sleep. But he kept them open, watching what was going on in front of him as if he were at the pictures.

'That's right,' Baker told him coldly. 'I win.'

'And what will you do with your victory?'

'I'm going to get me laddo there to casualty and make sure we leave the police a puzzle they'll never solve.'

'Perhaps.'

'I'm certain of it. I used to be one of them. But I'm sure your file told you that.'

'Of course.' Harker dipped his head in acknowledgement.

'And did it say what I did during the war?'

'Soldier?' the man guessed.

'Commando.' He glanced across at Markham. 'See if you can stand, Dan. I'll be done with this one very soon.'

Markham crawled to the wall, gasping from the pain. His hands touched the brick. Inch by inch, so slowly it seemed impossible, he pushed himself up. It hurt. Fuck, it hurt. Finally he was standing, panting, sweating hard, leaning back, closing his eyes against the dizziness.

CHAPTER TWENTY-THREE

'Just stay there.'

Markham nodded. He heard Baker's voice but he didn't open his eyes. Simply leaning against the bricks was all he could manage.

'You'll be my executioner?' Harker asked.

'You started that when you killed Dieter de Vries,' Baker told him. 'Vreiten or whoever he was.'

'He committed suicide. Wasn't that what they said?'

'So you're clever. It doesn't make you less of a killer.'

'And does murdering me bring justice?' Harker asked.

'For that poor bugger you're sitting next to, yes it does.'

'Then you'd better do your job, commando.'

Markham didn't want to see. All he heard was a sound like a quiet sigh. Then Baker was there, taking his arm and putting it around his neck to support him.

'Don't worry, we'll have you out of here in no time.'

He could feel the man reaching around and removing one of the guns.

'Just hang on to me,' Baker ordered. 'I've got your weapon.' He took out a handkerchief and wiped the pistol before dropping it back on the floor. Then the same with the one Harker had dropped. 'Right. Two guns, both with the prints gone. That should confuse everyone. Now, try to limp. Let me take the weight, all right?'

They moved slowly. Markham hung on to the bigger man, hopping each pace and letting the wounded leg drag. Step after step. Baker had the torch in one hand, lighting their way.

'You killed him.'

'Of course I did. Don't be daft.' He spoke through clenched teeth. Caught in deep shadow, his face looked determined. 'I told you I always preferred a knife.'

'What happened to you?'

'I was coming back when I saw you go in. I thought if I went in the other way we'd have a better chance of catching him. I was lucky, the door to the tunnel's round the back of the office building. No one saw me. Then I waited.'

They crossed the culvert then the opening of the tunnel leading to Bridge Street.

'Not long now,' Baker said. 'You're not too bad. A few more minutes and we'll have you in casualty.'

Each step seemed harder. Markham wanted to stop, to rest and catch his breath, but he knew the other man wouldn't let him. He wasn't even going to ask. Baker was older, large, out of shape. Yet he was the one doing the work, concentrating, forcing them on and taking the strain.

How long had they been moving? It could have been three minutes, it could have been twenty. The only thing he could think of was the next step, moving one more pace. His leg hurt. Every time it caught on something he wanted to scream, forcing himself to stifle it.

Finally they reached the ladder.

He looked up. Only a few feet but it seemed like a mountain. How was he going to climb that?

'I'll go first,' Baker said. 'Use your arms and your good leg. Pull yourself up, just one rung at a time. I'll be waiting at the top to haul you over.'

He was gone, taking the torch with him. For a minute Markham was in darkness, resting his hands on the cold metal.

'Start climbing.' The order came down to him and Baker moved the beam so he could see.

It was like being back at school, on the bars or the rope in the gym. Letting the shoulders do the work, dragging himself higher. One leg hanging free, the other resting on a rung to balance him.

Even before he was halfway up, his muscles ached. He started to raise his head, to glance up to the top.

'Don't,' Baker shouted. 'Keep facing straight ahead. You're doing well, Come on, Dan, you can make it. Slow and steady.'

Higher up and he needed to stop, to keep resting and give his muscles time before he moved on. Breathing, telling himself he could do it. One more, than another. A short break. He was soaked with sweat from the heavy effort, the shirt sticking to his skin.

'Only five more, Dan. Almost there now.'

One. Two. Stop for a few seconds to catch his breath. Three. Four. Then a pair of strong hands was gripping him tightly around the wrists and pulling him up and over the top of the ladder. Keeping hold of him when he simply wanted to collapse.

'Just a few more yards now and then it'll be fresh air.' He lit up the doorway with the beam. 'See? Almost there.'

By the time they came close he had no strength left. He was simply hanging on and letting Baker drag him. The door swung back and the grey November daylight flooded on to his face. The cold air was a shock, taking his breath away for a moment.

'Are you all right?'

He answered with a nod, fumbling for a cigarette, then his lighter. He could scarcely keep his hand still enough to light it. Baker was wiping the door handles, getting rid of their fingerprints, leaving the door slightly ajar.

'Stay here a minute. Enjoy your smoke.'

'Where are you going?'

'Wipe our prints off the ladder. So no one can ever show we've been here.'

Markham looked down at his trousers. The right leg had a dark stain that ran down to his calf.

As he inhaled, the smoke left him dizzy. It hadn't done that since he was fourteen. Three minutes and Baker returned.

'You wait here. I'll bring the Wolseley down.'

***

The bright lights in the Public Dispensary didn't allow any rest. He was lying on a trolley in a curtained-off cubicle, waiting to see the doctor.

'What should I tell them?' he'd asked as Baker drove to North Street and parked in the small, weeded space next to the building.

'Say you cut it on some scrap metal. And you got that graze on your face when you fell. Give them a false name,' he added.

'No one's going to believe a story like that.'

'They will, especially if you stick to it. Trust me on that. People believe what they want.'

'What about …?'

There was no doubt what he meant.

'In a few minutes the police are going to receive an anonymous call from a telephone box,' Baker told him. 'A man will tell them about the metal door on Bridge Street and say he thought he heard shots from inside. That'll bring them running.' He kept his hands tight on the steering wheel.

'They'll come and ask us questions.'

'Let them.' He turned his head. 'We don't know a damned thing about it. And we'll keep saying that.'

'And my leg?' Markham asked. 'They're not stupid.'

'They won't be able to prove it.' He kept his gaze steady. 'You hurt yourself on some sheet metal. Understand?'

Markham held his stare for a moment.

'Yes,' he answered finally.

'At least this way they'll find Trevor Peel.'

'He didn't deserve what happened.'

'He was in it, Dan. He made his choice in the first place, remember that. I've known a lot of people who didn't deserve what happened to them.' He shook his head slowly. 'That's life. Go on, get yourself in there and seen to. I'll be out here when you're done.'

Markham didn't move.

'What Harker said about Amanda Fox. Did you believe him?'

'I don't know,' Baker sighed. 'I hope he was lying. After I call 999 I'll ring the wife and make sure she's still there.'

***

That had been half an hour before. He kept glancing at his watch, seeing the time pass slowly. Finally a nurse appeared, cutting his trousers with a pair of scissors.

'My my, what have you done to yourself?' she asked as she peeled the fabric away.

'Scrap metal,' Markham replied. 'I slipped and it sliced me open.'

Just like Baker said, she didn't even question the fact, simply took a ball of cotton wool and poured iodine on to it.

'This is going to sting but it'll clean everything up for doctor.' Another quick, professional smile. He half-expected her to tell him to be brave.

Another five minutes and the man bustled in, white coat flapping around his body. He looked younger than Markham, with a fresh, baby face behind a pair of NHS glasses. He poked painfully at the wound, nodding to himself and saying nothing.

'No real damage,' he announced finally. 'You were lucky, Mr …' He smiled and glanced at the chart. 'Wilson. It missed the artery and the muscle. I'll stitch you up. It'll take a week or two to heal properly, but you'll be fine. There'll be a scar, but nothing too bad.'

'Thank you,' he said stupidly.

An injection to numb his leg, then he lay back, not wanting to watch the man work with his needle and thread. Another jab for tetanus.

'I'll give you some painkillers to last a day or two. Go to your GP in a week and have him take out the stiches and give you a follow-up on the tetanus,' the doctor told him mechanically.

They lent him a walking stick and he hobbled out on to North Street, trousers flapping wildly where they'd been cut. Baker's Wolseley was in the car park, the engine running.

Awkwardly, Markham climbed in.

'Did they fix you up?' he asked as he pulled out into traffic.

'No real damage.'

'You'll be running the hundred yards in no time.' He was heading away from town.

'Where are we going?'

'Alwoodley. Your Mrs Fox decided she was ready to go out for a walk this morning and never came back.'

'So Harker was right.'

'It looks that way. She's probably flown the nest but …' He shrugged. 'My fault. Last night I told her we were close to nabbing him.'

The car rushed along King Lane, all the way to the house.

The doors were locked. A few seconds with the picks and they were inside. The place felt empty, as if the life had been sucked out of it. In the bedroom clothes were tossed on the bed, the jewellery gone. Amanda Fox had made her run.

'What time did she leave your house?' Markham asked. He'd hobbled slowly around the place.

'About nine, Nancy said.'

He looked at his watch. It was after four. Plenty of time. She could be on a ferry to the Continent by now.

They drove back slowly.

'I believed her,' Markham said bleakly. As they searched he'd gone back over his conversations with her, to see if there was any clue he'd missed. Not a thing.

'You're not the only one. She had me convinced, too. And our Nancy. Played us all for fools. Had herself in the perfect place to know what we were doing and what was going on.' He slammed his palm against the dash. 'Bloody woman. She'd have had us dead without a care.'

'She was smarter than us.'

'Aye, she was,' Baker agreed. 'I wonder why she didn't run before, though. It's not as if she didn't have a chance.'

'Staying with you she knew what we were up to,' Markham said. 'How close we were getting. If we hadn't been able to find Harker it would probably have been safe for her to stay in England. Maybe she'd have headed up a new operation or something, I don't know.'

'Perhaps. She was good, I'll give her that. Took guts to hang on that long. But it doesn't make me feel less of a bloody idiot.' He drove in silence for a little while. 'Do you want me to drop you at home?'

'If you don't mind.' He didn't think he'd be able to drive for a few days.

'I wonder why Harker went back to the tunnel.'

'Maybe she didn't have the chance to tell him we were close. He did say he was expendable.' Or perhaps it was for the photograph of the young woman he'd hidden in his bedding.

'Maybe.' Baker grunted. 'Too late to worry now.' He parked behind the flats. 'They'll be out to see us tomorrow.'

'I'll be at home.'

'Just stick to the story. We know sod all about it.'

'I will.'

The stairs took effort, using the stick and balancing himself against the wall. Finally he was inside, home. Safe. It was all over.

Markham picked up the phone and asked for a number. It took a while until he was connected. He hung on, letting it ring. Even after someone answered, they still had to go and find her.

'Hello?' As soon as he heard Carla's voice he began to smile.

'I don't suppose you fancy Leeds this weekend, do you?'

'Why, Dan? Has something happened?' An edge of fear in her voice.

'Nothing too bad. I'm a bit banged up. I don't think I can drive up there, though. I've hurt my leg.'

'Yes,' she said quickly. 'Of course.'

'It's nothing too bad, honestly. I'll give you the full story when you're here. But it's over. Really over.'

'Good,' Carla said warily.

'It is,' he promised. 'I'm sorry, though, you'll have to take the bus from the station.'

She laughed.

'How do you think I usually get around, Dan?'

They talked for a few more minutes. By the time he put down the receiver he felt pleasantly warm, the ache gone from his body for a while.

He crumpled the old army trousers and threw them in the bin. Not even fit for rags now.

An evening of Thelonious Monk on the record player. Awkward, beautifully disjointed melodies to match his thoughts. The painkillers left him floating, but they couldn't block out the images of Trevor Peel. Or the memory of Harker.

***

'They've been here.' Baker's voice on the telephone was gruff. 'They're on their way to your flat. Remember what we agreed.'

'I haven't forgotten,' Markham told him. 'Don't worry.'

'How are you feeling?'

'Not too bad.' His leg was stiff; it hurt when he tried to put weight on it. The stitches looked red, angry and ugly. But he could limp around with help from the stick.

'I'll bring your car out later.'

'Thanks.'

★★★

Davidson and Molloy. Neither of them so pleasant this time, but they still couldn't shake off being gentlemen. However much they insisted, Markham denied knowing anything. There was a tunnel under Bridge Street? He didn't know that. No, they'd never found Harker. Or Mrs Fox.

'What happened to your leg?' Molloy asked.

'I cut it on some scrap metal.'

'That must have been nasty.' He didn't believe a word.

'I had some stitches. It'll heal.'

They went at him for an hour, changing tack every few minutes. One friendly, the other aggressive. All the techniques he'd learned back in military intelligence. He'd also been taught how to counter them. He didn't give them an inch. They had no proof and they knew it.

'One last thing,' Davidson said as they were preparing to leave. 'I believe you were looking for someone called Trevor Peel.'

'Yes, we'd arranged to meet but he never showed up. Why?'

The man stared at him. Markham returned his gaze.

'It doesn't matter.'

'We might want to talk to you again,' Molloy told him as they left, but he knew they'd never return. They'd had their chance and found nothing.

***

An hour later and it was Baker at his door, wheezing from the stairs and handing over the car keys.

'Did they get anything from you?'

'Of course not,' Markham told him.

'Good lad.' He paused. 'I'd better tell you, we've had another missing person case come in.'

'From your mates on the force again?'

Baker laughed.

'I'm just pulling your leg. There's been nothing at all. Get yourself well and I'll see you on Monday. We'll hash it all out then.'

The second post arrived as the big man was leaving. Inside an envelope, a small poster advertising Georgina's appearance at Studio 20. Written in pen, *Tickets going fast! Book now!*

He'd send her a good luck note. She didn't want him there, but he wished her well. Maybe this would be the start of good things for her.

***

Markham whiled away the rest of the day reading and dozing in the chair. Like an old man, he thought. He pottered around the flat, eventually turning on the lights against the darkness outside, looking out of the window, anticipation rising every time the bus stopped.

Finally she was there on the other side of the road, glancing up and waving as she saw him. Her red coat and beret were bright against the evening gloom. He smiled. There was hope yet.

ABOUT THE AUTHOR

CHRIS NICKSON is the author of the Richard Nottingham and Tom Harper series (Severn House). He is also the author of two historical crime fiction series for The Mystery Press: *The Crooked Spire* and *The Saltergate Psalter*, medieval mysteries set in fourteenth-century Chesterfield, and the Dan Markham series set in 1950s Leeds. Chris lives in Leeds.

PRAISE FOR

DARK BRIGGATE BLUES: A DAN MARKHAM MYSTERY

BY CHRIS NICKSON

'The book is a pacy, atmospheric and entertaining page-turner with a whole host of well-rounded characters'

Yorkshire Post

'[*Dark Briggate Blues* is] written with an obvious affection for the private investigator genre, this is a skilful take in an unusual setting. It has real depth which will keep you turning the pages'

Hull Daily Mail

'This is a tense thriller, all the more disturbing for the ordinariness of its setting among the smoky, rain-slicked streets of a northern industrial city. Nickson has captured the minutiae of the mid-20th century perfectly'

Historical Novel Society